Miguel's Secret Journal
The Four Corners of Earth

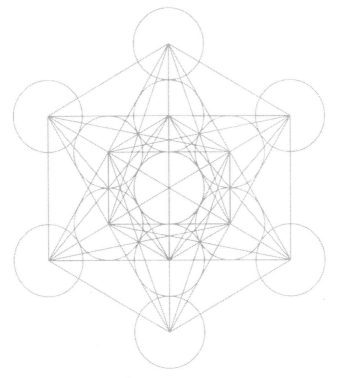

A. V. Zeppa
Book Two

D1527599

outskirtspress
DENVER, COLORADO

Miguel's Secret Journal The Four Corners of Earth
All Rights Reserved.

Outskirts Press, Inc.
http://www.outskirtspress.com

ISBN: 978-1-4787-0154-5

Outskirts Press and the "OP" logo are trademarks belonging to Outskirts Press, Inc.

PRINTED IN THE UNITED STATES OF AMERICA

"I saw four angels standing at the four corners of the earth"
                                                    Revelation 7:1

protecting the world with the energy of ten billion suns.
I saw four angels destroy the pain and darkness of pure hate
    effortlessly as they flew across the horizon to protect the
    ones who have gentle souls,
        those who have been forced to live alone because they
        are different;
        your time has now come.

Listen to the Haunting Melodies

Journal Entry 32

3 am Monday Morning
October 1st

I am saddened by the look in their eyes
and their repulsion of what I am.
I am stunned by the ease with which they hate.

I put my hands up and touch the wind
and I can feel the vibrations of earth
knowing I am one with truth.

I am saddened by those who have never known love
or artistic wonder
or the power of the written word
and how those words can change the hand of fate.

I am heartbroken by the thought that they never loved me
or even tried to see me,
it was like I didn't even exist,
but I am now here for all to see.

"Michael, are you awake? Wake up sleepy boy," he said, as he softly nudged me and kissed my shoulder. I love to hear Gabriel say those words. He had his arms wrapped around my body as we lay all comfy in bed.

"Yeah, I'm up," I whispered, as I stretched and gave him a kiss.

"I need to fly and I want to take you with me. Are you up for it?"

"Right now? You mean it?" I excitedly turned over and pulled his naked body on top of mine.

"Yes, I mean it. I want to show you how beautiful this world looks in the night sky, how peaceful it looks in the distance. I also want to show you how people are able to be themselves when they think no one is watching."

"Can I really fly?"

"Of course you can. Even in your human form you've always been able to, but you just couldn't figure it out. You dreamt about it a thousand times, and I tried to show you how by flying around your room hoping that you could see me somehow. But if you really think about it, flying is much more than just physically gliding through the air. What is so kool is that you've been flying around in your sketches and poetry for years. I wanted you to fly to me using your artistic soul because I couldn't break through the barrier God had created to separate us. I was hoping you would be able to break through it somehow. Michael, I was in total misery because we were apart, and I was so sad as I watched you live your human life knowing that God wouldn't let me be human too. I was angry because I couldn't do anything to

2

help you through your pain and loneliness. But I was always near, and I felt that you knew I was watching over you in some way. Your premonitions were real. You made me smile so many times as you created beautiful sketches and poetry. And every now and then you'd look around your room wondering what was going on because you knew something was there. I cried night after night because I couldn't break through, but I was giving you love and hope even though we weren't in the same worlds. I even went behind God's back and flew to earth as often as I could to be near you. There was no way he was going to stop me, no matter how he tried.

I told you that time has no meaning to us now, but the last fifteen years we were separated seemed like an eternity, and I couldn't make them go by any faster. To tell you the truth, I almost betrayed him because I thought he was being so cruel to us."

I felt numb as Gabriel told me everything. It got me angry that we were forced to be in a kind of purgatory for no good reason.

"Yeah, it was weird because I knew something was in my room, especially when people were violatin me. I didn't know it was you, but I swear I could almost see your face at times, which really kinda freaked me out at first, like I was goin crazy. But I got used to it after a while.

And when I was real sad or in a lotta pain I would silently call for you and I would feel your presence; it always calmed me down. I love you so much," I said, holding Gabriel's body tightly against mine.

3

"I love you too Michael. Are you ready?"

"Yeah, I've been waiting my whole life for this."

"Close your eyes and hold on."

We were instantly looking down at our naked bodies lying on the bed softly glowing and looking so peaceful. I felt like pure energy as I floated in the air trying to understand what I was actually doing. Everything felt strange, like all my emotions were colliding together, like I didn't exist anymore. I started feeling sad all of a sudden because I knew what it all meant.

"Why are you sad Michael?"

"I don't know. I guess I still want my human body. I still wanna be human. For some reason it feels like I'm dying and I'm scared. Does that make any kind of sense? Even with all the pain and sadness in my life, I love being human. It's worth fighting through all the shitty stuff because experiencing even a little love and happiness makes it all worthwhile. Man, I don't know what I'm feeling. I guess it just feels strange to only be energy and not have my body. I hope you know what I mean."

"Yeah, I do, because I've been enjoying my human form too. But you know we can still keep our bodies anytime we want. Look at your body and visually take a little bit of flesh into your mind and see what happens." All of a sudden both of us had our bodies again even though we were floating in the air. I grabbed Gabriel and kissed him =D

"Michael, we have no boundaries. We can do anything and be anything we want. We control everything around us. You are slowly getting your powers back. Can you feel them yet?"

"I think so. It just feels mad weird for me to be up here

looking down at us in bed," I said, as I looked at my swollen face, black eyes, cut lips, and bruised body.

Gabriel immediately surrounded me with love because he knew I was still feeling sad about what my mom had done to me.

"We look so innocent lying together."

"That's because we are innocent. We are just a couple of teenagers trying to find our way. Are you ready to fly?"

"Yeah, this is gunna be fun! =D

Can we go visit my sister? I wanna make sure she's all right. I really miss her."

And then all of a sudden we were shooting up through the floors and ceiling of the apartment building, and within seconds we were totally out of Earth's atmosphere thousands of miles in space. We were looking at this amazing blue world rotating peacefully in the darkness of the universe.

"How do you like the view from here Michael? I'll bet you've never been on a date like this before," Gabriel said, with a sly smile.

"This is crazy. How'd we get here so fast?" I asked. "I've never seen anything like it. Earth looks so beautiful."

Gabriel kinda laughed. "We are incalculable energy that can actually travel faster than the speed of light. We are similar to the same kind of energy that is the core of this universe, and all of the other universes still unknown to man. The only difference is that we are divine energy that has no boundaries and can never be destroyed by anything except other divine entities."

"I don't understand what you're saying. It sounds crazy."

"It's hard to explain, but we aren't energy that is tied to this universe, like everything else within it. We are made from the energy of divine light, a power so overwhelming that it has corrupted many angels throughout eternity. Many fallen angels are trying to destroy us, and will do anything in their power to see us die. I'm sure that sounds a little strange, but it's true.

Don't worry; once you make your complete transformation it will all make sense."

"Yeah, everything you're telling me and even what we're doing right now is some crazy stuff. I don't really understand what you're saying about how our energy works, but all I know is that I feel totally free for the first time in my life."

So anyway, there we were looking at the world from space, and I was looking at Gabriel and smiling. I thought about how the people I know would think I was a total craziod if I ever told them I was an angel. They'd lock me up in a second..lol

It's been nice how Gabriel is slowly helping me cope with everything because I'm really stressed out emotionally right now. I almost feel numb, ya know, like this is all a crazy dream and I'm gunna wake up and my old life's gunna return. It gets me panicky thinkin bout it O__o

As usual, my thoughts were all over the place as we silently hovered in space. I finally asked, "When will I be able to fly on my own?"

"Well, you're kind of doing it right now; I'm just helping you a little until it all comes back. When that exactly is, I'm not sure, but you'll know when it happens."

We were enjoying the view and talking about stuff, then all of a sudden my mind started feeling mad strange. I thought I was getting one of my bad headaches, but instead I started getting flashes of this intense white light streaming through my mind at about a zillion miles a second. Then images appeared of some humungous battle I was in. I saw Gabriel, CJ, Hunter and me protecting an intense light source from being destroyed. It started to make sense about me really being an angel; what I was seeing was my past. I could actually feel it in my mind. Maybe now I can start to accept why this is all happening.

"Hey, are you ok?" Gabriel asked.

Just as I was about to answer him, I felt something dark and powerful coming from somewhere far away in the universe. I could feel it racing towards us at an intense speed.

"Gabriel, I can feel something evil coming our way. I know you feel it too," I said, as I tried to look deeper into the universe to find whatever it was. Gabriel let out two intense beams of light from his eyes and scanned the heavens. He looked worried as he searched.

"He's coming Michael, and he wants to destroy you once and for all. He knows we're back and he's bringing as much force as he can gather."

I didn't say anything, but looked at that peaceful world sleeping in the night sky and knew we had to save it once again.

"He wants to kill you before you get your powers back. Somehow he knows you're vulnerable, so we are going to protect you until you have fully transformed. This is the very reason why you can't stay human much longer. Lucifer is going to try to destroy you, this world, and this universe once and for all."

"Gabriel, I'm not afraid of him. Even in my human form I'm

7

stronger that he will ever be because he doesn't understand the true power humans possess. But I'm going to show him, and then I'm going to do the most loving thing I can do; destroy him once and for all."

Gabriel smiled. "I know you are Michael. We'll do it together. Hey, let's go see your sister now." And then we were off, and in like a second we were in Rosanna's bedroom in Brooklyn watching her sleep like a little angel. She had a new stuffed bunny rabbit in her arms as she slept. My aunt was taking good care of her.

I gently floated above her and whispered in her ear that I was with her now. I kissed her cheek hoping she could feel it. Then we floated down and stood by her bed as I gently woke her up. Rosanna slowly opened her eyes and saw me and Gabriel smiling at her. I knelt down by the side of the bed as she looked at us sleepily. Then she smiled and jumped up to give me a big hug.

"Miguel, I missed you so much. I've been worried cuzz you were hurt real bad. Are you ok now?" she asked, as she continued hugging me.

"Yeah, I'm fine. Are you ok? Is Aunt Maria taking good care of you?"

"Yeah, she is. I miss mom, but I feel safer here."

"I miss you so much. I like your bunny rabbit," I said, gently petting it.

She smiled and put her little hand on top of mine. "Miguel, something's wrong. Am I dreaming? Are you and Gabriel really here? You look different."

I looked at Gabriel for a second trying to figure out what I was going to tell her.

"No, you aren't dreaming. And yes, I guess I am a little different now, but Gabriel and I are still the same. I want you to know that you can call for me anytime you want and I'll come to you."

All of a sudden Rosanna got panicky. "What's wrong? Did you die? Please don't be dead Miguel. Please don't leave me."

"I'm not dead Rosanna. I'm fine, really I am. I'm always gunna be here for you know matter what. I'd never leave you. Do you believe me?"

"Will you come and visit me every night until we go home?"

"Of course I will," I said, even though I knew there was no home to go to. I felt so bad for her knowing that our family was gone forever.

"Rosanna, let's not tell Aunt Maria about me visiting you right now. Will you keep it a secret?"

"Why don't you want her to know? Aunty is worried about you and wants to see you. She's not mad that you're gay if that's what you think. She loves you. She told me that we shouldn't judge people. Aunty was crying when she said that. I also heard her talking to one of her friends about you saying what a nice boy you are, and how you didn't deserve to be beaten for being gay." I was so happy to hear that. At least two people in my family love me.

"I'm glad she feels that way. I love Aunty, and I'm glad she's taking good care you, but I don't want to see her right now because I know she's still talking to mom. Let's keep this a secret, ok?"

"Ok Miguel, I promise. I like secrets."

Then Gabriel knelt down beside me. "Rosanna, how would

you like to come live with Miguel, my mom, and me in the next couple of weeks? I don't want you and your brother to be separated."

She smiled this huge smile and gave Gabriel the biggest hug.

"We have to go now, but I'll come see you again tomorrow night."

I tucked her back in bed and gave her a kiss. "Close your eyes now and dream some good dreams." Then Gabriel gently touched her cheek with his hand and she was instantly asleep.

"Hey, let's go fly around the city for a while cute one, and then I'm going to make love to you on top of the Chrysler Building while the whole universe watches."

Nite =p

Journal Entry 33
Tuesday, October 2nd
11:30 pm

Tragic Flaw

I don't mind
Shooting at the rhymes
It's ok
It's all a fucking maze.
Stop
Go
They're the ones who broke my heart
Me
You
I don't ever wanna know
I'm just full of fucking holes
It's a Tragic Flaw.

One by one
Blinded by the sun

Tell me why
It's all a fucking lie.
Me
You
Standing at the edge of dreams
Fast
Slow
I don't ever wanna know
Life is full of fucking holes
It's a Tragic Flaw

I've been crying a lot the last couple of days because I know things are never gunna be the same. I feel so sad right now, but I also realize that I gotta start moving on; I just have to figure out a way to do it.

I know it seems like it's all unreal with what is happening to me, or like it's some kind of crazy dream, but if you really think about it, ya know, everything; our lives, this world, this universe, the trillions of stars out there, all of it seems unreal.

Gabriel, CJ, and Hunter have been helping me get through all this crazy stuff.

CJ and Hunter came over to hang with us after school today. I need them to be close by.

My body is still real bruised and sore, but I can feel it starting to change in certain ways. It's really weird. I can't explain it, I just feel it inside. My body's been glowing on and off a lot more, like someone's flipping a switch inside me like ima light bulb :p

Even my angel wing tatts have been moving like crazy. They've been tickling my arms.

The guys smile every time it happens because they know I'm changing. They're also happy that I can fly now.

I went to see my sister again with Gabriel a little while ago and my aunt almost caught us because she heard my voice. She opened my sister's bedroom door thinking she'd find me and Rosanna together, but all she saw was Rosanna talking to her bunny rabbit. We were standing right in front of her, but she couldn't see us. Yeah, Gabriel made us invisible.

It was kinda funny because my aunt's face looked so frustrated, like she was losin her mind.

Rosanna just looked at her and smiled. CJ and Hunter laughed when I told them about it.

Ya know, every time I look at my three angels it makes me smile because they've been here for me. I honestly don't think I'd be alive right now if it wasn't for them.

We didn't have school on Monday, so I got to spend the whole day with Gabriel. It was nice not having anyone around to bother us. I can't believe we live together now =D

Gabriel decided he wanted us to tell his mom the truth about things, so that's what we did yesterday morning. We kinda shocked her. Let me take that back; we really shocked her. I can still see the look on her face. I felt happy we told her, but I also felt guilty because Gabriel isn't who she thought he was; a normal gay teenager, and her son.

Gabriel explained everything as gently as he could so it wouldn't upset his mom too much. The look on her face was total confusion at first, like she couldn't believe what he was saying. But he made it easy to understand when he asked her to look into his eyes. She looked into those haunting blue eyes and saw the other side. His mom could see where we came from and what our existence looked like. It overwhelmed her just like it did me at first, but I was happy that she could see that angels really do exist and that heaven is a real place, even though it's nothing like what people could ever picture it to be. They really do have it so wrong :/

His mom didn't say anything for the longest time. Then she started crying as she touched Gabriel's face. I could see how much she loved him and what it was all going to mean.

She whispered, "I see you and Miguel surrounded by beautiful white light, and I feel an overwhelming sense of love. Thank you for showing me."

She hugged Gabriel for the longest time. Then she hugged me. I told her, "You're helping to protect us while we're here. You may not know it, but you're also an angel because you're a mother who has loved and protected Gabriel from all of the bad things in this world. You have so much love in your heart. I've always wanted a mom like you."

She looked at my messed up face and gently put her hand on my cheek.

"Miguel, you are so brave. I know you are going to help this world because of the life you've had to live. It must have been horrible to live in an abusive situation." She looked at me with this look of guilt because she wasn't there to help me.

"It's not your fault," I quietly said. "It's just the way life turns out sometimes. This kind of stuff happens to kids all over the world. I wish there were more moms like you because there would be a lot more love and happiness in this world."

Gabriel explained that he chose her to be his mom because he could see how much love was in her heart, and because she wanted to have children but was having a hard time getting pregnant. Tears kept running down her face as he explained how he altered her life. Then I started crying too because I felt so bad for her. But Gabriel said that as far as he was concerned, she was his real mom. To her it seemed like she had really raised him for the last fifteen years. Gabriel had altered time so she actually believed she had. CJ and Hunter did the same thing to their earth parents too. It's just so hard to understand all this stuff, but it's the truth.

As Gabriel told his mom everything, I started wondering again why God decided to put me in such a terrible place with such fucked up parents. Why did he put me with people who looked right though me, who beat me and yelled at me and made me feel like a worthless piece of shit my whole life? Why would he let my mom's boyfriends violate me?

What lesson was I supposed to have learned by all this?

Why couldn't he have at least put me with people who would love me, like he did for Gabriel, CJ, and Hunter? I know I'm just supposed to understand and accept it, but I really wanna know why, and I wanna know why he won't talk to me yet. All I know is that we're gunna have it out, believe me! *I'm sorry again for the rant, but I can't stop thinking about all this stuff.*

After his mom came outta shock, she looked at us and smiled. "Both of you are gifts to the world, and I know you will make it a better place. I always knew you were special Gabriel.

I knew it because of how you've always viewed life with the wisdom of someone much older than your years." She continued, "I'm also proud of you both for coming out so everyone can see how much you love each other. Gay people are God's gift to the world because of the intelligence and artistic genius they've shared since the beginning of time. So are gay angels. I can see how much you love each other, and I will always help you any way I can."

Gabriel thanked her and then gently held her hand. Then he held mine as we connected our minds together. Gabriel was letting her see the world from our point of view. She smiled as the truth was there for her to see; she could feel all of the love in the universe just like us, and it made her happy knowing there was more than just this beautiful blue world.

Σ †

It's mad strange how Gabriel, CJ, and Hunter can alter time and people and anything else they want. I can't wait to be able to do this too :D

My existence as an angel has been coming back to me in different ways. It's been hitting me little by little while I'm awake and doing stuff, and also when I sleep. It's weird because I'll be talking with Gabriel and all of a sudden I close my eyes and see my life playing out just like a movie. And when I'm sleeping, my dreams physically let me experience past events. All of it's been flooding my brain like crazy, and it scares me knowing all of the battles we've had to fight to protect everything. I wish there was another way to fix all this mess insteada always having to fight. I know God is testing me with the crummy life I've lived because I've always had to fight to survive my own personal hell on earth.

Was I reborn a human for God's entertainment?

Did he create me only to be a shield? His shield?

Is fighting the only way to keep peace in this universe? On this earth?

Shit, I don't even know what I'm supposed to do yet; I feel lost with all this stuff happening. Whatever my purpose is, I'd like to win whatever battle I'm supposed to fight without violence. I just don't know how to do it yet :/

It always seems that violence can only be defeated by violence. I remember last year in math class this very cute guy was talkin about how he wished people could solve their problems without fighting or having to use armies. He wanted governments to abolish all of the armies in the world. I thought he was crazy because we gotta have armies. I didn't understand what he was trying to say, but now I do.

I'd love a world that could solve problems logically; maybe someday :/

Gabriel was reading my mind. "Michael, I don't think there is any other way because of who we're dealing with. Lucifer has always used deception and hate to bring out the worst in humans. This is a simple truth. People could easily conquer their negative temptations if they wanted to, but most choose the path of least resistance instead of a life of knowledge and integrity."

A kool thing happened Sunday night. I was in Gabriel's bed

17

tryin ta get some sleep, and he was in the living room reading, so I called to him to come get naked with me by connecting our thoughts. I heard him get off the couch and start walking towards the bedroom. I looked at the door waiting to see his smiling face, but he flew right through the wall and got into bed next to me. He held me in his arms and kissed me real gentle.

"Did you like my big entrance? I'm just showing off a little."

"Can you show off a little more for me?" I said, pulling him on top of me and grabbing his cute little ass. We made love all night long ;P

Everyone was staring at me in school today because my face and arms were still real fucked up looking. My face is still swollen and bruised, and my lips are still cut up and puffy. They're like twice the normal size. Even my arms and chest have some dark ugly bruises that hurt a lot when I touchem. Gabriel didn't want me going to school; he just wanted me to rest. That was so sweet of him, but I said, "I'm feeling ok, and I'd be lonely without you."

"Well, let me at least heal your wounds then. I feel so bad for you."

"I'm ok, it doesn't hurt too much, and besides, I think it's important for people at school to see what hatred looks like. You know something; I think this is how I'm supposed to start fighting back. We need to make this world aware of its own ignorance somehow."

"You're right Michael. I just feel so bad for you."

"All that matters to me is that we're together. What my

mom did to me is nothing compared to what's been happening to other gay people around the world. We've been outcasts forever. They've made us feel dirty and less than human. They've beaten, tortured, and murdered millions of us throughout time. Every person at school needs to see what bullying really looks like. I'm gunna wear these cuts and bruises with dignity because I want people to know I'm not afraid.

Ω π

When we got to school, Jacob, Jennifer, and Christal came running up and gave me big hugs. They felt so bad because of what my mom had done to me.

"Everything's kool now," I said.

Jacob asked, "You gunna be ok Miguel?"

"Yeah, it looks a lot worse than it really is. And besides, Gabriel's taking good care of me."

"We're here for you, so if you need anything just let us know."

"I know you guys are, and it means a lot to me."

As we talked, Luis and his boys came round the corner. Luis took one look at me and started laughing. "Hey faggot, you like rough sex or somethin? Looks like you got fucked real good.

Hey white boy, don't be so rough with your little Latino girlfriend."

"I guess you haven't learned anything yet," Gabriel said, getting between me and Luis.

"Listen bitch, I don't know what the fuck you been doin or how you is doin it, but I'm gunna figure it out, and then me and my niggas are gunna fuckin take care of you and your ugly girl-friend," Luis said, with a stupid smirk on his face. Then he looked at me and started actin even more thug by grabbing his crotch and stuff.

"Someday I'm gunna fuck you up real good so you won't never forget. If ya think your face is fucked up now, wait till I take you down. Your queer white boy won't be wit you all the time to save your ass. Ya know something, your ugly ass face looks good this way, and I'm gunna make sure it stays fucked up."

As Luis said all this shit, I kept staring into his eyes without blinking or looking away. It totally freaked him out. He stopped talking and just looked. I was trying to show him who I was, and I think he was seeing something because he suddenly leaned back and said, "Somethin ain't fuckin right. What da shit you tryin ta pull?"

He looked into my eyes again, and that's when I showed him how empty his life really was.

I was showing him his future, and it scared the shit outta him because it was nothing but darkness. Then all of a sudden his body started shaking all over the fucking place.

He didn't know what the fuck was goin on, and neither did I at first. Then I realized it was me that was making him spazz out. I decided to see if I could move him too; I could. I made him go all stiff as I slowly pushed his body up against the locker like he was a feather in the wind. I just thought it in my mind and it happened. Wow, I couldn't fucking believe it =D

I could feel my body getting stronger, and I could feel my an-gel wing tatts taking in all the energy around me. I was sucking in energy like a hungry animal; it was the most excellent feeling :D

Luis couldn't control his body at all; I had him paralyzed. I finally looked away after a few seconds and he fell to the ground. His friends were looking at him and then back at me real weird tryin ta figure out what was goin on. Gabriel had this huge smile on his face, but Jennifer, Jacob, and Christal had backed way away when Luis started shaking. The whole fucking situation must have looked mad strange. Luis gave me this frightened look as he slowly got up off the floor.

He finally got it together a little. "Come on my niggas, let's get the fuck outta here before we turn inta faggots." As they walked down the hall, Luis turned around and looked at me one more time.

My friends were speechless at what had just gone down. I was shocked too as I shyly looked at Gabriel realizing what I had just done. We just kind of stood there for a few seconds. No one but Gabriel knew that I was using powers I didn't even know I had.

"Well that was fucking strange," I said, to break the silence.

"You gotta tell someone what he's been doing to you Miguel, cuzz this bullying shit's gotta stop before you get hurt even more," Jacob said.

Jennifer and Christal agreed. "I'm gunna get my brother and his niggas to kick their fucking asses," Christal said, getting tight. "Believe me when I say that, cuzz my brother's like twenty-four and hangs with a crowd that knows how to get shit done, if ya know what I mean."

"I'll be ok guys, don't worry. It's just Luis bein Luis."

After everyone left for class, Gabriel gave me a gentle kiss on my swollen lips.

"I'm glad it's happening. Just follow your instincts and you'll be able to control your powers the way you need to. This is just the beginning. We are going to have a lot more trouble soon, and we need you to fully transform so you can lead us. But in the meantime I think I'm going to have to teach Luis and his little friends a lesson they'll never forget," Gabriel said, with that intense look in his eyes.

"Hey, don't worry about it; it's just his typical shit. He was just tryin ta act kool in front of his boys."

才 ♭

You should have seen the look on Mr. Atwood's face when I walked into class. I felt sorry for him because he looked so upset. "Miguel, what happened to you? Are you all right? Guys, come with me for a minute." Everyone in class was staring at me as we went out in the hall to talk. "Please tell me what happened. Did Luis do this to you?"

"No, it was my mom. She beat me after I came out to her," I said, looking down at the floor embarrassed as hell.

"I'm so sorry this happened to you Miguel. I feel responsible because I know how hard it is for parents to accept having a gay son or daughter. It's all my fault. We should have had a meeting just for parents to better prepare them for the gay community that is emerging here at school."

"Mister, it's not your fault. It's nobody's fault but my mom's."

Then Gabriel told him that she was arrested and charged

with assault and battery and child abuse, and that the judge had issued a restraining order saying she wasn't allowed within five hundred feet of me or my sister. Gabriel also told him that the judge wanted to put me in a foster home but changed his mind and said I could stay at his house.

"My mom signed some papers which makes her Miguel's temporary guardian for the time being."

I was mad embarrassed as I started spilling my guts to Mr. Atwood. "She's been hitting me my whole life, but this is the first time she actually wanted to kill me; I could see it in her eyes. I'm ok now. All this mess on my face is gunna heal. Even what I been feelin inside of me is gunna heal someday. Thanks for your concern mister."

Man, it was an emotional day, but I'm glad I went to school so everyone could see.

Nite…

Journal Entry 34
Wednesday, October 3rd
10 pm

It is easy to hate and it is difficult to love.
This is how the whole scheme of things works.

Confucius

I know it's never gunna stop. There's so much hatred around me and Gabriel right now, and I know it's only gunna get worse, especially after what happened today. Everyone seems to be coming at us from all directions now.

Once again it started as soon as we got to school this morning. Some guys were standing by the front doors calling us queers and cocksuckers as we walked in. Then our locker was vandalized with all sorts of gay hate shit written on it with markers and paint and stuff. They even carved the words *Faggot ass bitches* right into the door with something sharp. The door was bashed in so bad that we couldn't even open it up.

Someone splattered red paint to make it look like the locker door was dripping with blood, and there was a drawing of a knife going through a naked emo guy's blood-splattered chest.

Whoever drew it could actually draw because it looked just like me; I guess someone wants me dead now. Right under the picture of me getting stabbed was some weird saying that didn't make any sense. It was written real small. It said, "sicssicssics beast is come."

Gabriel looked at me looking at it, but didn't say anything. I didn't have a clue what it meant.

"This is what I've been expecting; they're starting to get bolder now."

Then he put his hand on the door, felt it for a second, and knew exactly who vandalized it.

"Luis bashed the door in and threw paint all over it, and two guys named Anthony and Donato wrote the gay slurs and drew the picture," Gabriel said, with a worried look.

"What is it? You got that look in your eyes like somethin's wrong."

"Yeah, something's not right about these guys. They aren't what they seem to be."

"What do you mean?"

"They've been sent here, and they have some power. We just need to find out how much power they actually have." Then Gabriel calmly put his hand up and stopped everyone in their tracks. He made time stand still.

"Follow me; I want to get a good look at these guys."

We walked down the hall, up two flights of stairs, and then

into the bathroom at the end of the hall, and there they were. Luis, his friends, and these two new Rican guys, all frozen stiff.

There were six ofem and they were in the middle of smoking a blunt and sniffing some kind of white powder shit that one of the new guys were passing out. It was mad strange to be able to get a close look at all of them.

I wasn't afraid or anything, just curious. But they gave me the creeps because I could feel how much hate was oozing from their bodies. They actually had a distinct smell. It was a combination of burning metal, burning tar, and rotten meat. It was disgusting O__o

Gabriel went right up to Anthony and Donato and shot white light from his eyes into their bodies. He illuminated their bodies so much that it looked like they were gunna start on fire any second.

It was mad kool seeing Gabriel take in everything these guys were made of and figure them out.

"What do you see?"

"It's just what I thought. They're disciples. Lucifer has sent them here to lay the ground work for his return. Fortunately they have limited powers."

"What are we gunna do?"

"We are just going to keep an eye on them as they blend in with all of the other thugs.

It's obvious what Lucifer is trying to do, and I'm sure he'll be sending more of them as he tries to get everything in place."

"I don't know what you mean. You're scaring me Gabriel."

"Everything's all right, but we need to let CJ and Hunter

know about this right away. They warned me this was going to happen."

Then Gabriel touched my shoulder and we were instantly transported back in front of our locker again. He put his hand up and everyone started moving like nothing had happened. People were laughing as they walked by looking at the gay slurs and our smashed to shit door.

We went to the principal's office to let him know what happened. He came back with us to our locker, took some pictures, and said he'd report it to the police and the Department of Education as a hate crime.

☮ ♒

Now that people know we're gay, it's interesting to see the reactions when me and Gabriel walk down the halls together. Some of the girls are nice to us and say hi and think it's cute when we hold hands and stuff, but the guys are so paranoid that they do everything they can to avoid looking at us, like they're afraid they might catch gayness or some corny shit. I was kind of doing an experiment today as we walked from class to class. I tried to make eye contact with guys in the hall, but every single one ofem, except my friends, either looked down or looked away real quick. It scares them to see two guys holding hands and showing affection towards each other.

Oh yeah, they look at us when they think we don't notice. They'll see me and Gabriel holding hands or kissing and have this look on their faces like they wanna throw up.

I know we scare em, and I wish we didn't. We're just two

guys who love each other, that's all. What's so bad about that? I wish everyone could see that lots of people love and care for others of the same sex in different ways. Not everything is sexual. Friends love friends, dads love their sons, and moms love their daughters. This is the glue that makes everything meaningful. I just wanna be able to love Gabriel out in the open because it isn't dirty or perverted or evil or wrong for a guy to love another guy, or for a girl to love another girl.

Me, Gabriel, Jacob, Roberto, Jennifer, and Christal went to Mr. Atwood's class at lunch today to make some GSA posters that we could put up in the halls. We want everyone to know that our club is going to be a place where people can have some fun and be themselves without any negative judgment. We went online to get some poster ideas from the GLSEN website, and found some kool sayings:

Homophobia is Gay

Gay Rights Are Civil Rights

Hate Is Not A Family Value

Love is Love   (I like this one a lot :D)

Celebrate Diversity

Hate Free Zone, and a lots others :D

Mister had poster board and all kinds of markers, charcoal pencils, and even some watercolor paints. It was mad kool being with my friends hanging out and making posters.

I really got into it and was drawing like a madman. It felt like all this energy was coming outta my body as I took the charcoal pencils and started drawing the seven of us together with a huge peace sign in the background. Whenever I draw, I always go to this place in my mind where nothing else matters. What I didn't realize was that everyone had stopped what they were doing and started watching me as I sketched. This was the first time I felt comfortable enough to let people see what I can do; it's been my secret world forever. Gabriel was smiling as he watched everyone watching me. Roberto was the first to say something as he looked at what I was sketching.

"Holy shit Miguel, I didn't know you could draw like that. That's fucking awesome man."

"What? Oh," I said, as I stopped and looked at everyone looking at me. I felt a little embarrassed, but Roberto made me smile as I thanked him. Then he stood right next to me and watched me finish bringing everyone to life on the poster-board. Mister liked that I put him in the sketch too. He said it was an honor to be included.

We finished most of the posters and decided we'd tape em up in the main halls right after school so everyone could see them. Hopefully we'll get some people to show up next Tuesday for our first GSA meeting. To tell you the truth, I'm worried that maybe no one is gunna come. Hopefully a few people will be brave enough to check it out.

ぬ 才

We put the posters up in the hallways after our last class and then watched people read them to see what kind of reaction we'd get. The girls were kool with the signs, but the guys hated them. "Fuck this shit, I'm gunna transfer and get the fuck outta this queer hole." One guy even took out a pen and wrote "fuck you faggots" on the Love is Love poster. How sad is that?

Jacob, Roberto, and Jennifer yelled at the guy to stop, but he told them to fuck off and then ran down the hall and out a side door.

After everyone left school, me and Gabriel went back to our locker so I could get my Trigonometry book. When we got there, the janitor guy was replacing our locker door and cleaning off all the red paint that was splattered everywhere. Mr. Atwood was coming out of his classroom, saw us, and came over to talk.

"I'm sorry this is happening. You two don't deserve this. How are you holding up Miguel?

I know you are going through a lot of emotional situations right now, but just be strong and don't let all that has happened get you discouraged. We will fight this together."

"Thanks mister. None of this bothers me too much, I just feel bad for anyone else who wants to come out around here, or who wants to be different in other ways. It's obvious some people wanna try and scare us with this stuff, but it isn't gunna work."

After I got my book, me and Gabriel walked out the front doors holding hands and talking. All of a sudden someone grabbed me by the arm real hard and tried to jerk me away from Gabriel. He was hiding by a wall and snuck up behind us. I couldn't believe it, it was my dad.

He had this look of pure evil in his eyes as he started yelling at me.

"Miguel, what da fuck you think you is doin? Get da fuck

away from that boy, NOW!" he yelled, as he grabbed hold of my whole body and tried to wrestle me to the ground.

I took one look at him and felt this rage inside of me that I've never felt before. I wanted to kill him right where he stood. I yelled at him to stop, but he kept his arms around my body and was squeezing me hard and hurting me. That's when I looked at him and went mad. Some kind of electricity or something came outta my body, and it electrocuted my dad. He let go of me, fell to the ground, and started shaking and jerking all over like he was having an epileptic fit.

I stood back and lifted his body off the ground just by looking at him. Then I sent him flying thirty feet through the air, slamming him against the school wall. Once again, all I had to do was think it, and it happened. Gabriel asked me to stop, but I couldn't. My angel wing tatts were drawing in energy from everywhere. Gabriel's Metatron Cubes were trying to stop the energy from entering my body, but I was more powerful than they were. Gabriel was trying to stop me from killing my dad as the two of us became locked in this weird battle of energy. I was totally outta control with anger and rage at what my dad was trying to do to me, and I was gunna kill him.

"Michael, you need to stop. Don't lower yourself to his level," Gabriel said, as he put his arms around me trying to calm me down. "It's ok Michael, he doesn't matter; I hope you can see this. He's never going to hurt you again."

I tried to get calm, but I couldn't because I didn't know how to. My whole body was shaking as I started crying. "Gabriel, I'm sorry. Please forgive me."

"It's ok Michael; everything is going to be ok." He kissed me and calmed me down.

"Thanks, I think I'm ok now." I wiped my eyes and then walked over to where my dad was lying on the ground and stood over him. He looked up at me with horror in his eyes. His face was a bloody mess from hitting the wall. It's the first time I ever saw him look scared. Then I let it all out.

"Do you like the way I look? You like all these cuts and bruises I got on my face?

They probably take you back to the good old days when you'd smile as you beat the shit outta me. I bet you got lots of good memories of hitting me and making me feel worthless, like I wasn't fit to be alive. My face is probably like a family photo album you keep in your mind, but I ain't never gunna let you touch me again because it's over. You aren't my dad anymore, and if you ever come near me or Gabriel again, I'll kill you."

Gabriel came over and put his arm around me and said, "Let's go home now."

Learning How To Feel

Ripples of a sun tide
felt beneath my shallow footsteps
walking in a moonbeam
that throws shadows like the wind.
help me wind
help me warmth
help me learn how to feel
so I can know what it feels like.

Infinity's emotional equations
ripple through the life force
bending space and time
revealing absolute truths
within their absolute rhymes.
Help me Binary Stars
help me 1.4 solar masses
shoot Heaven's power
like an arrow into my heart.
Please shoot your arrow into my heart
so I can know what it feels like to feel once again.

Journal Entry 35
Thursday, October 4th
10 pm

Walls

Bust those hurtful walls into oblivion
ride lightning to new beginnings
leave those fears for others to remember,
you have nothing to hide any longer.

Remember the fountain of youth
where innocence was a normal feeling
where there was no pain or sadness
and no one to steel your soul?
Well we can live there again.

Do not linger where ignorance makes its home
only those who are blind
and those who have never known love

live within these walls
these walls of fear
and **Hate**
and the tides of darkness,
remember their names.

They've tried to destroy everything that is you and I
so we must build our dreams in our own way
build them as high as you can
and never live in fear or torment again.
Bust those walls of **Hate** *into oblivion.*

When Gabriel and I got to school this morning, we went through the usual gay bashing shit and sex come-ons by guys who want us to suck their dicks. I really thought this would get old or boring by now, but I guess these guys really wanna have a gay experience. It's stupid because they think they're being funny, but to me it shows how insecure they really are.

Well anyway, we walked through the main hallway where we had hung our posters yesterday, and most ofem had been written on or ripped right off the walls. Every single poster had been vandalized except the sketch I did of all of us together. It was still on the wall without a scratch on it. I went up to it to get a closer look because something was different about it. It was definitely different from when I'd sketched it yesterday. It was mad weird because there was this intense look coming from all of our eyes, and I didn't remember doing the eyes that way. I couldn't figure it out until Gabriel said something.

"We're alive in your sketch. Michael, how did you do it?"

"How did I do what?"

"Somehow you protected your drawing so no one could destroy it. This drawing has a soul. Very kool cute one."

"I did what?"

"Look at it closely. It has the ability to protect itself. That is so original," Gabriel said, as he looked down at a humungous pile of dust underneath it. He started laughing.

"Michael, can you hear them?"

"Can I hear who? What are you talking about?"

"Listen closely and you'll be able to hear them."

All of a sudden I could hear screams and crying coming from the dust pile on the floor.

"Who's screaming?" I asked, all panicky.

Gabriel explained what I'd done. "Anyone who tries to destroy your sketch is turned to dust. There are six little screaming thugs in this particular pile. Man, I didn't know you had this particular ability already. I'm very proud of you."

I looked at him totally shocked. "You mean I killed em just because they touched my drawing."

"No, no. You've just put them in a kind of a purgatory until you decide to judge them.

Very clever. I would never have thought of that. Michael, it's simple; you get to choose if they live or die."

"I will bring thee to ashes upon the earth."

Ezekiel 28:18

I was totally stunned as I listened to them scream and cry for their lives.

"They must be scared. I don't wanna hurtem over a drawing that's supposed to bring people together. How do I change them back?"

"Let me help you."

We walked down the hall a little ways, turned around, then Gabriel held my hand and told me to think of the words *"You Are Forgiven"* in my mind. As soon as I did that, all ofem transformed from dust back into their sad pathetic little selves. It was the weirdest thing to see them go from dust back to people. Two ofem were those Rican thugs who had me cornered in the stairwell pulling my hair and slapping me around during the first week of school. All ofem were crying as they ran out of the school as fast as they could.

"Michael, you let them see what absolute death feels like. I can tell you right now that we will never have a problem with them again."

As I stood there in shock, Principal Rodriguez came out of his office and motioned to us to come talk to him. For some reason he makes me nervous; I always think I've done something wrong. I hoped he hadn't seen what had just happened :/

"Hi guys. Can you come with me for a minute? I think both of you are going to find this interesting."

"Sure mister," I said, as we followed him. Gabriel had this big smile on his face for some reason, but I was scared we were in trouble. When we walked into his office, there was Luis, Anthony, and Donato standing next to a security cop. I didn't know what the fuck to think.

Mr. Rodriguez said to them, "Ok gentlemen, here they are as you requested. What is it that you want to say?" The whole thing was mad wack as Luis started talking.

"Miguel, Gabriel, I'm sorry for rippin your posters and throwin em on the floor an shit." Then Anthony and Donato said, "We're sorry for drawin crap on em and writin stupid shit. As soon as we did it we felt like shit, so we went to a security cop and tol em what we done."

I couldn't believe what was coming outta their mouths. Something wasn't right about this whole thing. Their faces had this pained look as they said they were sorry. It was like they couldn't stop themselves from apologizing and being nice. We accepted their apologies. Then Mr. Rodriguez said they'd be serving a week's detention for malicious destruction of school property, and that he was writing this incident up as a hate crime and emotional bullying.

"I'm filing a report with the Board of Education and the police department."

Luis said, "Good, we wanna be punished for what we done."

I couldn't believe he said that because he had just told me the other day that he was gunna hurt me real bad when he got the chance. I didn't know what the fuck was goin on.

Gabriel just kept smiling through the whole thing. We finally left the office and headed to our locker.

"What the fuck just happened in there?"

"Well, you know how you unknowingly gave your sketch certain powers to retaliate against hatred? Well so did I. After seeing that guy write those offensive words on the Love is Love poster yesterday, I decided that anyone who tried to desecrate or destroy our posters in any way would automatically confess what they had done to the principal or a security guard."

"Wow =D   Those guys must be so pissed off right now," I said, laughing.

"The posters will automatically go back to their original state and hang themselves back on the wall from now on. I want to see how many people are going to vandalize them. It should keep the office busy for a while." We both laughed.

The rest of school was great for a change.

It hurts to know the truth
that innocence can be taken away in the blink of an eye
like some forgotten promise
that it would never happen again
or that it would be our little secret.
It hurts to know
that what they did to me
stained my already wounded soul,
it was so long ago when I was young.

After school got out, I had to go talk to a lady social worker who's been assigned to my family's case. Gabriel was worried that me talking to her was gunna get me upset again, so he didn't want me to go.

"I need to do this. I need to talk about it so I can free my mind from all the bad stuff that's been eating away at me for years. I also wanna stop this kind of shit from happening to other people in the same situation. It'll be nice to know someone's finally on my side and understands the hell I've been through. Gabriel, I've been silent way to long, so what I gotta do now is start fighting back any way I can.

"I definitely understand what you're saying, but I just can't stand to see you in so much pain and feeling so sad. Do you want me to come with you?"

"I want you to be there, but at the same time I think I need to do this by myself."

"Are you sure?"

"Yeah, I gotta do this thing alone. I gotta stopped feeling so pissed off inside about stuff. I'm not gunna let my mom's old boyfriends get away with violating me, and I'm never gunna let anyone treat me like a piece of shit ever again. That includes my mom, my dad, or any assholes at school who think being gay is wack. I'll be all right…Hey…"

"What cute one."

"Do you know I love you more than anything?"

"Are you sure?"

"Yeah I'm sure. Thanks for being here for me. Go hang with C J and Hunter. I'll see you in a couple of hours."

Gabriel held me in his arms and kissed me nice. It made me feel all warm inside. That's all I needed to give me the courage to get everything out in the open.

† ↘

I was scared at first when I got to the social services office. I was mad nervous, but it felt good to finally be able to tell someone about what's been happening to me; how my mom and dad beat the shit outta me for years, and how my mom's boyfriends tried to have sex with me. All ofem made me feel dirty and less than human. They made me wish I was dead.

The look on the lady's face said it all as she looked at my black eyes, my bruised cut up face, and when I told her about all the stuff they did to me. Her name is Mary, and she was real nice. She tried to make me feel as comfortable as possible as I started spilling my guts out. I could tell by the look in her eyes that she'd heard this same story a million times from other teenagers who've been beat to shit and violated just like me.

"Miguel, are you comfortable enough to talk about what's been going on?"

I didn't say anything for a few seconds as I looked down at the floor trying to figuring out how to begin. "Yeah, I think so." Then it all started coming outta me with emotion I've never felt before. It felt like I'd been buried alive and was doing everything I could to dig myself out of the ground to get some air.

"I've been slowly dying my whole life until I met my boyfriend Gabriel, fell in love, and got away from my dad, my mom, and her boyfriends. My mom and dad drank and did lots of drugs when they lived together. They've never known how to control their lives or their emotions. It's like they always hated everything and blamed everyone but themselves for their problems.

When they lived together they always fought and hit each other because they never had enough money, or they were doing too many drugs, or didn't have jobs, or whatever bullshit excuse they had. Then they'd take it out on me because I guess I was the reason their lives sucked. My dad never liked me and always let me know it. I don't know how many times he told me to my face that I was a fuckin piece of shit and a fuckin mistake; as he put it, 'You was a great fuck gone wrong.' He'd hit me with his belt, one that had this huge buckle on it, and it would leave marks on my legs and butt. He'd also slap the shit outta me with his hand or fist. It hurt so much. As I would cry, he would laugh, and my mom would never say anything or even try to stop him. He would even punch me in the stomach when he got real angry. I always felt like I was gunna die because I couldn't catch my breath. He was smart about it though because he always made sure to hit me on the parts of my body where no one could see what the hell he was doin.

A couple of times Miss Martinez, my fifth grade teacher, talked to me and asked if my mom or dad ever hit me. She asked because she saw that I had some bruises on my arms once and choke marks on my neck another time, but I told her that me and some friends were playing in the street and I got pushed against a car, and the choke marks were from wrestling with my cousin. From that point on she watched me real close for the rest of the year.

Well anyway, one day my dad started calling me a queer and a pussy boy when I was around eight years old. I didn't know why he was sayin that stuff. Hell, I didn't even know what it meant at the time, but I knew it had to be bad. I could never figure out how he knew I was gay when I was little because I didn't even know it till I was around twelve, and even then I couldn't admit it to myself. Then one day he just left my mom, me and my sister. I was nine when he left, and it made me so happy that he was gone, even though I loved him and wanted him to love me back. I thought I wouldn't get yelled at or hit so much after that, but my mom easily made up for it in a hurry. I'd just hide in my bedroom as much as I could to be safe and be away from everything, but that didn't work out to well. She'd come into my room, yell and hit me whenever she was drunk or stoned."

I had to stop talking for a few minutes because I started crying for some reason. It felt good to be telling Mary all this stuff, so I did't know why I was crying, but I was crying so hard my stomach hurt, and I started getting a real bad headache.

"Miguel, it's all right. We can take a break for a few minutes. Take all the time you need."

I looked down at the floor thinking about how I was gunna tell her how my mom's boyfriends violated me. It was the hardest thing I ever had to do; that's when I grabbed the trash can and puked my guts out. I was crying and puking as Mary put her arm around my shoulder and gently rubbed my back.

"It's ok Miguel. It's ok. Everything is going to be all right."

After I was done throwing up, she gave me some tissue and water so I could get the puke taste outta my mouth.

"I feel like such an ass right now. I'm sorry I made your office smell so bad."

"It's ok. Just sit back and close your eyes for a few minutes. We can stop if you like."

"No, I don't want to. I need to get this all out, even if I puke up all my organs, I need to get it out," I told her, as I sat back and closed my eyes.

She took the trash can out and came back a few minutes later with a couple of sodas. I was glad of that because I was real thirsty.

"I think I'm ready to talk some more. I need to tell you about two of my mom's boyfriends. They violated me. They touched me and tried to have sex with me. I've never told anyone about this except Gabriel. The first time it happened was about three years ago. I was twelve when Jerel touched me. It was one of those crazy nights where my mom and him were gettin high and drunk. They had their stupid Latin music up real loud and I couldn't sleep because of all the noise they were making. Well my mom partied too hard and passed out. I was trying to hold my pee, but I finally had to go to the bathroom and saw her out of it on the couch as Jerel sat next to her smoking a blunt. He was toking and giving me this wack look as I walked by to go to the bathroom. I tried not to look at him cuzz I was afraid he was gunna yell at me like he would usually do. I made it back to my bedroom without him sayin anything and finally fell asleep.

But a little while later I woke up all of a sudden for some reason. It was like somethin was letting me know I was gunna get hurt. The hairs on my arms stood straight up as I lie there as still and quiet as I could. It was real quiet and I was hardly breathing. I was tryin my hardest to disappear. Then I heard the hallway floor squeaking as I heard footsteps slowly coming down the hall. It got quiet again for a couple minutes. I was so scared because I knew something bad was gunna happen to me. I heard footsteps again and could see a shadow in the dim light under my door. I knew it was him. Then I heard the door knob start turning as the door clicked open. Jerel slowly opened it as the door eerily squeaked, like it was warning me. He quietly walked in and closed the door behind him. I was so fuckin scared I didn't know what to do. I wanted to scream, but I knew my mom was out of it, so I pretended to be asleep, hoping that he'd go away, but he didn't. It felt like the whole world had stopped dead in its tracks and left me there to die. All I could hear was my fan going and his heavy breathing as he came closer to my bed. I could smell his stinky beer and weed breath as he leaned over my bed and stood there looking at me. I had my eyes closed as tight as I could, but I could still see him in my mind's eye, like I was having an out of body experience or something. I swear to fucking God I was tryin like mad to leave my body, but I just couldn't do it, so I rolled over to my side still pretending to be asleep as I started crying. And that's when I felt him touch my shoulder and arm with his filthy hand. He started slowly stroking my arm like he was petting an animal, and I was trembling in that dark tomb not knowing what was going to happen next. I tried to scream at the top of my lungs, but nothin came out. Then he kinda grabbed my arm and slowly pushed my body to make me lay on my back. I didn't have nothin on but my underwear as his hand slid across my chest and then down to my boxers. I was so scared that I peed myself and peed all over his hand as he touched my dick. He quickly moved his hand away and cursed at me saying, 'You fuckin little shit.' Then he stood up and left. As he was leaving I opened my eyes a little and saw that he was completely naked and his dick was hard. I started sobbing as I grabbed my pillow and put it over my face so he wouldn't hear me. I cried the rest of the night because he was still in the apartment. I lay there in my piss for hours not moving an inch because I was fucking scared that he was gunna come back and touch me again. I felt so cold and lonely as I stared up at the ceiling wanting to die.

But then all of a sudden I felt some kind of weird energy all around me. I thought I was goin fuckin crazy, but this energy, or thing, or whatever it was, calmed me down for some reason. It's hard to describe, but I knew something was in my room with me because my body started to feel warm. It felt like it was circling my bed protecting me. I know you think I'm crazy, but I think it saved me from being violated again that night.

I don't know what time I finally fell asleep, but when I woke up I changed my underwear, took off my sheets and tried to hide em so my mom wouldn't see that I peed my bed. Then I sat in the farthest corner of my bedroom and just stared at my door hoping Jerel was gone. A couple of weeks later my mom and him had a big fight, so he stopped coming over."

"Miguel, you were so brave. There are so many evil people in this world, and what Jerel did to you is the worst kind of evil. A lot of times the person who is being sexually abused thinks it is their fault. You know it wasn't your fault, don't you?"

"Yeah, I do now, but at the time I didn't know what to think. All I knew was that things didn't feel right from the first moment Jerel started comin over. I could always feel him looking at me even when I wasn't in the room, like he had x-ray eyes. I hated to be anywhere near him because he would call me out and argue so that I had to talk to him. He would always say, 'You isn't rep-sectin me boy, but you will real soon.' I knew what he meant; I could see it in his eyes."

"Did any of your mother's other boyfriends sexually violate you?"

"Yeah. About a year later. My mom had another boyfriend. Orlando was different from all of my mom's other boyfriends because he was like ten years younger than her. I think he was maybe like twenty or so. I really liked him because he was real nice to me and stuff.

He would take me to the movies, buy me any kind of food I wanted, and even play video games and wrestle with me and stuff when my mom was working. It was like having a big brother.

Well anyway, one day after school when my mom was wor-kin and my sister was at her friend's house, Orlando came over to watch TV with me. We were sitting on the couch laughing at a show we were watching, when all of a sudden he started to tickle me. Then we started to wrestle like we usually did, but this time it was different because he got on top of me and I could feel his hard dick against my body. He was pressing his dick against me and rubbing it on me. He had me pinned down so I couldn't move, and he was tryin to kiss me on the lips, and I was yelling for him to get the fuck off of me, but he wouldn't let me up. He was kissing my neck as I tried and tried to get out from under him. Then he tried to take my jeans off, and that's when I started kicking him and screaming at the top of my lungs. All of a sudden he got off me and I saw that his jeans were down to his knees and his dick was sticking out of his boxers. He pulled his jeans up real quick and told me if I ever said anything to my mom, he'd kill me. Then he left.

I ran to my bedroom and locked the door, then I hid under my bed and cried. I never told my mom or anyone what happened because I knew he'd kill me."

"What happened after that?"

"He came over a few more times over the next month, but didn't come near me. And then he finally broke up with my mom."

All of a sudden I started crying hard again and couldn't stop. Mary came over and put her arm around my shoulder telling me everything would be all right. She let me cry.

Mary wants me to come back in a couple of weeks so we can talk some more.

Friday Morning 3am

Hey, It's Only Me
I've fallen in my dreams
I've ripped at all my seams
You've tried to see me there
But I'm not anywhere
Hey, it's only me
Hey, it's only me.

You've reached into my soul
And tried to steal it all
You think you're almost there

But you're not anywhere
Hey, it's only me
Hey, it's only me.

Time will show
That I was the one who really cared
Rip at my seams
Open me up
I don't mind.
Hey, it's only me
   Hey, it's only me
      Hey, it's only me
         Hey, it's only me

Sometimes when my mind starts floating away, I close my eyes and fall back into my nightmare life where my flesh was being violated to the point where I was rotting away like raw meat that's been left on the kitchen counter for days.

I'm hiding in the shadows so they can't find me, but I got nowhere to go, nowhere to hide, except under the bed where all the monsters live, and they try to make me bleed too.

Then I see those human hands reaching under the bed trying to grab me, and those dirty hands are grabbing and pulling, and the monsters are clawing my skin and pulling, and I'm screaming as my body starts ripping apart. I can see the pool of blood oozing out from under the bed, knowing that half of my body belongs to the monsters, and half to the humans; no difference really. Then I open my eyes and look at the ceiling fan going round and round as Gabriel lies next to me with his arms hugging and protecting me.

"Are you all right Michael? I know it must be painful."

"Yeah, I'm ok. I need to remove this stuff from my mind, and the only way I know how is to face it head-on. It's making me stronger because I'm learning how to forgive."

Journal Entry 36
Friday, October 5th
9 pm

It's been a crazy week O__o   I can't believe everything that's happened, but I think things are getting better; at least I hope so.

Had Drama Club after school today, and we had a blast rehearsing lines for the play. Jacob was bein all corny doing all this overacting drama stuff. It was mad funny =D

Then Roberto and Jennifer started acting all crazy too. They pretended to be little kids fighting over a candy bar as they yelled back and forth, "That's mines, no that's mines, no that's mines," and tryin to get it from each other. =p

Gabriel helped me rehearse some lines for one of the characters I might get to play.

Can't wait to see which part I get. I just hope I don't have too much to memorize.

Miss Linda got pizza and soda for us, which was very kool because everyone's always hungry like every hour of the day..lol

We talked and laughed about crazy stuff as we ate. I was even hungry for once. Maybe I'll finally gain some weight :/

Roberto came over and sat next to me as we ate. I really like him; he's such a nice guy. Roberto didn't say anything at first; he just quickly turned his head and smiled at me like he was being shy or something, which is totally not like him at all. I was glad he felt comfortable being around me though, because I've made a lot more enemies this week now that everyone knows I'm a gay boy.

It hasn't been an easy week. My face and body are proof of that :/

So there I was with Roberto on one side and Gabriel on the other. All of a sudden Roberto turns to me again and asks if I'd like to go over to his house after rehearsal and hangout.

"Miguel, you wanna come over and play video games when we're done here? I got the latest Xbox game, From Dust. It's mad kool cuzz you get to be a god. You know, you get to play God and you control the destiny of the world. You can really fuck it up if you want, or make it a paradise. It's your choice," He said, with this huge grin on his face.

I kinda did a quick look over to Gabriel for a second to see he reaction.

"That sounds awesome, but I can't today, I got some stuff I gotta do."

Roberto's smile quickly disappeared. But then Gabriel said, "Miguel, that sounds like fun.

You guys should hang today." I looked at him totally stunned because we haven't really been apart since he came to be with me.

"Are you sure? Weren't we gunna, ya know... :/ "

"No, it's all right, we can do that later. I was going to go hang with CJ and Hunter in the Village in a little while anyway."

I gave him this discreet look like what the fuck is goin on? Was he tryin to get rid of me because he's already sick of me? Man, I got mad insecure all of a sudden.

Then Gabriel started communicating with me through our minds.

"Go have some fun cute one. I have something important I have to do with CJ and Hunter, something you can't help us with because you haven't fully transformed yet. I'll explain it all to you later. You know I love you, so go have fun."

"Ok, but I'm gunna really miss you."

Then I turned to Roberto and said, "Yeah, I'd love to hang."

"Kool. Can't wait to show you the game." His smile returned.

After rehearsal was over, we walked out to the street and hung out by the graffiti covered wall near the subway entrance for a while. We were bullshitting about what Jacob's friend Amado put on Facebook the other night. Amado posted that he had snuck into his living room after his mom and dad went to sleep and watched some hot sex on the porn channel they secretly subscribe to. He was laughing about it because they think he doesn't know about it ;p

Well Amado and three of his friends were posting stuff about naked women and jerking off and stuff. Then some girls they know saw his wall and posted that they were being gross immature assholes. Then Amado posts back, "You bitches can come over and help us jerk off anytime."

It's kinda funny and sad all at the same time what some people write on their wall O__o

Well anyway, Gabriel was ready to take off, so he kissed me all sexy nice in front of everyone. Jacob said, "Look at the hot emo boys makin out. Let me take a video of you guys kissing!"

Gabriel smiled and said, "Ok, no problem." I looked at him weird for a second and then smiled back. Jacob took out his iPhone and said, "GO"

We started kissing again as everyone watched. Jacob was slowly walking all around us getting as many angles as he could as we kissed and touched each other. I was gettin so fucking worked up that I lifted up Gabriel's t-shirt and gently caressed his stomach and chest. I wanted to get naked with him right there on the sidewalk. OMG it was so hot as our tongues danced together for everyone to see. I was licking his snake bites and those full pouty lips like there was no tomorrow ;p It was so sexy hot kissing Gabriel like that in front of all my friends. I don't know how long we kissed, but we slowly stopped and just looked into each other's eyes for the longest time.

I thought to myself how I wished everyone could know what real love feels like.

"Man, that was hot," Jacob said. All the girls were smiling at us with this 'awe that's so cute look' in their eyes. "I'm puttin this on YouTube; cute emo guys makin out. Smokin hot."

Gabriel gave me one last kiss and said, "I'll see you tonight," and then started walking down the street. I watched him go into a crowd and disappear. When I turned around and looked back at Roberto, I noticed that he looked real sad.

"Are you all right? Is anything wrong? I asked.

I was thinking that he probably thought it was gross to see two guys making out.

"Na, I'm ok. You ready to have some fun?"

"Yeah! I haven't played any video games in like forever. From Dust sounds mad kool."

We said goodbye to everyone and started walking to Roberto's apartment.

As we walked, I thought how strange it felt not to be with Gabriel. It felt like I was lost or something. But it was also very kool getting to know Roberto better. Normally he has a certain way of talking where he kinda puts up this invisible shield so people can't get to know him well. It's the same thing I've been doing for years, but I could tell he was just being himself with me. He started talking about what had happened to me last weekend.

"I'm sorry about you getting hurt after coming out to your mom. She really sounds like one fucked up bitch. Don't take that wrong, but she really has to be fucked up to do that to you."

"Yeah, it wasn't too good what happened. My mom has shit loads of stuff wrong with her.

I thought she was gunna kill me. I had to put a chair under the doorknob to jam the fucking door so she couldn't get at me again. Then the cops came and busted the door open and found me lying on the floor all bloody and beat to shit. Blood was all over the floor, on my bed sheets, furniture, and even on a lot of my sketches. She broke my nose, which made me bleed all over the fucking place. Man, I don't know how many times she punched me in the face. Shit, I couldn't even feel nothing after a few punches. She even smashed my mirror to shit too. After a while, some ambulance guys came into my bedroom with this rolling bed thingy and lifted me onto it. They looked around my room with these real sad looks on their faces, then they looked at me and said I was gunna be ok. They wheeled me into the living room where they had my mom in handcuffs. She was yelling all sorts of nasty shit at the cops. My sister was crying and came running to me thinking I was dead or something. I told her as best I could that I was gunna be ok, but she was grabbing onto the side of the bed and wouldn't let go. The ambulance guy said she could come with me to the hospital. She calmed down because we could stay together. It was one fucked up night to say the least. I don't ever wanna go through that again."

"Well, I think you were brave doing what you did, you know, coming out to the whole school, and to your mom. I know I could never do that."

"Yeah, I guess. It's just that I got tired of it all. I was tired of feeling ashamed just because I'm gay. But ya know, it's the best thing I've ever done because now I can just be me. You could do it too if you were gay. You have so much confidence; I wish I had more. I'm still mad shy and get nervous about all sorts of stuff." Roberto didn't say too much after that.

No one was home when we got to Roberto's apartment. He said his mom and dad work all kinds of crazy hours and he doesn't have any brothers or sisters, so he's by himself a lot.

"What's it like being an only child?" I asked.

"It sucks. I wish I had like seven brothers and sisters so my mom and dad would let me breathe once in a while. They're always after me to do my homework and telling me what to do all the time. They even try to tell me what to read an shit. I get like straight A's and that seems like it still isn't good enough for em. I fuckin hate it sometimes because I'm afraid that if I breathe the wrong way they'll get into my shit. They wanna plan my whole fucking life out, but I'm not gunna let em. My dad is way over the top most of the time. I get the feeling he's trying to compete with me for some reason. I don't get it."

We got some chips and sodas from the kitchen and then went to his bedroom to set the game up. As Roberto was messing around with the wires, I asked, "What's it like to be so smart? It's like you know everything and aren't afraid to say what's on your mind in class to make your point. It's mad kool what you do. I wish I could be more like that."

"Thanks, but I don't think I'm that smart. It's just easy for me to remember stuff, and I like to read all sorts of shit I find interesting. I love reading about mythology and anything supernatural. That's why I'm into Japanese anime and the Greek gods and all the hero stuff in video games. I kinda wish they were real because life gets so boring sometimes. It's like it connects me to this world like nothing else can. I know I probably sound like a total jerk off geek, but it's who I am, and I don't give a shit what anybody else thinks. That's why I always get my ass in trouble; I say what's on my mind, and most people don't like that. But I'm gunna tell the truth no matter who it hurts, even though it ends up hurting me most of the time. I can see the fucking games people play. I'm always thirty steps in front ofem, and they don't have a fucking clue.

People are so fucking stupid it makes me laugh. I'm so bored at school because no one ever challenges me. Most of the teachers hate my guts because I won't shut up, and I always know the answers to their questions. But Atwood's kool. I think he's the first teacher that actually likes me. He knows when I'm playing around with the whole class with my wack sense of humor, and I think he likes it when I do that because I always see him smile when the rest of the class doesn't have a clue what I'm doing. He actually gets it. You know what I mean?"

"Yeah, Atwood's kool. He helped me with coming out, and he helped get the GSA club going."

It was kool that Roberto was telling me stuff that probably none of his other friends know about him. We finally started playing From Dust. It was awesome! We decided to be two competing gods for the same world, and things got intense. Roberto was trying to fuck it up, and I was trying to make it a paradise. He had armies with all these hi-tech weapon systems taking over country after country as I tried to use logic to reason with his leaders. He fucking took over the world in no time because as Roberto said, "The guy with the biggest toys always kicks ass. Your reasoning is only gunna get you killed every time Miguel. You should know that by now."

I really sucked at this game, but I was still having a great time.

Then things got real serious because Roberto told me something that really surprised me.

After we finished playing, we started watching this Anime

called Death Note. I sat next to him on the floor eating potato chips trying to figure out the basic plot. A couple of minutes into the show Roberto turned to me and said, "Miguel, can I tell you something? And will you promise not to get mad at me for what I'm gunna say?"

My mouth was full of chips, so I tried to swallow them fast so I could talk.

"Yeah, I won't get mad. Why would I get mad at you?"

Then he kinda cleared his voice in a nervous way and looked me in the eyes.

"Miguel, I'm bi. You know, bisexual, and I have a huge crush on you. I really like you a lot and was hoping that you might like me too. I know you and Gabriel are boyfriends, but I really like you and was hoping you might give me a chance."

I was totally shocked and didn't know what to say. I just kinda stared at him for a few seconds. Then I got it together. "I really like you too, but I really like Gabriel a lot and I don't think we're gunna break up anytime soon."

Roberto got this real sad look on his face when I said that; I think I hurt his feelings.

"I think you're a really cute guy, and if there was no Gabriel in my life, I'd definitely wanna be your boyfriend because I think we have a lot in common. I hope you're not mad at me. You're one of the nicest guys I've ever met." I leaned over and gave him a hug, then I kissed him on the cheek because it looked like he was gunna cry. He looked at me with his sad brown eyes.

"I'm not mad at you, I could never be mad at you Miguel. Please don't be mad at me. I still wanna be friends with you and with Gabriel too. He's lucky to have you, I hope you know that."

"I'm lucky I met him, and I'm lucky to have you as a friend."

"Miguel, I've never been able to tell anyone I'm bi, but I knew I could tell you because you'd understand. It feels good to be able to be myself for even just a few minutes. I feel so stupid right now. I'm sorry, please don't hate me."

I felt so bad for him because I knew exactly what he was going through. People like us always have to hide. "I don't hate you. It makes me feel good that you like me that way. I like it that you're honest about stuff. It must have been hard for you tell me, but I'm glad you did. I won't say anything to anybody if you don't want me to."

"Thanks. I don't think I'm ready to come out. Everything about this is just so fucking complicated, I hate it."

"Roberto, I just want you to know that I'm here for you anytime, and so is Gabriel."

I gave him another hug, and then things got serious real fast; I kissed him on the lips, and it was for more than a few seconds. My emotions were all over the place when I finally stopped and looked him in the eyes. He looked kinda shocked for a second, but then smiled that beautiful smile of his.

"Thank you for liking me. It means a lot," I whispered.

I had my arm around him as his head fell against my chest. We didn't say anything for a long time, and it was nice. I was trying to take away some of his sadness and some of my guilt.

I decided to give him a little part of who I am so he could feel the love I feel. I transferred some of my energy into him, and when I did this, his whole body got real warm and started glowing. He slowly lifted his head up and looked at me weird for a second, and then smiled, like he knew exactly what I was doing.

It was a special moment I'll never forget.

I Wish You Could See
We live in such a sad and deceitful world
where we have to pretend to be happy and brave
showing no fear on the outside
but shivering from a cold heartless world on the inside
as we desperately try to find connections that are real.

I've lost my family forever because of what I am
just because I told the truth
but it was time to be the real me
instead of some shallow carbon entity
that once walked in the shadows of Hell.

My friend is now trying to be who he really is
and he is reaching out for my love
and I hope he can feel the love I have for him
because he is connected to me.
It's just the real him and the real me
that's the way it was always meant to be.

Why must we hide behind the cloak of intolerance?
The real him and the real me aren't as bad as it seems
I wish you could see.

After I left Roberto's apartment, I decided to walk home instead of taking the train because I needed to think about some stuff. I'm getting scared about how my life is gunna change soon.

I don't think I wanna leave all of this behind; I love being human. I don't know how I'm gunna deal with the change, or if I even want it to happen. Man, I'm just so confused right now.

It was nice to walk and be by myself for a little while.

I finally made it home, and just as I rounded the corner to the apartment building, Gabriel appeared out of nowhere, put his arms around me, and kissed me.

"Michael, I really missed you."

I held him in my arms as tight as I could and kissed him for the longest time.

"I missed you so much," I said, as I started to cry.

"Michael, what's wrong? What happened?"

I felt so overwhelmed as Gabriel held me. "Everything is just so fucking confusing. My family's disappeared, I'm an angel and have to save the world, like I can save the world when I can't even deal with my own life right now. I'm no hero Gabriel. I'm just a guy who's trying to make it in this world, and I'm being told I can't be human anymore. Why can't I be both?"

"Michael, it's ok to have these feelings. It's all new to you. We'll figure it out, so don't be upset. Let's go inside and get something to eat, and then we can relax and talk."

My Wish
I am crying
knowing that I have to leave this world

and I don't want to leave
because I'm still human
even though I have wings.

But I guess I must learn to see
and look a little closer
because we all have wings
and we can fly as far as we dare
as far as our love will take us.

My wish is for you to see
that we are all humans who have wings.
And one day
each one of you will realize this
and each one of you will be free.

We were snuggled up on the couch after dinner with the lights down low. Gabriel had this awesome song on called High Hopes by Pink Floyd. It sounded so sad. I connected with the words even though I didn't know what they meant exactly. The guy's voice was so emotional that I actually stopped kissing Gabriel and listened to him sing. Gabriel explained the meaning.

"The lyrics reveal an important truth about this world. It's about the loss of innocence people once had in their childhood. You know, the freedom to dream and imagine and just be a kid. But then as they grow up, it's taken all away by of the realities of life. Most people end up conforming because it is easier; it's their way of hiding from one's true potential."

"That's what is so fucked up. Society tries to make us into something we're not," I said, angrily.

"Yeah, but people do have a choice not to conform or give in. Think about Einstein and Beethoven and Shakespeare and others throughout history. They changed the course of history because they conformed to nothing but their own passions."

We continued listening to the rest of the song as I lay back and put my head in Gabriel's lap with my eyes closed. I kept them closed as I started quietly telling him about what happened at Roberto's.

"Roberto came out to me today. He told me he's bisexual, and that he likes me, and wants me to be his boyfriend. I felt so bad for him because I know what it's like to feel that way and not be able to do anything about it. It's always so fucking complicated for some reason."

Gabriel was gently stroking my hair. I opened my eyes and saw him smiling at me.

"What did you say to him?"

"I told him it was nice that he liked me, and that he felt comfortable enough to tell me. I also said that if you weren't my boyfriend that I would want him to be my boyfriend. Then I hugged and kissed him twice because he looked so sad. I hope you're not mad at me."

"Why would I be mad at you Michael? You did the right thing. It must have been very hard for Roberto to tell you how he felt. I knew he liked you a couple of weeks ago when we went

64

to our first Drama Club meeting. He kept staring at you when he thought no one was looking. I thought it was cute because I could see he had a huge crush on you.

You know something? You're starting to change the world already because you made Roberto feel like he could be himself. He didn't have to hide because he knew you'd understand. This is why we're here."

"Yeah, I think this is the way it's supposed to happen. But how do we get everyone to do that without letting the world know we're angels? You wanna know something else? I wanted to tell Roberto who we are in the worst way because I felt like I wasn't being truthful with him, but I held back. I wanted to talk to you about it first. Do you think it would be all right to tell him?"

"I don't think we should do that just yet, but if you had told him, he would have believed you. I can tell that Roberto is a guy who understands more than most people.

As we talked, my phone started buzzing. I took it out of my pocket to see who it was. It was Jacob, so I answered it.

"Hey you hot emo boy! I did something really bad, and I feel terrible about it. You know that video I took of you guys kissing today? Well it's goin crazy ass viral with like six thousand hits in the last hour alone. It's had over thirty thousand hits since I posted it this afternoon.

It's mad crazy. Everyone on YouTube is commenting how hot it is, but someone at school saw it and put the video on Facebook, and now a bunch of assholes are putting wack comments about you guys bein gross faggots and how they're gunna kick your ass when they see you at school on Monday. I'm so sorry I put it online. Please forgive me Miguel. I never meant for this to hurt you. I really like you guys, you're my best friends."

"It's ok Jacob, don't worry about it. Everything's gunna be all right." Gabriel just smiled and said, "I guess we're celebrities now."

Jacob was really upset. "I'll help you fight anyone who tries to hurt you."

There was silence for a few seconds. "Are you still there?" I asked.

"Yeah, I'm here. I need to tell you something."

Then he told me what I already knew. "Miguel, I'm a gay boy too. I wanted to tell you as soon as you came out, but I was afraid. I don't wanna hide anymore either, and I have you to thank."

Wow! I couldn't believe what was happening; two of my best friends came out on the same day.

It made me feel like everything was gunna be ok =D

Journal entry 37
Sunday, October 6th
8 am

A lotta stuff was on my mind last night and I needed Gabriel, CJ, and Hunter to help me figure some of it out. I kept thinkin bout everything that's been happening to us at school, my dad trying to take me away from Gabriel, what happened with Roberto, and all the changes my body's been going through. Everything's changing faster than I can deal with right now, and I need help.

Something else also happened that I really like; I haven't felt sleepy at all. You know, I don't need to sleep anymore. I'm never tired. Me and Gabriel just lay in bed and talk and make love; that's been the best thing so far.

He says angels don't need to sleep. He just puts himself in a dream-like state of meditation with his eyes closed. "Meditation helps me stay in harmony with celestial energy. Michael, this is what you are starting to experience. We don't require the same things the human body needs in order to survive. We can exist within our own energy, so we never need to sleep. There is no physical depletion of energy and no boundaries within our existence."

"I'm glad we have no boundaries because I wanna stay here until we fix this place once and for all. I want the world to be everything it was supposed to be, and I know the four of us can make it happen."

"I know we can Michael, that's why you were reborn as a human. You understand more than anyone else the pain and suffering people have to live with every day. You have had to sacrifice your life to better understand what needs to be done. You were also chosen because you are the most important angel that has ever existed, and I'm the luckiest angel in existence because you chose to love me.

"No, you got it all wrong. I'm the lucky one. Nothing would matter to me if we weren't together."

It must of been around 2 am or so. We were lying in bed kissing and getting all sexy, but my mind was going like a thousand miles a second, and I couldn't stop it. Gabriel could tell I wasn't really into making love. "What's on your mind Michael?"

"I wanna go flying. I thought we could fly around the city and see some stuff, then go see my sister, and then hang with CJ and Hunter. I'm getting these strange feelings, and I can't figure out why. I think all of us need to be together right now."

"That sounds like fun. We need to talk to them about Anthony and Donato. And you also need to know what we were doing yesterday while you and Roberto were hanging out."

"Yeah, I meant to ask you about that. You had me all confused, but I'm happy the way things turned out."

"I'm sorry for the mystery, but I knew you'd have a great time with Roberto. Whether you know it or not, hanging out together is important for both of you," Gabriel said, with this serious but empathetic look.

"Yeah, I agree. Let's go to the Village today. I want Roberto to come with us. He needs to be with us too. I know It's important. Does that make any sense?"

"Yeah, it does. I'm feeling the same thing you are. We all need to get to know each other a bit more intimately. Inbox Roberto and see if he can come with us, and then let's go flying."

"Kool. Hey, we might as well see what people have been posting about our video on Facebook. I also wanna see if we're still getting lots of hits on YouTube..lol I feel bad because Jacob's so upset."

I checked out YouTube first and saw that we had over one hundred thousand hits. I was shocked to say the least. =) I guess people like to watch emo boys make out..lol

Then I went on Facebook and found all sorts of shitty comments about us, which is typical for the Bronx. I decided to check Maya's page and couldn't believe it, she actually attached a link to our video on her wall with some stupid gay bashing jokes. She had like over three hundred comments from people at school about it too. The first two were from her and Luis.

She wrote, "Gay jokes aren't funny. I mean, cum on guys."

Then Luis wrote, "Gay jokes aren't funny, butt fuck it."

It was cruel what they were posting. It doesn't feel too good reading that stuff, but I'm learning how not to care so much. They got the problem, not me. I went back on YouTube and read some of the comments there. Lots of people posted nice things about us sayin we were cute and stuff. It's nice to know so many people from all over the world are on our side and like the video.

"You know Michael, even though some people are posting ignorant comments, we are making an important impact at school because we are getting the issue of discrimination against gay people out in the open. It's going to be a battle though because insecure people try and make themselves feel better by knocking down others who are perceived as weak or different. We scare the hell out of them because we are being honest. It's that simple.

"Yeah, I know exactly what you're saying. I see how insecure and scared people are at school whenever I try to look them in the eyes. I can't believe so many straight people are afraid of gay people. We have to figure out some way to deal with all the negative stuff that I can actually smell on those thugs who really do wanna hurt us."

"Michael, you're right, they are afraid. But I'm afraid too because you could get hurt. So I have to do everything in my power to make sure nothing happens to you until you've fully transformed. Let's go see CJ and Hunter and plan this thing."

"I'll call Roberto in the morning to see if he wants to hang."

Without saying another word, we flew to see my sister and then to Greenwich Village.

THE FOUR CORNERS OF EARTH

It's mad kool to see the city from the sky, and to be able to fly all on my own.

When we got to CJ's, both of them were waiting for us. We hugged and then went out on the terrace so they could scan the universe. I'm starting to see stuff a long ways away now, so I was trying with all my might to figure out where Lucifer was. I couldn't see him, but I could feel his presence, and so could the guys.

I was getting a little frustrated trying to see stuff, so Gabriel came over and put his arm around me and told me not to worry. Then he suggested that CJ and Hunter should come live with us and transfer to our school. I really liked that idea because we would finally be together.

"We will use this apartment for human interaction and as a second front when the time comes to do battle," Hunter said, as he kept scanning the universe.

He's really scary sometimes because he's so quiet and intense. He has this look about him where you know he could kill at any second. He wants to destroy anything evil.

CJ said that sounded like a great idea. "Yeah, I've been pretty bored at school lately waiting for you two to get your honeymoon over with. We need to be together to take care of the business we were sent here to do."

So it was all settled within a matter of minutes about what we needed to do.

Ω Σ

11:50 pm

Roberto was psyched that I wanted him to hang with us. He said he'd been thinking about me all night because of what had happened between us. We had a nice talk, which made both of relax about stuff. He came over around noon and had lunch with us before we headed to the Village. When Gabriel answered the door, and I could tell Roberto was nervous.

"Hey Gabriel," he said, looking down at the floor, and then shyly at him.

"Hi Roberto, I'm really happy you came over," Gabriel said, giving him a hug.

Roberto looked over Gabriel's shoulder at me; I gave him a big smile and then hugged both of them together. Roberto knew what it meant because he whispered, "Thanks Gabriel. Thank you Miguel, I really need this right now." It was nice because we knew everything was good between us.

Gabriel introduced his mom to Roberto, and then we went into the living room to talk and listen to some music. Gabriel's mom insisted that she make lunch for us. Roberto was looking around at all the nice furniture and electronic stuff everywhere. "This place is sick."

Gabriel thanked him for the compliment.

After we ate, we headed to the Village to see the guys. I was a little worried because CJ and Hunter can be intimidating as hell when they wanna be, but I was sure Roberto could hold his own with them. He couldn't believe it when we got to their apartment building on 5th Avenue. Roberto just shook his head and laughed, "Man, do I feel poor."

"Hey, don't worry about it. They're just like us really, except they have rich parents, that's the only difference. They're real nice guys. You're gunna like em a lot," I said.

It was funny to see Roberto being so quiet as we rode the elevator up to the seventeenth floor. We could hear music coming from the apartment as we walked down the hall. Just as Gabriel was just about to knock, the double doors opened automatically. CJ and Hunter were in the living room fencing. It was O D kool cuzz they were really going at it. They said hi to us and started cracking jokes about being ninjas in a video game as their swords were intensely flying around each other. I still can't believe how good they are with those things. =D

Roberto had the biggest smile on his face as he watched. Gabriel put his arm around me and smiled knowing Roberto was already having a great time watching them battle each other. They finally stopped and called a draw. CJ and Hunter took their gear off as Roberto looked around the apartment amazed. He slowly walked over to the picture window and stood there looking out at the city. CJ walked over to Roberto and asked if he liked the view. He shook his head up and down.

"My name's CJ. You must be Roberto. It's nice to meet you."

"Hey CJ, nice to meet you too."

"Lemme show you around." He took Roberto on a tour of the apartment and then out to the terrace. This gave Gabriel and Hunter a chance to tell me what they were up to yesterday.

Hunter kind of paced the living room for a few seconds and then started telling me everything.

"Michael, you're in a lot of danger right now because you are still part human; I'm very angry about this. I went to see God to ask why he won't let you transform back into an archangel immediately. I'm pissed off about what he's been doing to you, because if we aren't resourceful enough, you could be destroyed. Well, do you know what he told me? He just calmly said that Gabriel, CJ, and I know what we need to do to protect you until the time is right. I just don't get him sometimes. It's like he plays these little games with us to see where our breaking point is. He really makes me angry."

Man, I've never seen Hunter this mad before. His eyes were glowing like supernovas as his pupils changed to glowing white light. Gabriel asked him to calm down before he blew up the whole apartment building. Hunter's eyes were glowing and glaring at us, but then finally returned to normal.

"Hunter, thanks for protecting me and for talking to him. I'm angry too, but I know I have to accept what's happening even if I don't understand everything yet."

"No problem Michael, that's what we're here for. I promise to do everything I can to protect you, even though you may not agree with how I occasionally do it."

"Thanks," I said, wondering what he meant by that comment.

Then Gabriel said that I'm being protected with Metatron Cubes. They strategically placed them around the Milky Way, the Solar System, and the Earth while I was hanging with Roberto yesterday.

I still don't really know how they work, but I know they are powerful things.

As we talked, CJ and Roberto were out on the terrace

talking. I wondered what they were talking about because it looked like they were having a serious conversation.

I hoped CJ wasn't scaring Roberto in some way. Gabriel decided to tap into their conversation so we could listen. What they were talking about shocked me and excited me all at the same time. I got pretty emotional as I listened; they made me feel so loved.

"How did you meet Miguel and Gabriel?"

"They came to a Drama Club meeting one day and decided to join. Both ofem scared the shit outta me cuzz you know, they're a little weird looking. I had never seen people like them up close. But something strange happened. I couldn't stop looking at em, especially Miguel, and I started feeling emotions inside of me that I couldn't understand or control. I don't know how to explain it, but it was mad weird the whole time they were there. I couldn't take my eyes of Miguel, and it felt good to be near him. Man, I don't know, but I feel intense things whenever we're together."

"I can see you like him a lot."

Roberto looked away kind of sad after CJ said that.

"You like Miguel, don't you?" Roberto didn't say anything again, he just looked out at the city.

"Do you love him?"

Roberto slowly turned and looked CJ in the eyes. "Yeah, I do. I love him a lot. I've never met anyone like him. He gives me goose bumps whenever I'm near him. I love everything about him.

He's quiet and shy. I love the way his bangs cover his eyes, and when he smiles, it makes me wanna be with him forever.

You probably think I'm fucking crazy cuzz we only just met, but I really love him and I don't know what to do about it because he loves Gabriel."

"I understand where you're coming from because I love Miguel too."

CJ shocked me when he said that. I watched CJ and Roberto stare at each other in silence. Then I looked at Gabriel and Hunter totally confused. I didn't know CJ liked me like that. Hunter whispered, "Keep listening."

"Roberto, you need to know that Miguel is a very special person. There's really no one else like him in this world. You need to know that. He possesses love and truth in a very special way. You can feel it whenever you're near him. The reason why you love him is because you have many of the same qualities he has. That makes you special too. But the thing is, he loves Gabriel with all his heart. He loves us too, but just in a different way. They were meant to be together, and we have to accept this reality even though it hurts. So if you love him as much as I do, you can't put any pressure on him to be your boyfriend. Do you think you can do that?"

Roberto didn't respond to the question.

They made me feel special with what they were saying, but I told Gabriel I didn't wanna listen anymore. He apologized. "CJ is just trying to help Roberto deal with his intense feelings for you because he's in the same situation."

Gabriel kissed the tears on my face and then hugged me nice. I wondered if he was mad because CJ and Roberto have those kinds of feelings for me, but Gabriel just smiled.

"Michael, whether you know it or not, you have this effect that makes everybody have intense feelings for you. They either love you or are afraid of you. There seems to be no middle ground."

CJ and Roberto came back into the great room a few minutes later. Both ofem were smiling, so that made me relax. CJ put some music on and then ordered Chinese food. I asked Roberto if he wanted to play video games, and of course he said yeah, so we hooked up CJ's Wii and the four of us spent the afternoon and evening listening to The Beatles, Young The Giant, and Green Day as we played Smash Bros. =D

Journal entry 38
Sunday, October 7th
11pm

Sometimes the world takes you on roller coaster rides
that twist and turn and spin you upside down
then dives from a perfect infinite sky
back to earth speeding towards the ground
pulling up at the very last second
just to let you know that you are still alive.
You ride to those moments in your mind
and look with new eyes
at places you've always been able to feel
but just could never see.

Have you ever had those moments where you know things are gunna be ok? Or those times where nothing needs to be said to someone you love, and they understand?

That's what I really liked about yesterday when we hung out at CJ's.

We were playing video games shoulder to shoulder having a blast as all of us battled to win. At one point I looked at everyone and thought how lucky I was to have these guys in my life. I actually stopped playing for a few seconds to take it all in so I'd remember the moment forever.

Here was the kool thing; all ofem suddenly turned and looked at me at the same time and smiled because they knew what I was thinking; Even Roberto seemed to know too. He bumped my shoulder for me to keep playing =D

I smiled back and played for a few more minutes, then got up and went out to the terrace because I was getting emotional. Sorry, I'm just real sensitive right now. I know I sound like a big baby :'/ but I can't help it.

"What's wrong with Miguel? Is he all right?" Roberto asked, as I closed the sliding glass door behind me.

"He's fine. He's just happy we are all together and having fun. It means a lot to him," Gabriel said. "Miguel just wants to be alone right now. He's been through a lot in the last week, but he'll be ok, just give him a few minutes." Roberto had this concerned look on his face, but I turned and smiled at him from the terrace, and he kinda smiled back with a questioning look.

It was nice to stand outside and look at the city as the wind hit my face. It made me feel connected. I looked down at the park and watched little kids, parents, and teenagers talking and laughing and bonding like they're supposed to. I could also hear a couple of musicians playing a guitar and a cello; it was nice because it seemed like I was listening to a soundtrack for what I was watching. Seeing all of this from high above made me appreciate the little moments of my life that have made me who I am, I just wish I had more of the good ones before I change.

After a while, I watched the guys through the glass doors having fun, and I knew how lucky I was. It felt good to put stuff in the right place.

The other thing I liked about yesterday was the train ride home. Gabriel was holding my hand and Roberto was kind of tired; none of us said anything. It seemed like we were in a dream-like state as the train wheels made this rhythmic sound as it went down the tracks. It actually put Roberto to sleep. His head fell against my shoulder, which made me smile because I knew he was comfortable being with us, and I knew he was gunna be all right. Gabriel kissed my cheek and then put his head on my other shoulder for the rest of the way home. These are moments that are the most important to me because they are real.

Ok. Today was one of those days that were kinda crazy. It's like one emotional thing after another, and I'm wondering when this shit's gunna stop O__o

Everything started off wavy because CJ and Hunter had finally moved in with us. It was O D the way it happened. We were in our bedroom listening to music and talking about the GSA meeting coming up this week, when all of a sudden we heard some banging and stuff in the guest room.

Gabriel smiled. "I think they're here."

Then Hunter and CJ walked through the wall, smiled at us, and asked how it was going.

THE FOUR CORNERS OF EARTH

CJ had this half smile with a dirty looking grin. "I hope we aren't intruding, I'd hate to walk in on the two of you naked and well, you know ;p" Hunter punched CJ on the shoulder and told him to cut it out..lol

I jumped up and gave both of them big hugs.

"I'm really happy you guys are here. Can't wait to go to school together. It's gunna be type fire. When are you gunna move your stuff here?"

"Everything's here," Hunter said. "Check it out." The four of us walked through the wall and into their space. I couldn't fucking believe it. The room was like ten times its normal size. It had a living room with all the latest electronic toys, two bedrooms, a kitchen, and a humongous bathroom. It was only like a twelve-by-twelve room before.

"How'd you make the room so huge?"

"Remember Michael, we can alter everything around us. Do you want me to make our room bigger? I'll make it any way you like," Gabriel offered.

"No, I love it just the way it is. I don't ever wanna change it because it's our special place. I want it to be the same forever."

"We made a nice space for you and Gabriel at my place too. Michael, you said you wanted to live in the Village with Gabriel someday, well that day is now here. We can split our time between both places," CJ said.

"Thanks guys, this means a lot. Can we check it out in a little while? I wanna fly around the Bronx and show you the neighborhood, although I don't think you're gunna like it much."

All of a sudden things got serious :/

"Michael, we need to talk to you about what happened when your father tried to take you away from Gabriel the other day," CJ said, with this serious look on his face.

Hunter got angry at CJ. "I would have done the same fucking thing, except I'd have killed him."

I looked at Gabriel like, what the fuck's goin on? They scared me because they were arguing about what I had done. I thought I did the right thing like Gabriel told me to do; I walked away.

"CJ, why are you mad at me? There was no way my dad was gunna take me away from Gabriel. No fucking way! And I did the right thing by walking away before I killed him."

"Yes Michael, you did. But there are some things you need to know about handling the powers you are acquiring until you fully transform back. Actually, you have very little of your powers, and yet you almost killed your father because you were out of control. You let your human emotions get in the way."

"Well, I am human, and my dad hates my guts. He's never wanted me to be happy."

"Let's all sit down and talk this out rationally," Gabriel said, as he put his arm around my shoulder and took me over to the couch. CJ was gunna start talking again, but Gabriel stopped him. I guess he wanted to be the one to tell me stuff.

"Michael, once you have all of your powers back, you will be the most powerful entity known in any realm other than God himself. When he created you, he gave you attributes no other angel possesses, and this gift must be used with wisdom. I know you're angry and hurt about what your father has done to you in this life, but it shouldn't make you hate him or want to kill him as much as you do. You have been given an incredible gift by being a human. This is very special. You have also learned many things in your short life. Even though your life has been difficult, you have become a brilliant artist. You discovered your strengths and weaknesses by realizing that it was ok to be gay. You had to deal with some very evil people who were supposed to have loved you, but instead tried to destroy you for their own pleasure. You have survived because you have love and compassion inside of you like no one else. So what we are asking is that you think things through before you react, because we don't know if we can stop you. Michael, you told me that you are learning how to forgive, but you've been doing that your whole life; that is a true gift. Don't hate your father because of his ignorance. He has to live with being lonely and unloved for the rest of his life. In a way, he is already dead."

I didn't say anything as I looked at Gabriel and the guys, but I knew he was right.

CJ got up and spoke again. "Gabriel's right, if you let hatred overtake you, I don't know what will happen, but I know it won't be good. When you had your father up in the air, you were drawing energy into your body at such an alarming rate that we had to help Gabriel contain what you were doing with several Metatron Cubes. We've never experienced what your body was doing because none of us have ever been human. An angel becoming a human, and then an angel again is all new to us. The only thing we can think of is that it must be another level of power God wants you to have, something we have no knowledge of. Look, we know it's been an emotional time for you, but we love you and are here for you, and know that no one is ever going to take you away from Gabriel."

I started crying. I felt so bad that I put them through this. I didn't mean to, I just thought bad stuff was gunna happen to me, like never seeing Gabriel again if my dad took me away.

CJ and Hunter came over and sat next to me and said everything was gunna be all right.

"Once you are the archangel, you will use your powers in ways that might seem cruel to humans, you know, to help them understand that they can't harm other people. You've seen us do this with Luis and his gang, Gabriel used his powers to get rid of your mom's boyfriend, and all the others who have tried to harm us. You are using the power you have right now to stop people from being cruel, and that's ok, you just have to know when enough is enough," Hunter said.

I couldn't believe he was saying that because I know how intense he is about everything.

"Yeah, I know what you're thinking Michael. You may see us do things that will make you wonder, but until you fully transform, we are going to protect you anyway we can."

"I know this won't be hard for you, because even though you are only partially an angel, you are pure love. You show it every day," Gabriel said, as he kissed me nice.

"Hey, will you show us around the Bronx now?" CJ said, bumping my shoulder and smiling.

"Yeah I'd love to," I said, wiping the tears off my face.

"Let's walk insteada flying, that way we can see the real Bronx."

"Sounds good to me," they said.

Just as we were about to leave, Gabriel's Metatron Cubes started going crazy. All of a sudden we could hear someone screaming at the top of their lungs in front of the building.

"Michael, it's your mom. She's here to try and make you go with her," Gabriel said.

I looked at him all panicky. I flashed backed to when she was beating the shit outta me. It felt like I was gunna have a panic attack. I went to the window to see if it was really her. My face hasn't even healed yet, and now she wants to hurt me all over again. I was trying real hard to keep my emotions smooth, but it was hard because I started feeling the energy all around begin to enter my body again. The guys looked at me like what the fuck is gunna happen now, but I was able to control what I was feeling even as I let some of the energy into my body.

"It's ok, I won't let her get to me." They looked like they weren't so sure.

"Let's go down there so I can get her straight about some stuff."

We walked outside and saw the doorman trying to calm her down. When she saw me she said, "There he is. He my fuckin son and he don't belong here no way. They got him all fucked up wit dis queer shit. They been brainwashin my boy. You gotta let me take him now cuzz he's fucked up in the head. Look at the way these boys got him lookin an shit. You gotta see it's wrong, so get your fuckin hands off me mutha fucka."

I stood there with the guys listening to her pathetic words.

"Mom, you have to leave now. You know you're not supposed

to be near me. I'm not going anywhere with you ever again. This is my home now, and nothing is ever gunna change this fact, or the fact that I'm gay. I still love you and hope you'll get some help because you're real lost. If you can ever figure stuff out, then you'll be able move on like I have. It's over mom."

Man, she lost it then. She kicked the doorman and jerked herself loose from his hands, and then she started running at me with hate in her eyes. It was those same eyes I saw last week as I lay there all bloody on my bedroom floor. I just put my hand up and stopped her dead in her tracks. Then I lifted her off the ground and held her in mid-air so she couldn't move.

Gabriel grabbed hold of my shoulder as the three of them wondered what I was gunna do next.

The doorman tried to run inside to call the cops, but Hunter froze him in his tracks and put him to sleep so he couldn't see what was happening.

"Gabriel, I'm ok. I'm not going to hurt her. I just want her to understand a couple of things."

I held Gabriel's hand and looked up at her with a big smile on my face.

"Mom, I love Gabriel more than anything. He's my boyfriend and that's never gunna change.

You gotta understand that I'm gay, that I was born this way, and that I'll always be gay. I love who I am and you should love me too, but you don't, and I can't do anything about it except to move on. This is my home now, and it's gunna be Rosanna's in a couple of weeks too. I want you to look at me real close, because I'm not just a kid who is gunna take shit from you or anyone else.

I'm showing you that I'm different, and maybe someday you'll understand how I can do what I'm doing to you right now."

The four of us looked at her hovering in the air as she looked back at us in horror.

"Now I'm going to put you back down and let you walk away. I don't want to hear one word from you or I'll hurt you like you hurt me, and I mean it."

Then I let put her gently on the ground and unfroze her body. I stood there waiting to see what see was gunna do. She looked at me like I was a ghost or something, and then turned and walked real fast down the street without looking back. I realized at that moment that I didn't have a mom or dad anymore.

"Michael, I'm very proud of you. You did the right thing even though you are still angry and hurt," Gabriel said, as he put his arm around me.

I was proud of myself too because I really did want her to feel the same pain I've felt for years, but instead, I just told her the truth and that was painful enough. I didn't cry either; I felt calm and happy inside because I knew I was finally moving on.

"You want to go take that walk now?" CJ asked.

"Yeah, that sounds good. I wanna get something to eat too."

Hunter went over to the doorman and woke him up. The guy walked back into the building without saying a word. "I erased this little incident from his mind," he said, with a sly grin.

✦ <

It was kool showing the guys around. No one bothered us for a change; although we knew a lot of Rican thugs were watchin us as we went from block to block. They were definitely sizing us up. I'm sure they wondered what the hell a bunch of emo guys were doing in their hood.

Well anyways, after we got something to eat, we flew to the Village so CJ and Hunter could show us our new bedroom. It was awesome =D It was exactly like our bedroom in the Bronx.

"We know how special your private space is to both of you, so we thought hey, why not have one here too."

"Thanks guys. This means so much to me."

We decided to spend the night there. I made love to Gabriel all night long ;P

Journal Entry 39

Monday, October 8th
11pm

Card tricks and sleight of hand
are realities of indignity,
a fool's desperation.
Time angles away
as light bends around the sun
such a general relativity
a cosmological constant
quietly showing the way.
So try not to miss the next train
because time never stays,
time never stays.

Ok. Man, I don't know where to begin =p :/ :D

So much stuff happened when we got to school today. I still can't believe it.

Lots of shit went down in the halls because there are four of us now. Some Ricans were callin us emo faggot cutters and sayin all we wanna do is kiss and suck off all the straight boys at school.

I guess they saw the video of me and Gabriel. Guys were walkin by us all day making kissing sounds and grabbing their crotches like they were protecting their junk. Roberto and Jacob hung with us, and they were getting shit too. Fortunately it didn't bother them too much. At least I know who my friends are.

Hunter went ballistic a couple of times today to the point where I thought he was gunna kill someone :/   And then the weirdest thing of all happened to me when I was hanging by my locker; I started hearing voices in my head :/

$$\rightarrow \ \leq \ \oint$$

It all started when we tried to walk through the front doors of school this morning.

Some assholes started gettin tight when they saw us come through the front gates.

"My niggas, what da fuck is dis fuckin shit comin at us? You fags breedin now? Dis fuckin shit's gunna stop cuzz me and my niggas ain't wantin no mo mutha fuckin queers comin here."

It must have looked like an invasion to them..lmfao Yeah, we were as emo looking as you could get this morning =) Well anyways, we tried to walk by without saying anything, but like ten thug wannabes decided to block the doors, which was the wrong thing to do. I looked at Hunter and could see his eyes starting to go white with rage. CJ asked them real nice, "Would you mind stepping aside so we can go inside?"

Well this guy named Cesar wasn't havin it. "You faggots can

use another fuckin door cuzz only straight mutha fuckas are goin through these doors."

Hunter turned to me and asked, "Who the fuck is this little bitch?"

Then he quickly put his hand up to them while he was still looking at me. Every thug who was blocking the doors was slammed into them so hard it shattered all the fucking windows and bent the doors in. Then Hunter turned to look at them and smiled as they lay on the ground all fucked up. Other students who were watching what just went down tried to get the hell outta there real fast, but CJ stopped em where they stood, freezing everyone in place. Me and Gabriel stood there watching as CJ and Hunter handled everyone like they were playing a video game.

Hunter motioned with his hand again and pushed the assholes aside so we could walk into the school. The doors were so fucked up they wouldn't open, so CJ backed up and said, "We would like to enter." The doors flew open and were ripped off their hinges like they weighed nothing at all. They fell on Cesar and his friends.

"Oh, pardon me. I didn't mean to hurt you," CJ said, smiling that sly smile of his.

As we walked in, Hunter stopped, looked down, and then grabbed Cesar by the hair, whipping his head around so he was looking Hunter right in the eyes. He told him something in a language I've never heard, and then gave Cesar an electric jolt that made his whole body go spazz. He let go of Cesar and looked at the rest of those guys and calmly said, "Have a nice day pussys."

As we walked through the lobby, CJ unfroze everyone, and then went up to the security cops and told them that Cesar and his friends messed up the front doors. "You need to report this kind of vandalism to the proper authorities."

"Well, I can see we are off to another normal day at school," Gabriel said, shaking his head.

CJ and Hunter had to go to the office to get their schedules, so Gabriel and I headed to our locker. When we got there, I went to grab for the lock and put my arm right through the locker door. Yeah, my arm went right through it like it wasn't even there. I looked around real quick to see if anyone had seen what I'd just done.

Gabriel Smiled, "Hey cute one, look what you can do. You can go through solid objects on your own now."

"You mean I didn't walk through the wall on my own yesterday? Man, I thought I was doin it all by myself."

"We kind of helped you; I hope you're not mad. Hey, why don't we disappear for a while so I can make love to you again." ;p

"I wish we could because you're making me mad horny," I said, as I kissed Gabriel's beautiful pouty lips and tried to hide my woody from everyone.

"Michael, I'm glad you can do this now because it means you're getting closer."

Just as we were about to kiss again, the guys walked up. "Can't you two stop kissing for two seconds," CJ said, bumping us and smiling.

"Did you get your schedules?" I asked. Hunter started

opening up the locker next to ours. I looked at him weird because that locker belonged to Seiko, this kool Asian girl who's crazy gifted at piano.

"Don't worry Michael, I just moved everyone down one locker so we could be next to you guys. No one will know," he said, as he shoved some books inside and then started looking down the hall to see what was up.

Things were already intense, and I could tell something was bugging Hunter big time. He definitely was in the mood to do some hunting. I could feel it coming outta his body. Believe me, he's the kind of archangel you want on your side when all hell's breaking loose, if ya know what I mean. Gabriel and CJ were trying to keep him calm because they knew he was out for blood. All of sudden Jacob yelled to us from down the hall. He ran up to us along with Roberto, Jennifer, and Kristal. They gave us big hugs. Jacob got all crazy shy all of a sudden when he went to hug Hunter. He hesitated for a moment, but Hunter grabbed him and gave him a nice long hug. When they let go of each other they were both smiling. It was so cute to see them both crushing ;p

"What are you guys doing here?" Jacob asked.

"We decided to transfer here because we thought it'd be fun to go to school in the Bronx. We are going to live with Miguel and Gabriel during the week, and then we'll go back to Greenwich Village on the weekends," Hunter said.

"That's fucking kool. You guys gotta join Drama Club so we can all hang out together."

"We can't act for shit, but we can do backstage stuff. We're pretty good at doing things in the shadows," CJ said.

"I'm really happy you guys are goin to school here," Jacob said.

I still couldn't believe how shy Jacob was being; he's never like that. He's so crushin.

Roberto was bein all shy too when he said hi to me. "I had a lot of fun this weekend. Thanks for letting me hang with you."

"I had fun too. We need to do more of that," I said.

All of a sudden Jennifer and Kristal playfully punched me and Gabriel. "What? You guys partied and did't invite us?" Jennifer said, pretending to be mad. "Don't worry, we're planning to have a party next weekend at my place, and all of you are invited," CJ said.

"You mean in Greenwich Village?" Jennifer asked.

"Yeah, my parents are going to be out of town, so I thought I'd have a few people over."

"Jennifer, you gotta see where he lives. It's fucking awesome," Roberto said, with this huge grin.

As we were hanging, I suddenly started hearing all kinds of voices in my head. It scared the shit outta me. I put my hands up to my ears to try and stop it. Everyone stopped talking and looked at me weird, especially Gabriel.

"Miguel, are you ok?"

"I don't know," I said, as I backed up against the locker.

Gabriel put his arm around me and walked me down the hall. Roberto tried to help, but I told him, "I'll be ok. Go back and hang."

We walked around the corner so we could be alone. I didn't say anything for a few seconds as I looked down the hall, and that's when I figured it out.

"I can hear what everyone's thinking." Gabriel just smiled.

"I'm serious. It's driving me crazy with all these voices in my head. How do I make it stop?"

Gabriel kissed me on the cheek. "Michael, close your eyes and try to lower the volume in your head. All you have to do is to learn how to control this ability and you'll be able to turn it on and off. It's just going to take a little practice."

I closed my eyes and tried to get my mind quiet, and it kinda worked.

"Just relax, you can do this," Gabriel said, as he hugged me.

I opened my eyes and looked around at everyone. When I looked at someone directly, I could tune everyone else out and just hear what that person was thinking. It was kool in a way, but I also felt like the stuff I was hearing was none of my business. You'd be surprised what people are thinking '___'

Everyone asked if I was ok when we went back to our locker.

"Yeah, I was just feeling a little dizzy. I'm ok now."

CJ asked Gabriel, "It happened, didn't it."

"Yes." Then CJ and Hunter gave me big hugs.

"What happened?" Roberto asked, totally confused.

"Everything's kool," I said, giving Roberto a look I hoped he'd understand.

Then all of us headed to class.

All day long I listened and practiced turning it on and off. That's about the best way to explain it I guess. I just pretended that I had a switch in my mind that I could flip on and off, and it worked. I realized how lonely and insecure people really are whenever I did listen; just like I used to be. I've always thought about how most people seem so confident, but a lot of it is just good acting. I guess that Shakespeare guy had it right about the world being a stage O__o

It's like when we're between classes and everyone's posing and putting on shows to get attention. Everyone seems like they got it together, but when I listen to their thoughts, they are wishing they were more popular, more confident, or better looking. No one's ever satisfied, and this is sad because we're lucky to be who we are. We put on these fake masks all the time because we're afraid. Pretending in real life is a waste of time.

Then I started thinking about how the whole fucking world is now living in cyberspace.

People create themselves in ways that aren't real. It's just more pretending. There's a lotta frustrated emotions out there. A lotta people are sad and angry about life.

It's a fucking gift! Don't you get it? :/

Interacting in cyberspace has created a strange sense of belonging. We are alienating ourselves from each other big time; it's the new human reality.

I guess I'm just really ranting right now.

Another thing I figured out while I listened is that like ninety-nine percent of what we do every day is try to love someone, and have that someone love us back. It seems so fucking simple, but it's the hardest thing to make happen. I've been given this gift of being an archangel, and I'd love to help everyone find love, but I don't know how to do it. Maybe one way to find love is to start being truthful with each other and then see what happens. It seems simple to me.

♪ 🎵

There was something else bothering me all day as I sat in class; I couldn't get it out of my mind. Last night I was lying in bed meditating, and all sorts of images were coming at me a gazillion miles a second. I could tell Gabriel was helping to channel my past into my brain.

I saw the four of us fighting a battle against Lucifer and his army of fallen angels. What I noticed most was just how brave Gabriel, CJ, and Hunter really are. Tears ran down my cheeks as I watched. Gabriel put his hand in mine and showed me something that really shocked me. He showed me how Hunter and Lucifer were created at the same time, from the same divine energy source. They were inseparable and loved each other very much, but Lucifer's arrogance and deceit destroyed their special bond. Hunter tried everything in his power to help Lucifer stay pure, but it was no use. Lucifer wanted to destroy God and enslave all living things throughout all existence.

Gabriel whispered, "Hunter wants to destroy Lucifer as badly as you do. It's personal."

That information made me realize I can't stay human, that my life has only been a temporary holding place for something more meaningful. I told him I was ready.

"Gabriel, I want it to happen because I'm really not afraid anymore," I said, even though I was crying. "I've always felt trapped in this body, and being able to leave it anytime I want is gunna be ok now."

"Michael, you and I will finally be as we've always been. We were created at the same time in the same way Hunter and Lucifer were, but the love we have for each other has never been broken."

Gabriel decided to show me the biggest battle of our existence; saving heaven and earth from being taken over by Lucifer. I was leading God's army of angels to set the ultimate trap for Lucifer. We had his army cornered on the edge of an event horizon. After three days of fighting, Hunter was ready to destroy Lucifer once and for all, but I stopped him. There was an echoing silence as all of the other angels stared at the two of us waiting for the final order to be given. I reminded Hunter that Lucifer was destined to live in his own hell for eternity; that God had predetermined this, and I had to make sure it happened. Lucifer was caught in our trap, but Hunter realized that Hell would not stop him from spreading his hatred throughout space and time, especially this universe and this world.

"Michael, Hell is not going to stop him, I know this from experience. You have to believe me. He is a true enemy and must be destroyed."

I tried to reason with Hunter, but I could see he wasn't listening to me anymore, so I decided to paralyze every courageous angel in my army, Hunter included. Then I sent Lucifer and his fallen angels into the depths of Hell for eternity just as I was instructed to do. After they disappeared into that intense inferno of pain and suffering, I saw Hunter's angry eyes glaring at me as he floated paralyzed and helpless.

All of a sudden I woke out of this memory in a cold sweat because I could see intense beams of white light racing out of Hunter's eye sockets destroying everything in their path. I knew he was trying to find where I was so he could destroy me.

I sat up with my body drenched in sweat as tears ran down my face. I thought I was gunna have a panic attack. After I calmed down a little, I looked over at Gabriel hoping he would help me deal with this, but he kept his eyes closed and said nothing. I wanted him to look at me and tell me he loved me, and that I did the right thing, but he didn't. It seemed like Gabriel was mad at me too, and that made me cry even harder.

I kept wondering if he thought I'd done the right thing. I could feel Hunter's anger and resentment deep inside of me, like the whole thing had just happened.

I know he hasn't forgiven me, and in some ways, I think I should have let him destroy Lucifer when we had the chance. The creation of Hell has only caused more pain and suffering for the human race.

"It's all right Michael, you did the right thing. You had to do it," Gabriel finally whispered. He sat up and gave me a nice long hug.

♥ Ω

I've gotten to know Hunter a lot better through the memories. Now I understand why he's so intense. Hunter was feeling all the shitting energy in the halls as we stood by our lockers right after 4th period. We were talking and getting ready to go to our next class, when I suddenly felt something bad happening in the next hall.

"Luis is hurting someone real bad. We gotta help this kid."

"Can you see what he's doing?" CJ asked.

"Yeah. Let's go."

CJ put his hand up and everything froze in place. Then the four of us walked through the locker wall. It was the strangest feeling to being doing it on my own now. It was weird because I could hear the particles making strange noises. I swear I could feel every atom bouncing around inside my body. We came out of the wall in the other hall and walked up to Luis, Anthony, Donato, and two other guys I've never seen before. Everyone stood frozen in place. Hunter Shot beams of white light into all of their bodies to see who was who. Their bodies lit up just like when Gabriel did it last week. "They're Lucifer's little shit disciples," Hunter growled.

"Luis is starting to change. He's getting stronger. They are changing him," Gabriel said, knowing what this meant.

"What do you mean he's changing?" I asked.

"It's the powder Luis has been snorting. It's a substance Lucifer has used on humans for centuries. It makes them physically stronger, and it makes their hatred so intense that they begin killing for pleasure. This powder kills the concepts of right and wrong. Luis is slowly turning into an evil killing machine. What this powder does is take the hatred that is already inside someone and magnify it tenfold. This stuff will make Luis or anyone else who snorts it seem invincible. It also gets them hooked, so they'll do anything to keep snorting it. Anthony and

Donato already have Luis hooked and they're trying to get as many haters as they can on the stuff so they will have an army of mortals to help Lucifer destroy the earth. We have to make sure Lucifer doesn't get through the traps we've set up. We think South Bronx is going to be his entry point back into this world. Michael, he wants kill you in the worst way," CJ said.

I didn't say anything, not because I was scared, but because I was trying to figure out what to do. The whole thing seemed like a bad dream, like my whole world was being torn apart again. And I thought my mom beating the shit outta me was bad. Now I got fucking Lucifer coming to kill me. I was trying my hardest to find the strength to do the right thing and not run away. Gabriel put his hand on my shoulder for reassurance.

"Don't worry Michael, we will fight him together."

I looked at Luis who had this poor helpless kid pushed up against the locker with one hand around his neck, and his other in the kid's pocket trying to steal money, or a phone, or something. The other four were standing in front of him so teachers couldn't see what Luis was doing. Hunter stared at Luis for a second and then smiled. "Well CJ, what should we do about this little situation?"

Hunter stood in front of Luis and unfroze him and his boys. Luis didn't know what the fuck was happening because we had come out of nowhere. Gabriel and I stood back as Luis and Lucifer's disciples got a little taste of Hunter and CJ.

The guy they were picking on was a little skinny kid no more than five-foot four or so. Hunter grabbed Luis's collar and jerked him away. It was fucking weird because the kid stayed frozen in place against the locker. Luis looked fucking scared outta his mind as he faced Hunter.

"What the fuck do you think you're doing bitch?" Hunter said, as his eyes burned into Luis's. Hunter lifted Luis off the ground just by looking at him. Then he shoved Luis against the locker repeatedly with such force that his head bounced around like his neck was broken. The back of his head kept hitting the hinge of the locker door over and over, making him bleed all over the place, just like Luis did to me a few weeks ago.

As this was happening, CJ put his hand up in front of Luis's new friends and slammed them into the lockers across from us. It didn't seemed to hurt em at all. They got up right away and looked at CJ with stupid grins on their faces. CJ put his hand towards them again. They were lifted off the ground and brought right back in front of him. "I don't fucking like you," he calmly said.

"You think this is funny? Well let's have some laughs then." All of a sudden the wall across from the lockers started cracking open just like an earthquake does to the ground. The whole school was shaking as the wall slowly opened up completely, revealing an intense inferno of fire. I could hear people screaming in pain as it echoed through the hallway. Then CJ smiled and said goodbye to Anthony, Donato and the other two Disciples. He sent them flying through the opening and back to Hell. As soon as they flew through that fiery opening, it immediately closed up and disappeared.

"I thought I'd send Lucifer a present," CJ said, laughing.

Everything was happening so fast that I didn't know what to

do, but I wanted Hunter to stop hurting Luis because I thought he was killing him.

I yelled at Hunter to stop, but Gabriel grabbed me by the arm and told me not to interfere.

Gabriel held onto me as I watched in horror. There was a huge pool of blood on the floor as Hunter kept banging Luis's head. Luis was now unconscious with blood also coming out of his mouth and nose. It was creepy sounding because I could hear each drop of his blood hit the floor, like it was amplified a thousand times louder than normal. I screamed at Hunter to stop; all of a sudden he did. He held Luis's body up in the air as he turned to look at me. Our eyes locked onto each other like we were in some kind of mental battle. I asked him to teach Luis a lesson some other way and let him live.

"This is not what we're about," I screamed.

Hunter looked at Luis, and then back at me. He walked over to Luis's body and touched his chest. Luis instantly became conscious. He looked at Hunter with absolute fear in his eyes.

"Take a look at the blood on the floor. It is your blood. I want you to see what the future has in store for you if you continue to bully people weaker than you," Hunter told him.

Luis looked at the floor as his body shook with fear.

"I should let you bleed to death so you can feel the pain you're causing. I want you to know something; you are totally irrelevant in the scheme of things."

Then Hunter took a step back as Luis slowly floated down until they were face to face. He grabbed Luis by his shirt and said, "I'd love to rip you in half right now, but I think I'm going to wait for the perfect moment. I'm going to make you feel pain like you've never felt before. What you're feeling right now is nothing compared to your final destiny."

All of a sudden these intense white beams of light came out of Hunter's eyes and started burning through the lockers, the walls, the ceiling, and then the sky as Luis fell onto the bloody floor crying uncontrollably. I yelled as loud as I could, "Stop it Hunter, stop it right now!" I tried to tackle him, but Gabriel and CJ grabbed me and held me back.

I yelled, "Lemme go. Lemme go." I couldn't stand the feeling of hate that was overtaking us.

"Hunter, if you kill him this way, then we are no better than Lucifer."

All of a sudden Hunter stopped, turned around and looked at me with a look that could kill. Then he turned back to Luis, picked him up and whispered in his ear, "We will continue this at some other time." In an instant, time unfroze and everything was back to normal as we stood in front of the guy getting picked on. Luis ran down the hall as fast as he could. The guy being beat up looked so frightened as he backed away from us.

"What's your name," Hunter asked.

"Ramon," he said, with a tremble in his voice.

"Everything is all right now. We aren't going to hurt you. Are you ok? Tell us what happened."

"That guy running and a bunch of his friends were banging my head against the locker and punching me. They were tryin to steal my phone. They've been picking on me since school started.

They told me if I tell on em, they'd fuck me up real good," he said, staring at the floor looking real nervous.

"Hey don't worry, he won't be bothering you anymore," Hunter said. Then he introduced all of us. "If anybody picks on you again, let us know, Ok?"

"Ok. Thanks. Maybe we could hang out sometime," Ramon said, nervously.

"That would be kool," Hunter said.

"We're having a Gay-Straight Alliance meeting tomorrow after school. Do you wanna come? We could hang out and introduce you to some of our friends," I said.

"Yeah that'd be awesome. What time is it gunna start?"

"At three. It's in room 310."

"Kool. Thanks again for helping me."

I couldn't believe how calm everyone was with all the shit that just went down. It was so fucking weird as I looked around not seeing any blood on the floor, no cracked walls, no Hell staring me in the face, and Lucifer's disciples gone. I think I was still in shock when Hunter put his arm around my shoulder and smiled.

"Michael, I told you that I might do things that will upset you from time to time, but you just have to trust me. Oh, and one other thing, I'm not mad at you for anything that has happened in the past. I hope you know that."

"Thanks, I needed to hear that from you."

"I don't think the Metatron Cubes we've set up are going to stop Lucifer. He must have some new powers we don't know about," Gabriel theorized.

"That's all right, it's just going to make this journey a little more interesting," CJ said, as we walked down the hall to our next class.

What a day '___'

Nite

Journal Entry 40
Tuesday, October 9th
10:30 pm

You think you know how I feel
or how I should view this world
trying to make me look through your eyes
and wear your disguise
like some fucking badge of honor.

You spew your bullshit, envy, and hate
like blind philosophers reaching into nothingness
you are merely a performer on a stage filled with idiots
acting only to gain power.

You think you're a witness to the decay of individualism
but you will never know
because
even though you think you can feel life's ridges with your finger tips
or read between the lines
those ridges are the DNA of me and them
not you
and you will never know how I feel.

Men's enemies are not demons, but human beings like himself.

Lao Tzu

We had our first GSA meeting at school today, and it got mad intense cuzz people were trying to stop it from happening. They had security cops standing outside the classroom where our meeting was, and they had cops in front of the school where crazy parents and religious jerks were yelling shit as they protested against us. They were all out there. You shoulda seen it O__o

This crazy black preacher guy had a bullhorn and was yelling crap like he was givin a sermon on Sunday morning. A Catholic priest was there with a bunch of Latino moms and their kids holding up anti-gay signs. The sad thing was that alotta those moms didn't look much older than me, and I could tell at least half ofem were pregnant.

Then there were those Jewish guys with beards and crazy hats on their heads all dressed in black. They had their books out as they chanted together doing weird dance moves or whatever it is they do. There were also some crazy Muslim guys I always see yelling shit on 3rd Ave. They were praying and yelling anti-gay crap at us through their own bullhorn.

It kinda made me smile though, because all us queers were the one's bringing these religious groups together..lol It's just too bad they were hating on us O__o

The Principal finally had to go out and warn em because he was afraid it was gunna get violent. It was just all so stupid what they were doing. At one point they were even tryin ta get into the school, and the cops actually had to physically stop them from coming in.

Principal Rodriguez said they could only protest on the sidewalk, and if they tried to come into the school again, he would have them arrested. It was kool seeing him take a strong stand by supporting us. Well that threat didn't go over to good, and I thought for sure someone was gunna get hurt :/

Me and the guys were looking out the front windows to see how bad it was. We were on the fourth floor, so we had a good view. The black preacher guy was yelling stuff about homos going to Hell. "God will punish all you homosexuals. You are going to burn in Hell because you are sinners. You must repent now before it's too late."

All of those so-called religious people were yelling stuff about how evil we were. There must have been at least a hundred people protesting. They waved signs that said we were homos, perverted, mentally ill fags, and doing the devil's work. They don't have a clue what they're talking about. CJ shook his head. "They think they know the truth, but they're so far away from it. This is exactly why this planet is so fucked up."

"Yeah, it's sad to see so many people that think they have all the answers," Gabriel said.

I couldn't believe how many students were protesting too. The last thing I wanted was for our club was to make people hate each other, but I know we're doing the right thing no matter what anybody thinks. All of a sudden I saw Maya and Luis with their friends right in the middle of the crowd holding signs and yelling "Queer sex is sin" and "Homos burn in Hell" over and over. I also noticed three Ricans I'd never seen before standing next to Luis.

One ofem had a sign with a picture of an emo boy with devil horns and fangs and blood running down his chin. Under the picture was the word SATAN in bloody red paint. The letters had drip marks to make them look like they were bleeding too.

How lame :/ This other guy was holding a sign with a drawing of an emo boy cutting his arms with a razor and bleeding all over the place. I knew the drawings were meant to be me and Gabriel.

Then all of a sudden those three Ricans looked up at us and glared. I turned to Hunter knowing what he was gunna do. He shot beams of light into their bodies with such force that they flew backwards at least fifty feet, slamming into a parked car. All the protesters ducked down real quick, then turned around to see what the fuck was goin on because it sounded like a gunshot when they hit the car. It was a strange thing to watch because these guys got up like they weren't even hurt, and then walked back into the crowd. They looked up at us, smiled, and gave us the finger.

"They are Lucifer's. I don't think he liked what you did to the others," Gabriel said, laughing.

CJ smiled. "Well I guess I get to have some more fun. They do have a little more power, but they're nothing more than a pimple that will be popped soon."

Gabriel's eyes went white for a second. "Let's keep them around for a little while to see what they're up to. We just need to keep Michael away from them." CJ and Hunter agreed.

"Don't worry about me, I'll be ok."

"I know, but we have to be careful," Gabriel said.

Then he had an idea..lol He started making out with me right in the window so everyone could see. Luis looked up and saw us kissing. He yelled, "There they are, Them fags is kissin!" Everyone looked up and started yelling and waving their signs. The preacher guy yelled through his bullhorn, "You boys are sinners and you will burn in Hell." Then everyone started chanting "BURN IN HELL, BURN IN HELL, BURN IN HELL," over and over. Luis and his friends decided to throw their signs on the ground and stomp all over em. We kept on kissing to show them how much we love each other, and that we weren't afraid of them.

Then CJ and Hunter started kissing too as all the religious guys screamed more anti-gay stuff into their bullhorns. We listened to everyone's thoughts; it was sad to hear so much anger and hatred. Reading their minds also made me realize how afraid of life they are. They enjoy bullying us because it makes them think they're doing God's work; it makes them think it is their ticket into Heaven.

✝ ✝

Sometimes
I wish I could shut out the whole world and make it go away
so I wouldn't have to feel the pain
of the stares and taunts so easily thrown,
but that would be the easy way out,
so I'm done with you.
Why would you want to hurt another human being like that?
What special pleasure do you get
out of making someone feel terrible that they're alive?
I wish I lived in a world
where no one would criticize me for being different,

for being me.
But you will never say that it is ok to be who I am
because it scares you to the point that you fear me
and hate me,
this is your ignorant tool
to try and destroy people like me just to make yourself feel better.
All I have to say to this is, FUCK YOU!
Yeah, FUCK YOU!
because I'm not gunna run away from you ever again
and you aren't gunna make me feel like shit
just because you feel like shit.
Yeah, this is what your hatred is all about.
You are so simple it makes me sick.
You think you have all the answers
but you don't even know the questions,
and this is sad,
so sad.

We finally got bored and walked back to the meeting room to get things ready. I wanted our first meeting to be the best it could be. It was kool that we got to use a classroom that was recently turned into a meeting place for people who need to chill when they can't control their emotions. It has carpeting, a couple of leather couches, nice leather chairs, a Smart Board to show movies, YouTube videos, and educational stuff. It's the perfect place to have the GSA.

Principal Rodriguez even had pizza and soda delivered for our first meeting. It was real nice of him to do that. All of us get hungry like every twenty minutes, and pizza makes everyone happy =D

I wondered how many people were actually gunna show up because of all the shit we've been getting since we came out. I was curious to see who'd be brave enough to come. I wouldn't be surprised if no one showed up with all the protesting goin on in front of the school.

Some people were still hanging out in the halls and looking out the windows watching all the shit out front. I could tell none of them were interested in coming to our meeting. All this intimidation shit is sick; it's gunna keep away the people who need this the most. The other thing about the GSA is that we need straight people to be there too, and I can see it's gunna be almost impossible now.

It seems like when anything's considered gay, people get this look on their face like "Hey, I could be branded a queer if anyone sees me with real gay people." Or if there's something a guy likes that isn't macho, then they're considered gay too. I think lesbians have it worse sometimes because straight guys think it's sexy when two girls kiss or hold hands, and some guys even think they're gunna change em straight insteada just accepting them for who they are. It's all so stupid sometimes. All I know is that people have to watch their every move or else they're called queer or lesbo, or whatever. O____o

This kind of pressure makes everyone self-conscious of every move they make so they don't make a 'gay' mistake in front of their friends. I even see gay bashing on Facebook between friends, and I don't know why. If a guy says something nice to one of his guy friends, the response is always "No homo right?" It's so fucking stupid that guys can't even show real emotions to their friends. So many guys have real sex issues as far as I'm concerned :/

I think a lotta so-called straight guys question their own sexuality in one way or another.

I think they use gay slurs to test the gay waters. Like it turns them on in some weird way when they tell their friends, "Hey faggot, suck my dick," or some other stupid gay slur. All I know is that people should be able to tell same sex friends that they like them or even love them without it being considered sexual. Just get past that shit, ok?

⚥ ⚠

It was around 2:50 when Mr. Atwood came by to see if we had everything ready. The meeting was supposed to start at 3:00, but there was no sign of anyone yet. This had me worried.

"Hey mister, I don't think anyone's gunna show up with all that stuff happening outside. What are we gunna do?"

"Don't worry Miguel, give it a few minutes. You might be surprised. I just want you to know that I'm proud of all of you for being so brave. You are doing something that is changing the dynamic of the entire school, and sometimes it can be painful at first."

Then mister told us about a new student who was asking about the GSA Club. Mister said he wanted to join. "I think he may show up for your meeting. I need to tell you something, but you have to keep it confidential, okay?"

"Sure."

"His name is Sergio, and he is what we call a safety transfer.

What this means is that he was being harassed to the point where his teachers and the school administration feared for his safety. They felt they couldn't adequately protect him, so they transferred him here because our school is less violent. Please make him feel welcome any way you can. He's a great kid with a lot to offer."

"Sure mister. Can't wait to meet him."

It was 3:05 and no one had shown up yet. The cop was even wondering why it was so quiet. We were standing outside the door so we could introduce ourselves if people decided to come.

All of a sudden we saw this real skinny guy on his skateboard round the corner and zoom down the hall towards us. It was mad funny because he was just sorta standing straight up with this big smile on his face. He looked totally emo and had kool looking black and red spiky hair. He looked just like us =D It was type fire seeing another emo guy at school.

Man, he was comin down the hall so fast that I thought he was gunna run into the wall for a second, but he pulled up and stopped perfectly right in front of us.

"Hey, my name's Sergio. Am I late for the meeting?"

"No, you're just in time. I'm Miguel, and this is Gabriel, CJ, and Hunter. Nice to meet you."

I looked over at CJ, who had a look I've seen a million times on people with crushes; oh man did he have one ;p

Mister told Sergio nicely that he didn't wanna see him skate down the hall anymore.

"I'm sorry, but I didn't wanna miss the meeting," He said, as he picked up his skateboard.

"I had to make a quick decision with all that protesting goin on outside cuzz of the way they were all lookin and yellin at me, so I just skated around em real fast. The cops were laughing as I headed towards them. They opened the door so I could keep on going."

Mister smiled and shook his head.

Just as we were about to go into the classroom, we started hearing a bunch of talking down the hall. I could see the cop getting a little nervous, but I knew who it was before they even came round the corner. It was Roberto, Jacob, and everyone else from Drama Club. There were even some people I've never met before with em. Even Ramon came to the meeting. He had this huge smile on his face as he walked in. You don't know how happy I was to see them =D

Everyone was talking and laughing as they gave us hugs. Roberto gave me a nice hug when he saw me. Hunter put his arm around Ramon and thanked him for coming.

Sergio had this huge smile on his face as he started meeting everyone. It turned into an instant partido. I could tell Mr. Atwood was happy to see a good turnout.

Gabriel went over to talk to a couple of new girls who were standing around looking a little nervous. He introduced himself and made them feel welcome.

I stood by the door with Roberto. We watched CJ and Hunter talking with Sergio and Jacob. They looked so cute together ;p

"I think they're crushing," Roberto said, with this little grin.

"Yeah, they definitely are."

Then I told Roberto to get some pizza before it was all gone. "I'll wait here to see if anyone else shows up." I watched Roberto out of the corner of my eye as he stood by the window eating all alone. He looked so sad. Gabriel sensed it too, so he went over and started talking to him about some new video games. That got him smiling. It was a nice start to our first GSA meeting =D

I could see that no one else was gunna show up, so I finally closed the door so I could get the meeting started. After I got everyone's attention, I thanked them for showing up and supporting the GSA Club.

"I'm really proud of everyone who's here because I know you're not letting what's going on outside scare you. I want to thank Mr. Atwood and Principal Rodriguez for all the food, and for letting us use this great space."

I was trying so hard not to stutter :/ Just as I was ready to start talking about our goals for the club, the door opened and two guys that I would never in a million years expect to be anywhere near a GSA meeting, walked in. They're really popular, and they just happen to be the best b-ball players on the varsity team. I got mad nervous because I thought they were gunna harass us, or maybe pick a fight or something. They were O D tall, like at least six-foot-six. I swear they even had to duck a little as they came through the door. Everyone got quiet as they stood there. I didn't know what was gunna happen. Then I started feeling sorry for them because they looked real nervous, and even a little shy. Gabriel broke the silence and introduced himself.

"Hey, thanks for coming to the meeting. My name is Gabriel, and this is Miguel."

"Hey, I'm Marco, and this is Alex. Do you mind if we sit in on your meeting?" he asked, with some nervousness in his voice. Everyone was looking at each other, but not saying anything, so Sergio finally broke the ice. "Hey, there's room next to me," he said, as he squished over and made room on the couch. Marco smiled and said thanks. I think some people were thinking the same thing I was; are they gay? Wouldn't that be something to have two of the biggest stars on the b-ball team turn out to be gay? :D Gabriel gave me a little smile.

I finally got things started again. I told everyone that I wanted to start each meeting by going around the room and have people say how their week has been, and then if they wanted to share anything that was bothering them, they could.

"I think this is important because we need to be able to get to know each other honestly and openly. Let's make a rule; everything that we talk about here should stay between us. We have to help each other anyway we can."

All of sudden Marco raised his hand and asked if he could start first.

I smiled. "Yeah, that would be great."

He kinda hesitated for a moment as he looked down at his hands.

"I came here because I want to help you guys any way I can." He got quiet again for a few seconds. I could see his eyes starting to get emotional as he looked at me, and then back at everyone else. "My older brother Ronaldo committed suicide seven years ago because of all the shit that went down when people found out he was gay. Even though he took his own life, he was a real brave guy. When he finally got the courage to be honest, he came out to my mom and dad. They didn't like it at all, and really went after him about being, as they said, 'a fuckin queer.' And when he told a couple of his friends, they turned on him and told everyone at school. All the guys got into his shit until he couldn't take no more."

Marco stopped talking again because he was fighting back tears. No one said a word or moved an inch.

"At home there was lots of yelling and screaming goin on all the time. My dad would yell at Ronaldo saying he wasn't queer; that he was just confused and too young to know what the hell he was. They just couldn't accept him, and it hurt him real bad. Ronaldo was only trying to be honest with everyone. Then one day he just got quiet about everything. My parents were trying to fix him, you know, trying to make him straight, but he just let em talk and yell. Even though I was only ten, I knew he was hurting real bad. I knew he felt numb and alone because he had been abandoned by his friends, and by his own mom and dad. Then one day he started giving all his stuff away to me and a couple of his friends who were still willing to talk to him. I thought he was just being the nice guy he always was."

Marco stopped talking again as the tears started.

"I'm sorry, but this is really hard for me. I've kept this stuff inside for a long time and I need to get it out. It was a Monday. I came home from school and I felt something really strange, like an odd cold feeling as I stood in the living room listening to the sound of water dripping in the hall bathroom. It didn't sound normal; I knew something was wrong. I slowly walked down the hall calling Ronaldo's name. It was so quiet, and I felt all alone, but for some reason I knew Ronaldo was in there, I just knew it. When I finally opened the door, I looked down and saw all the blood and Ronaldo lying on the floor. I screamed at him to wake up as I got down on my knees and started shaking him, but he wouldn't wake up. I just held him in my arms and told him everything was gunna be ok. I don't remember what happened after that because everything went dark. All I know is that I really miss him. He was my best friend, and I loved him more than anything. So the reason I'm here is because I don't want this kind of thing to happen to anyone else."

Then he looked at me and Gabriel. "I know how hard it must have been for you guys to come out in front of the whole school. I wish my brother could have been on that stage with you. It takes a lotta guts to do what you did, so Alex and I want to join the GSA Club and support you any way we can."

I couldn't believe how brave Marco was by sharing something so personal. I wiped the tears from my eyes and thanked him. Then everyone started to applaud.

Marco is one of the bravest people I know because he's standing up for what is right.

Sergio raised his hand next. "Hey everyone, my name's Sergio. I'm new here. I've only been here a couple of days, but I already think it's the best school I've ever gone to. I had to leave my old school because I was being picked on pretty bad. I got bullied all the time. Everyone thought I was gay, which I am, but I never told anyone, not even my friends. I couldn't take being punched and pushed around and being called a faggot loser any longer. A lotta guys even said they'd help me slit my wrists if I wasn't man enough to do it myself."

Then Sergio stood up and pulled his t-shirt over his head. Everyone stared in disbelief. His back and stomach were all bruised; and I mean dark bruises that looked just like mine did. Then he showed us all these little cuts on each arm, and a bunch of little scars where other cuts had healed.

"All these bruises are from people punching me at school. And yeah, I cut. I hate it when I cut, but it's the only way I've been able to deal with all the shit."

Then he started crying. I went over and hugged him and said he was gunna be safe here.

"No one's ever gunna hurt you again. We'll protect you."

CJ got up and helped him put his shirt back on. I looked over at Mr. Atwood, who had this real pained look on his face. He knew what I was thinking. Every single person at the meeting shared something important about themselves that made us realize we aren't alone.

Roberto and Jacob were brave enough to come out in front of everyone. Carmen and Julie, the two new girls, came out too. Some of our straight members talked about the shitty life they have at home, and how they feel trapped by stuff they can't control.

Then Jennifer told us something that surprised me; she's been branded as a runaway by the police because she's left home so many times. Her mom is a lot like my mom. She does a lotta drugs and drinks a lot and has tons of boyfriends, and they're always trying to hit on her. Jennifer never feels safe. I can't believe how fucked up this world is :/

I never knew how much sharing our bad stuff could bring us so close together. It's really messed up when the people who have brought us into this world are trying to fuck us up. And if that isn't bad enough, we got people we don't even know trying to do the same thing, like those protestors and the school bullies. When it got to my turn to share, Gabriel looked at me and connected with my mind because he knew what I wanted to tell everyone.

"Michael, you can't tell them who we are. I know you think we're lying to them, but they wouldn't be able to comprehend it, at least not yet"

"I know, but I think it's important to be truthful."

Gabriel, CJ, and Hunter had these worried looks on their faces as I started talking.

"First of all I wanna thank everyone for being brave enough to come to the meeting. It means a lot to me. You know, we might have all these scars, and certain people may think we're all screwed up, but we are the ones who are gunna make this world a better place.

Everyone here knows my story by now, and you might think I'm brave, but that's so far from the truth. If it wasn't for Gabriel, CJ, Hunter, and Mr. Atwood, I don't think I'd be alive right now, and I mean that. There's some other stuff I need to tell everyone when the time is right because I think it's important to be as honest as I can, but I can't tell you yet. I hope you understand.

But please know I'll be there for any of you anytime you need to talk, scream, cry, or even if you need a place to crash for a few nights. You know all that negative shit goin on outside right now?And all the stuff that happens to us every day? Well it's never gunna break the bond that's happened between us today."

Children of the chosen
  come see how it will be
    it has been written in the golden book
      at the beginning of the beginning
        of a long lost dream.
          So there is no reason to hide any longer
            no reason to stand in the dark
              because if you look real close
                our story is being written on the pages in-between.

As we got ready to end the meeting, the principal walked in and asked all of us to sit down for a minute. He looked worried.

"I want to let you know that the news trucks have shown up and they're interviewing parents and students about your club, and it's getting pretty heated. It has become a very negative atmosphere down there at the moment, but they would like to interview some of you, particularly you Miguel. Would you mind if they came up here and did an interview? I told them I'd at least ask."

Gabriel looked at me wondering what I was gunna say. I looked around at everyone looking at me, and then said, "Yeah, I'll talk to them, but I don't want them coming up here because some people aren't out to their friends or parents yet, and because I don't want any of our straight members to get picked on if the whole world knows they're part of the GSA. I'll go down there and talk to em."

Sergio got up and stood by me, Gabriel, CJ, and Hunter and said, "I'm not afraid of them, I'm going with you."

"I'm not afraid either. This hate's gotta stop. I'm going too," Roberto said, as he got up and stood next to us. Then every single person silently got up and stood with us.

"Mr. Rodriguez, we're ready to go down there now," I said, with a big smile on my face.

We walked out the front doors looking at all the protesters yelling and waving their anti-gay signs. As we walked towards the front gate to meet with the reporters, a kool thing happened; we started holding hands as a show of unity. Me, Gabriel and Roberto, Hunter and Jacob, CJ and Sergio, Marco and Alex, and then everyone else. We had formed a human chain =D

All of the reporters were standing at the entrance with us on one side, and everyone else on the other. The looks on all those angry faces when they saw Marco and Alex with us was unbelievable; it was like they were witnessing an earthquake or some stupid shit. People started calling both of them queers. They got louder and louder as we walked closer. There were more cops by this time because the crowd got so big. Mr. Rodriguez and Mr. Atwood tried to calm everyone down, but it was no use. We just stood there facing them hand in hand with smiles on our faces.

Then Gabriel looked at the crowd with his piercing blue eyes, and everyone went dead silent. That whole angry crowd stood there silently not being able to speak or move. The look on the principal and Mr. Atwood's faces made me smile because they didn't know what was going on. We walked up to the gate where the reporters were standing.

"Which one of you is Miguel Montag?"

"I am. I'd like you to meet the members of the Gay Straight Alliance Club.

Mr. Rodriguez said that you wanted to ask us a few questions. What do you want to ask?"

"Do you think your club is unifying the school, or tearing it apart?"

"I think our club is making everyone aware that each person in the world is different and unique; that being gay is an ok thing; that having straight friends who support us is important. We have a right to be here, and to be who we are without hiding from an angry straight world. This is what our club is all about. If some people wanna keep hating on us, I guess that's their choice, but it isn't gunna stop us from what we are trying to accomplish with our club. You know, it's all about being tolerant about stuff, kind of like a clock without hands; looking at things with an open mind and no boundaries. We are the way we are, and nothing can change this fact."

"Do you think that you are in any danger at school because you're gay?"

"Yeah, we get picked on every day by a lotta people. It isn't any fun being called a faggot or queer, or other stuff I can't say here, but we aren't gunna let bullying stop us from being who we are. look at us. Are we so different that it makes all of them hate us like they do? We aren't evil, we're just teenagers trying to find our way. They can protest all they want, but we aren't going anywhere because this is our school too."

"Do you think someone is going to get hurt because or your club?"

At this point Principal Rodriguez stepped in and answered that question.

"I'm proud of these students for standing up to people who want to try and stop this club from meeting. They have every right by state and federal laws to form this club in our school.

I support them one-hundred percent, and we are doing everything we can to make this school a safe educational environment."

I looked at that crowd and could see real hatred in their eyes as they stood there silent and paralyzed.

"We're gunna go home now. I hope I answered your questions."

Mr. Rodriguez asked us to go back into the school because he was concerned for our safety, but I said, "We are going out the front gate like we do every day. We'll be ok mister."

Gabriel looked at the crowd again and made them close their eyes. The cops lined up like a fence so we could walk out. It was totally silent as we walk through the gate and down the street. After we got about a block away, Gabriel turned around and reset time back about twenty minutes, and then released the crowd. They started protesting again thinking we were still in the school having the meeting...lmfao

Nite!

126

Journal Entry 41
Wednesday, October 10th
11:45 pm

"At that time shall Michael stand up, the great prince
which standeth for the children of the people.

Daniel 12:1

With a charcoal pencil in my hand
and my eyes closed
I can see what isn't shown
and can draw what can't be seen
I can feel it within the heartbeat of a million dreams.
The lines appear
seemingly parallel
but not so quick
look a little closer
look with your eyes closed.
I shade the hemispheres of existence
where angles shape me
in space and time
and where vibrations take hold of my hand
and show me the way.

After the GSA meeting yesterday, we went home to relax for a change. I didn't wanna go anywhere. Gabriel's mom made us a nice dinner as sort of a celebration for our first meeting. It was so nice of her to do that. After we ate, we went to CJ and Hunter's room to relax and be creative. I was drawing like a madman because I was so inspired by what happened at school. For once it felt like we were making a difference.

Jacob called about a half hour ago and said to turn on the news right away. I couldn't believe we made the news. Hunter turned the TV on, and there we were. It was crazy seeing all those people yelling and waving their gay bashing signs at us, and it was really weird to see myself talking on TV. It looked like everything was outta control until the crowd went dead silent just before I started talking. The crowd looked so funny all frozen stiff. The only thing they could move were their eyes. It was eerie looking as the cameras scanned the crowd. I think the reporters were wondering what the hell was goin on because I'm sure they wanted everyone protesting as loud as they could for that added effect. The other thing I noticed was that our bodies had a slight glow around them. This concerned me a lot.

Gabriel smiled. "Don't worry about it, no one will figure it out. You know something Michael, you are starting to change things, I hope you can see that. And one other thing, you look so cute on TV. I know all the gay guys in New York City are going to be after you now," he said, as he started tickling me.

After the reporters interviewed us, they went back to interviewing parents, students, and the religious people. The preacher guy told the reporter about our YouTube video, which of course they showed a few seconds of. As they showed it, one parent yelled out, "Look at those two boys kissing like that. They got their hands all over each other. It's immoral and disgusting. They got no sense. We don't want this homosexual stuff goin on in our school. These homos don't belong, and we ain't gunna let em alone until they close down that stupid club of theirs. Did you see them tauntin us a few minutes ago? All ofem was holdin hands right in front of us. They even brainwashed our two best basketball players. We ain't haven no homos on our basketball team, it ain't right."

Then one of the Muslim guys starts spewing his shit. "These teenagers are dangerous to society because they are going against everything Allah teaches. They must submit to Allah now."

Then the preacher guy jumps in. "This homo club has to be shut down now! The school is allowing this kind of perverted behavior. These homosexual teenagers are trying to make it okay to be promiscuous. I can't imagine what they are going to put on YouTube next."

I just sat on the couch shaking my head, but was happy our story made the news. Maybe people will see how discriminatory everyone is being by hating on us. I felt so bad for Marco and Alex because they put themselves on the line for us. I hope they don't hate me after they find out about this. I'm sure they'll find out pretty soon.

"Don't worry Michael; they aren't going to hate you. Marco and Alex would never let anyone intimidate them. One good thing has come out of this; we have everyone's attention now. And by the way, you guys look so hot kissing on TV ^_^ I'm sure your video is gunna get a lot more hits tonight," CJ said.

All of a sudden my Facebook page started going crazy ass wild as everyone started

posting on my wall and in-boxing me. It was an interesting night to say the least.

$$\Sigma \, \odot \, \Omega$$

When we got to school this morning Mr. Atwood saw the four of us in the hall and asked us to stop by his room for a minute. Man, I thought we were in trouble because of the TV thing.

"Hey guys, I just want to tell you that you've made a real impact with the interview you gave. The office has received over two-hundred phone calls so far this morning from people all over the city. Most of them support what you are trying to accomplish. You should be proud of this," he said, as I stood there stunned. "The down side is that we've also received quite a few negative calls from angry parents insisting that the school shut your club down. But don't worry about that because ninety percent of the faculty supports what you're doing, and the law is on your side. I'm very proud of all of you."

"Thanks mister. It's good to hear that because I didn't think it went too well after they showed me and Gabriel kissing," I said, looking down at the floor embarrassed.

"Yes, that was an interesting video. Who posted it?"

Gabriel jumped in. "I did. I had Jacob take the video because I wanted everyone to see that two guys kissing is an ok thing. There's nothing wrong with showing how much we love each other."

It was nice that Gabriel was protecting Jacob so he wouldn't get into trouble.

"Miguel, on another subject, I have some good news for you regarding your artistic talent. I showed some of your drawings to a good friend of mine, Andrew Abrar, who happens to be a prestigious art professor at New York University. He was very impressed with what he saw and wants you to stop by after school tomorrow so he can meet you. They have a program called Project Explore for gifted high school students, and he thinks it would be the perfect situation for you. He told me that you are extremely talented. He wants to work with you."

Wow, I couldn't believe a professor actually liked my drawings. It made me feel special, even though I'm probably not going to able to go because of what I am. That thought made me sad because I'll be missing out on this kind of stuff. Gabriel was reading my mind and reminded me, "Remember Michael, you can do anything you want. You can be an angel and an artist too." I discreetly looked at Gabriel and smiled knowing I could keep doing what I love.

"Thanks for recommending me mister. I can't believe I'll actually be going to NYU." =D

"Here's the application to fill out. Professor Abrar also gave me an application for the scholarship that is available as well. Everything will be paid for. You'll meet with him and other art students on Thursdays after school, and on Saturdays. He limits his art classes to six or seven students. Miguel, you should be very proud of your gift. I know you are going to go far in life."

"Thanks for saying that. Mister, do you know Hunter can draw better than I can? I was kinda wondering if you'd look at his stuff and recommend him too."

"I'd be happy to. Hunter, would you bring me some of your sketches?"

"Sure thing mister, but I'm not nearly as good as Miguel," He said, looking a little embarrassed. I couldn't believe Hunter was actually blushing...lol

♈ ☮

We went back to our lockers to hang for a few minutes, and that's when Marco and Alex walked up with a few of his b-ball buds and said hi. I nervously looked at him as I said hi back, and then quickly looked away.

CJ got the conversation going. "Hey Marco, did you see yourself on TV last night?"

"Yeah I did, and I think it was fucking awesome. We stood up to em and really got our message across. All those people made fools of themselves talkin shit and actin so high and mighty, like they're perfect. I mean, did you see who was in that crowd? Man, I could tell you stories about some of those parents..lmfao Miguel, you did a great job explaining all that stuff about the GSA."

I was so afraid of what Marco was gunna say. I don't think I breathed the whole time he talked, but I did finally exhale. "Man, I thought you were gunna be pissed at us for being caught up in this thing," I said. He came over and put his arm around me right in front of all his friends.

"Miguel, we gotta hangout and get to know each other better. I told you I'm with you all the way on this, and I want you to know we got your back. Ok?"

"Thanks Marco, I appreciate it."

† ओ ♪

All day long girls came up to us saying they saw us on TV and that we looked kool and stuff. I wasn't used to this kindness at all because I've been picked on by so many people since school started. Even at the restaurant where we always eat, the waitresses said they saw us on TV and support what we're doing. They even gave us free sodas today :)

We were having lunch with our usual crowd when all of a sudden CJ and Hunter got up and said they'd see us back at school in a few. I wondered what was going on. Gabriel leaned over, kissed me, and then whispered, "They're checking on Luis and Lucifer's trolls. Hunter got some intense vibes that something's going on. Don't worry about it, they'll take care of it."

Man, it seems like we can never relax for even one minute without something happening.

"I'm still worried. I don't want anything bad to happen to them. Maybe we should go and help in case something bad happens."

Gabriel smiled his sexy smile. "Do you really think they need our help? They'll be fine. Remember, we have to protect you, and that's what they are doing."

I kissed Gabriel nice and then put my forehead on his and closed my eyes so we could connect in private. Even though

133

everyone was around us talking and laughing and stuff, we were far away sharing our thoughts.

We hung out by our lockers after school talking about how quiet it had been all day. Not one Rican thug said anything nasty to us. This had me worried, like maybe they're regrouping or some shit to figure out a new way to get us.

I asked CJ and Hunter about them checking on Luis and Lucifer's disciples.

"So what did you guys find out? What's going on?"

"Something just didn't feel right, so I just needed to see what was going on. It's no big deal," CJ said.

"We're just hyper sensitive about everything because of what's at stake. What you are going through is all new to us, so we want to make sure that our plans are all in place," Hunter added.

Now they really had me worried because I knew more shit was gunna happen soon O__o

Seiko walked up to her locker just as we were getting ready to go to Drama Club.

"Hey, I saw you guys on TV last night. That was so kool to stand up to all those jerks like that. Miguel, it's great to see that you're changing things around here. Last year sucked because all the assholes were running everything and intimidating everyone. You guys have them getting crazy tight. That's so kool."

"Thanks Seiko. You were like the first person to say hi to me and make feel like I belonged here. It was so crazy when school started. It's still crazy, but at least things seem to be getting better."

"Hey, do you guys want to stop by the music room and watch us play? We're practicing Tchaikovsky's Piano Concerto no. 1 in B-flat minor."

"Wow, that'd be kool. I love Tchaikovsky, but we have play practice today," I said, looking totally disappointed.

"I've got an idea," Gabriel said. "We'll stop by during our break."

CJ and Hunter said they were looking forward to hearing her play. "Miguel has told us you're an amazing pianist," CJ said.

Seiko playfully hit my arm because I embarrassed her. "I'm ok I guess, but I have a long way to go. You guys can meet the other musicians too. They're really nice, a little strange sometimes, but nice. I also want to let you guys know that we wanted to come to the GSA meeting yesterday, but we had to work on the concerto because we have a competition coming up in a couple of weeks. We're like practicing every day" :/

"Don't worry, just come to the meetings whenever you can. We appreciate the support. We'll see you in a little while," I said, as Seiko got some sheet music out of her locker.

"Hey, do you mind if we walk with you? The music room is on the way to the auditorium."

"Yeah, I'd like that."

✡ ♯

All everyone talked about for the first ten minutes at rehearsal was us being on TV. They were saying how kool it was that the GSA Club is making such a huge impact.

Roberto made me feel a little embarrassed because he said I made that whole crowd go quiet when I was talking to the reporters. "Miguel, you really handled that intense situation like I've never seen. It felt good standing up to all those morons."

"Thanks, but I couldn't have done any of it without all of you," I said, as I started to get emotional. Gabriel held my hand to calm me down. "If we all stay together on this thing, we can defeat them, and maybe help those angry people to have more love in their hearts."

It got quiet for a second, and that's when Roberto kind of laughed a nervous laugh and said, "My parents saw us on TV, so I decided to come out to them last night, and it didn't go so well. My dad was telling me all sorts of stupid shit that didn't make any sense, and my mom was crying, but at least she didn't say anything hurtful like my dad did.. It was mad weird to finally tell them the truth even though I think they were both having massive heart attacks."

"Is everything ok?" I asked.

"Yeah. Ya know, I think once it sinks into their brains and they have time to think about it, things will get better. I'm still dealing with being bisexual, so I know it isn't an easy thing for them. Thanks for helping me with this Miguel."

I went over and gave Roberto an emotional hug. Then everyone else came over and we did a group hug; I had lots of tears going by this time :')

♥ = ♥

Play practice was fun today. We practiced improv techniques again. It's hard to do sometimes. Everyone is supposed to listen and be aware of what the other actors are doing, and then go off script and see where it goes. It keeps me sharp trying to come up with clever things to say and different ways to use my body. Most of the time our improv turns out funny, but out of this acting I'm able to figure out different ways of responding to the script and other actors with more depth. It's also been helping me with my stuttering. I'm getting more relaxed in front of people now, and I think acting is helping because I don't stutter as much.

We did improv for about an hour using parts of the script from our play, and then we took a fifteen minute break. Me, Gabriel, CJ, Hunter, Jacob, and Roberto went to watch Seiko play piano. We could hear her as we walked towards the music room. Her playing sounded awesome. The hallway gave the piano an echo effect; it sounded like it was coming from another world.

I had a big smile on my face when we walked in because everyone there reminded me of us ^__^ Seiko was playing an intense piece as we stood in the doorway and watched. She was into it with her body moving to the emotion that was channeled from her mind to her fingertips.

After Seiko finished, she looked up and saw us standing there. She smiled and then introduced us to the other musicians.

"I'd like you to meet everyone from the Ananta Music Club," Seiko said.

"That's a very kool name for a club. It means infinite; without end, doesn't it?" Gabriel asked.

"Yeah, how did you know that."

"I guess you could say I'm interested in the infinite mysteries of the universe."

"Yeah, me too," Seiko said, looking at Gabriel weird. Then she continued introducing people. "Those two on classical guitars are Drake and Sergio. Sergio is our newest member. He just joined today.

"Hey Sergio," CJ said, with a smile like I've never seen ;p

"Do you guys know each other?"

"Yeah, we do. Sergio came to the GSA meeting yesterday," I said.

CJ quickly walked across the room and sat next to him. Sergio gave CJ a hug and then started playing a song with Drake. I felt bad for Gabriel because he should be in this club playing guitar with those guys. In the back of the room was a stage with drums, amps, mics, electric guitars, keyboards, and a P.A. System. The room had everything a musician could want =D

Seiko continued introducing everyone. "This is Razi, Tala, Kerri, Vega, Erik, and the guy over there on the cello is Brandon, but he likes to be called Shadow."

"As in Shadow the Hedgehog?" Gabriel asked.

"How'd you guess?" he said, with a little grin. Then he started playing the Hedgehog theme song All of Me on his cello. Drake started playing the guitar part and everyone else jumped in and played along. It sounded O D to hear a classical version. After they stopped, Gabriel walked over to talk to Shadow.

"That sounded awesome. You're an incredible cellist. I think your name fits you perfectly."

Shadow smiled a nervous smile. I got the feeling he was guarding himself, like we were aliens invading his world. I couldn't tell if he liked us or not.

"I really like the Hedgehog because he can distort space and time using chaos control.

Wouldn't that be kool to really be able to do that?" Gabriel asked.

Then Shadow smiled a little more. "Yeah it would. It would also be kool to have one of those chaos emeralds and be able to live in an artificially created universe. Sometimes I actually think we do live in one."

"Yeah, I know what you mean."

"Is it real?"

"Is what real?" Gabriel asked.

"Your accent. It sounds like you just got off the train at Kings Cross."

"As a matter of fact I did just get off a train there in a manner of speaking. And yeah, it's real.

I lived in London for nine years with my parents.

Shadow was giving Gabriel this really weird look as they talked, like he was playing some kind of mind game or something. Then Gabriel gave Shadow this sly smile that scared him for some reason. I could see it in his eyes because he quickly looked away. But then he got the nerve to look at Gabriel again. He started playing a song on the cello as he let the music flow out of his body. I closed my eyes and let the music fill my mind. I couldn't believe all the talent that was in this room. It was very kool getting to know everyone.

CJ invited all ofem to the party on Saturday. They said they'd try to be there. Man, I can't wait to have everyone together and have some fun =D

We finally headed back to rehearsal and practiced more improv. Seiko and her friends inspired me to be more focused with my acting, and about other stuff. I'm real nervous about meeting the art professor tomorrow, but I can't wait to see what NYU is all about.

It turned out to be a good day =D

•

Journal Entry 42
Thursday, October 11th
11:45 pm

I never believed in destiny
only random pain and broken dreams
and the voices of loneliness
that would haunt my world of shame.
I always thought that I was the guilty one
for being called a sin
for being called a stain on humanity
as they threw me to the curb
with the garbage on Tuesday morning in the rain.
So I ask
how can I be the chosen one
if I am sin personified
or a stain on humanity
or garbage in the rain?
I am haunted by the concepts of good and evil
and guilt and shame
but from my hand to the canvass
I begin.

At CJ's apartment on the terrace
  overlooking Washington square Park
    2:45am

"Are they all going to die?"

"I don't know. Right now we have no idea how this is going to turn out. Destiny is a funny thing when there aren't any rules."

"Then why are we fighting so hard if it doesn't matter in the end?"

"I think this is where love, compassion, and truth become important no matter what the outcome may be."

"Have you ever thought about what it would be like if there was no God or Lucifer or us?

What would happen if people were left on their own, and somehow they knew it?

Could they survive with that truth? That reality?"

"I don't have the answer, but it's an interesting equation."

"I just don't want it to turn out like the last world we tried to save."

"Michael, you remember what happened last time?"

"Yeah, I do. It came back to me while I was mediating tonight, and it made me sad because we had so much love and hope for them, but they threw it all away."

$$\Omega \; \Lambda$$

We didn't say anything for a while as we both looked down at the park. It felt magical as the lamp posts illuminated the shadows and the tree limbs danced with the wind.

I tried to let my mind go as I silently pieced stuff together.

"Gabriel, I'm real nervous about meeting that professor tomorrow. I don't think I'm as good as everyone says. What if it's all a mistake and he thinks I suck?"

"Don't be nervous Michael, just be yourself and show him what you can do. You're an amazing artist. This is not a mistake. Do you want me to go with you tomorrow?"

"Yeah, I would. I know I'm gunna stutter like mad if you're not there."

"Don't worry, just be yourself and everything will be fine. I think your stuttering is cute. It's part of who you are on earth," Gabriel said, as he kissed me.

♫ ♥

Not one thug said anything nasty to us this morning when we walked through the front gates at school. They were actually ignoring us as they stood by a side wall hanging out. I wondered if this was some new kind of strategy or something, so I started reading their minds, and all they were thinking about was how much they hated us and how they wished we were dead. Most of these guys don't think too deep. Besides them hating us, they were thinking about having sex, getting high, and trying to look all swag for their girls. '__' I had to stop listening because it was such a waste of time O__o I also wondered where Luis and his posse were. I haven't seen him or Lucifer's disciples at school since the protest. I know something's up.

We had to go through the lunch room doors because some worker guys were putting on the new front doors that we messed up the other day..lol We decided to stop by Atwood's class to talk. "Good morning guys. I just made a pot of coffee. Help yourselves."

"Thanks mister." CJ and Hunter went over to get some for all of us.

"Miguel, did you fill out the application and scholarship paperwork?"

"Yeah, I did. Mister, I'm real nervous about meeting your professor friend today."

"Don't worry; Professor Abrar is a very nice guy. He is very impressed with your artistic abilities. I had dinner with him the other night and he told me that your sketches have a very sophisticated quality for someone your age."

Wow! I couldn't believe what I was hearing. Gabriel had this "I told you so" look on his face.

"Thanks for letting me know that. That makes me feel a lot better."

"Mister, can I ask you something else?"

"Sure, ask away."

"What's New York University like? Ya know, going to a college like that? Is everyone a genius or something? If they are, I'm gunna feel mad stupid because I'm not like that. I'm not smart."

"Don't ever say that Miguel. You're one of the smartest students I know. Being smart isn't measured by test scores and grades alone. Intelligence is a complex variable that contains layers of thought, insight, and a curiosity about everything that we're a part of. Miguel, you can see things very few people can see, and that is a real gift."

144

"Thanks for saying that mister."

I finally felt calm and a little more sure of myself as we sat there drinking coffee.

Hunter asked mister to explain book one of Paradise Lost. I listened closely because Atwood sees stuff too, and that made me kind of wonder if he could see the truth about us.

ぽ ㄢ

We were hanging out at our lockers before first period and I noticed Shadow standing a little ways down the hall looking at us every now and then. He was hanging out with Drake and Erik.

I didn't wanna do it, but I decided to listen to him; I couldn't believe what he was thinking.

I put my arm around Gabriel. "I think someone's crushing on you."

"Oh really? Are you getting jealous cute one?" he asked.

"So who do you think likes me?"

"It's Shadow. He's hanging with Drake and Erik down the hall, and every time I look at him, he's looking at us. Actually he's looking at you. I can tell he's mad shy and wants to talk to you."

"I don't think he's gay," Gabriel said.

"You're right. He's straight, but he's still crushing on you because you connected with him yesterday. He wants to be friends but doesn't know how to tell you. I think that's so cute."

"Well, let's get him unshy then."

Shadow had his back to us as he talked to Drake and Erik. Gabriel made him turn around and look our way. Shadow looked at us for a second and then looked down at the floor real quick.

145

Gabriel smiled and then walked over and said hi to him. He brought all three of them back to our locker to hang. Things were a little awkward at first, but then we started talking about music and video games and stuff. Gabriel complimented Shadow again on his cello playing, which made him smile a very cute smile ;p

"Are you guys coming to our party on Saturday?" CJ asked.

"I am," Said Drake.

Shadow and Erik said they were gunna be there too.

"Kool."

Then Drake asked, "Do you guys wanna hang with us at lunch today? We don't go to the cafeteria because of all the shit that happens there. We hang out in the music room and prac-tice. We play Yugioh every now and then too. And we play other types of music too, not just classical. We love playing Beatles, Green Day, Linkin Park, and Black Veil Brides songs."

"Yeah, we'd love to hang out with you guys. I love Green Day and anything screamo," I said, with a huge smile on my face.

"I'd love to jam with you guys sometime. I play guitar and sing," Gabriel said.

"Kool. You wanna jam today?" Shadow asked, all excited.

"Yeah, that sounds great."

"I can sing screamo," CJ said, as he started singing the screa-mo part of Knives and Pens and jumping around like a madman =D

I looked at him totally shocked because I didn't know he could sing like that. So did everyone else in the hall..lmfao

"What the fuck, that's wavy," I said.

"Hey thanks."

146

We hung out for a few more minutes and then headed to Atwood's class.

We had a great time at lunch getting to know everyone better. CJ and Sergio immediately hooked up. They look very cute together. If Sergio only knew..lol =D

It was amazing to see Gabriel play guitar in a band. He looked so hot playing and jumping around all crazy. I almost couldn't control myself because he got me all worked up ;p

They started out playing Knives and Pens, and it sounded sick, like they'd been playing together for years. Gabriel sang the main part and CJ sang the screamo part. It sounded fucking awesome! Then they played Nothing Good Has Happened Yet by We Are The Ocean. Gabriel knows how much I love that song, and I could tell he was singing it to me. CJ sang the screamo part to that song too, and he jumped around just like the guy in the video. Sergio couldn't take his eyes off CJ ;p

I couldn't believe all that talent was in one room! Gabriel, Drake, and Sergio were playing guitars, Shadow played bass, Razi played drums, and Erik played keyboard. Seiko wasn't at school today for some reason. Hunter and I sat there listening as each of us sketched them playing. It's amazing how music brings people together. I love how it enters my brain and makes me realize that we're part of something unique, that we're all connected through these beautiful sound waves. Life without music would be cold and empty.

♪ Ω ♪

I was sitting by the window daydreaming during eighth period feeling nervous about meeting Professor Abrar. I knew I
shouldn't be all wound up, but I was. I felt like I wouldn't fit in
with all those smart rich kids. I was hiding behind my bangs and
hoody like I was trying to make myself disappear once again. My
leg was bouncin up and down like mad as I closed my eyes and
tried to find that inner strength that's gotten me through years
of bullshit. I was finally able to relax a little. When I opened my
eyes, I looked around at everyone and saw how bored and tired
they looked. Some people had their heads down or were secretly texting and updating their statuses on line. It was like all ofem
had nothing that sparked any kind of inner passion. It seemed like
they just wanted to get out of school so they could go home and
sleep or veg out to escape their boring lives. It's such a waste
when people don't use the potential they have. Thinking about
this made me realize that I have an opportunity of a lifetime by
going to New York University.

※ ↗

We hung out for a while by our lockers after school. I had
some time to kill before me and Gabriel had to leave. We were
taking the fast way to NYU anyways :D

I'm gunna be missing play practice on Thursdays from now
on, but Miss Linda said it was ok.

I talked with the guys. "You know, not seeing Luis or those
disciples for the last couple days has me worried. It's been way
too quiet. I know something's up. I can feel it."

"Michael, don't worry, we have it under control," Hunter said.

"Are you sure? I'm feeling something's not right big time. It's felt weird all day."

"I know what you mean. To be honest, they're regrouping and trying to find a way to take us on," Gabriel said.

"Yeah, they're running scared. That's what weak people do," CJ said, leaning against his locker smiling. "We're going to head to drama practice now. Good luck Michael. We're very proud of you. Have fun," Hunter said.

CJ hugged me and whispered, "Show them what you're made of Michael."

I don't know why, but I got real nervous again as we walked from Washington Square Park to the Tisch School of The Arts building. That's the place where I'm supposed to go for my class. Gabriel was so nice to me as he held my hand and gave me reassurance.

"Michael, you're really lucky to get to experience all of this. I wish God had made me human so I could understand the feelings you have right now. It's very kool that you have this artistic ability. The amazing thing is, it is your human side that has this talent. That's what makes you so unique. It's what Mr. Atwood and this professor are seeing."

"Thanks. My drawing and painting have been the only things that have kept me sane, that is until you came to be with me. I wish you could be human with me. If I had the power, I'd make you human so we could go through all this stuff together in the same way."

When we got to the front of the building, I turned and hugged Gabriel as tight as I could. I wanted to leave and make love to him insteada going in. I put my forehead on his, closed my eyes, and tried with all my might to give Gabriel part of my human side.

"Time to go in cute one."

I felt lost as we walked into the lobby to find out what floor the professor was on.

All the students in the building looked a lot older than me, which made feel like a little kid :(

Well anyway, we finally found the art studio. It was awesome =D I hesitantly walked in and saw this guy working on a painting. I thought I'd died and gone to heaven because it felt liked I belonged there. We walked over to watch him paint. He was in the corner with a huge canvas hung up at all these different angles. He looked at me for a second, smiled, and then kept on painting. It was really weird because he had two brushes in each hand and had his body right up to the canvas with his arms stretched out as far as he could while he painted. It looked uncomfortable, but I could immediately see what he was doing. The center of the painting was detailed and intricate, and the edges were blurry looking and abstract, like he was reaching for something beyond reality. I stood there smiling because he was reaching beyond what people refuse to believe exists.

"How do you like it?"

The voice startled me for a second. "It's awesome," I said.

"You must be Miguel Montag."

"Y-yes I am," I said, stuttering.

"I'm Professor Abrar." He walked to the painting and studied it for a second, then he turned around and looked me right in the eyes.

"You glow Miguel, and so does your friend."

"Hi, my name's Gabriel. It's nice to meet you professor."

"It's nice to meet both of you. Gabriel, you're from London?"

"Yes. I guess my accent does give me away."

Man, he scared the shit outta me when he said we glowed, and the way he questioned Gabriel.

I thought for sure he knew what we were. I tried to change the subject.

"This place is a dream come true for me. To tell you the truth, I'm mad nervous right now."

"What do you think of Donovan's painting?"

"It's incredible. I've never seen anything like it."

Donovan stopped painting and introduced himself. He seemed real nice.

"Would you like to do some sketching or painting?" Professor Abrar asked. "I want you to feel at home because I already know you belong here."

He pointed to an empty area right across from Donovan and said it was now mine.

"It's been waiting for you Miguel. Have fun."

This guy was wack, but Gabriel let me know everything was ok. I thanked the professor, took off my book bag, and got started.

"I'm going to go check out the rest of the building so you can concentrate," Gabriel said.

"I don't want you to go."

"You'll be fine. I want to check out the film department. I'll wait for you in the lobby."

He gave me a kiss and left. Then the professor told me to relax and just have some fun.

"I want you to get used to your new environment. Whether you know it or not, you were meant to be here Miguel. I'll be back in a little while." And then he was gone.

▲ ☻

A couple of hours went by like it was five minutes. I was so into it that I didn't notice that Donovan was watching me. I painted an abstract and sketched a portrait of Gabriel using a technique I've used for years. I close my eyes and let my mind connect with my hand.

Donovan watched as Gabriel came to life on paper. I was having an out of body experience, so I could see what was happening. The professor was watching me from the other side of the room. He had this strange look on his face. It kinda creeped me out a little, but all of a sudden I knew what to paint. It felt like I was seeing into a different world, so I zoomed back into my body and went at it.

Donovan came over after I had finished. He looked at the painting and the portrait of Gabriel. "Incredible! They're awesome Miguel," he said, smiling.

"Thanks. It was fun."

The portrait of Gabriel was perfect. There was so much love in his eyes. The portrait was letting me know that he was protecting me even when we weren't in the same room.

The professor came over and put his hand on my shoulder. "Miguel, very good indeed."

"I can't believe you did this portrait with your eyes closed. When did you learn how to draw like that?" Donovan asked.

"I don't know. I've been doing it that way since I was a little kid. I could always just see stuff in my mind and then draw it."

I felt mad embarrassed for some reason because both of them were staring at me.

"What's the painting about?" Donavan asked.

I looked at the professor and could tell that he wanted to know too.

"I call it Pandemonium. I didn't know what to paint at first, and then something came over me, and I knew what I had to do. Is it ok?"

"It's awesome Miguel. I love the reds against the darkness, and the brush strokes give it a sense of imbalance. It's strange though because I feel like there's something in the canvas. I've never felt this kind of thing before when I've looked at someone's work. It feels like it's trying to come alive. All I know is that you need to keep doing what you're doing."

"Thanks Donovan. That's really a nice thing to say. I still have a lot to learn."

"I think you're well on your Miguel," The professor said.

Gabriel was waiting for me as I came out of the elevator.

"Well, how was your first day at NYU cute one?"

"All right I guess."

"What's wrong?"

"I don't know. I can't put my finger on it, but something felt really strange. I even stepped out of my body so I could try and see what it was, but I couldn't see anything. I guess I'm just overreacting."

"Trust your instincts Michael. What you were feeling up there is real, believe me."

"The professor's a little strange, but I really like Donovan. He's so fucking talented. He can see stuff like we can. It was oozing outta him as he painted. I can't wait to get back here on Saturday."

"Are you ready to go home?"

"Yeah, I wanna have a nice dinner, and then I'm gunna get you naked and make love to you all night long ;p

Journal Entry 43
Saturday, October 13th
3 am

Guiding my mind to see it all more clearly
never letting go, always looking around the next corner.
Over untold centuries I've searched and searched
to feel what it is like to be real.
Honesty and virtue now seem like relics of the past
I could never doubt them, or the love I feel deep inside.
Show me the real meaning beyond these simplistic visions
even in the darkness we can go the distance if we try,
always know that in your heart.
Understand how it's connected
just like planets around a sun
time is nothing more than light bending in the wind.
On a restless ocean I disappear over that distant horizon
nearer to knowing my new reality.

It seems like I know what I'm doing with everything that's happening, but it also feels like I still can't find my way. The last few weeks have been like one of those scary dreams where your eyes can't focus and everything's blurry, and somebody's chasing you, and you're trying to run away, but your legs feel heavy, like you're stuck in slow motion, and then you wake up just as they are about to catch you. Gabriel always knows when I'm feeling this way, so he holds me real close to let me know he's there.

I'm trying to leave all the shit behind, but as I do that, I'm also leaving behind the few good moments I've had; I don't like that feeling.

Gabriel, CJ, and Hunter have been watching me real close the past few days. I don't know if that's a good or bad thing; I just can't put my finger on it. It's like I'm living in a mystery world and I don't know how the fuck it's all gunna turn out. When I try to read their minds to know more stuff, they shut me out. I know they're reading my mind all the time, and I can't stop em no matter how hard I try. I don't think it's fair, and they know it.

I know they love me and are protecting me, and I really do appreciate it, but I hate being in the dark on all the shit happening in this world, and the other world I can't quite get to yet.

I don't know why it's taking so fucking long to change. It's like I'm being played with on some kind of cosmic stage.

cogito ergo sum

And whenever you give your word, say the truth.

al-An'aam   6:152

We went to visit my sister around 4 am yesterday because she called for me.

156

I knew it had to be important, so we were there in a flash. She was sitting up in bed waiting for us when we got there.

"Hey Rosanna. What's the matter? You sounded upset. Is everything ok?" I asked, as I gave her a hug and a kiss.

"I miss you is all."

"Don't worry, you're gunna come live with me and Gabriel in a couple weeks after all the paper work goes through. I'm trying to make it happen fast."

"Miguel, I wanna tell you something, so don't get mad at me, ok?"

"I won't get mad."

"I think I wanna stay here and live with Aunt Maria for a while. Is that ok with you?"

"Are you sure? Why do you wanna stay here?"

Rosanna looked at me for a second with her sad eyes, and then hugged me real tight.

"I think I need to stay with aunty for a while and let you and Gabriel be together. I know you're special now, and so is Gabriel because of all this stuff you can do. You can hear me when you're far away, and you come to see me whenever I need you."

I looked at her with so much love in my heart. I wanted to tell her the truth so bad, but couldn't.

"Rosanna, I'm still the same brother you had a couple of weeks ago. You know that don't you?"

"I know you are, but I also know there's magic in you. Is it ok for me to live here? Will you still visit me when I'm lonely?"

I sat down on the bed next to her and hugged her real tight again. We sat there knowing this was what we both needed to do right now. I thought about her getting hurt with all the hate that's swirling around me, so living with my aunt is a way to protect her.

"I'll be here the second you call me, ok? Pretty soon I'll take you around the city in my special way and we'll have a lotta fun. I wanna show you where I live now, and I want you to meet my new friends from school."

"Miguel, are you happy?"

"Yeah, I'm the happiest I've ever been."

"Do you love Gabriel?"

"Yes, very much."

"I'm glad you love each other," she said, looking at both of us.

It makes me happy that she's ok with me being gay. Rosanna has never judged me, not even once.

We were at our lockers this morning hanging out with Sergio, Jacob, Jennifer, and Shadow, and I got to thinking about making some sort of statement to let all the homophobes know that we're not gunna hide or be intimidated. I wanted to get all of our new friends together in the most fucked up social spot in school; the cafeteria O__o

Hunter immediately stopped talking with Jacob, turned to me, and said, "It's done Miguel."

Everyone looked at him weird for a second because it came out of the blue.

"What's done?" Jacob asked, looking a little put-off, like he was mad that Hunter got distracted while they were talking.

"Just a sketch I was working on last night. I forgot to let Miguel know that I finished it. We were drawing together and Miguel went to bed early."

"Thanks," I said, as I looked at everyone looking at us. Gabriel and CJ smiled, and then started talking again like it was no big deal. I changed the subject real quick.

"Have you seen Roberto?" I asked Jennifer.

"No, not yet. He usually comes in a few minutes late. Why?"

"It's no big deal, I just wanted to ask him something."

I had a worried feeling for some reason, and I needed to know that Roberto was ok. Gabriel looked at me and squeezed my hand to let me know everything was kool.

Anyway, it was great just to hang and talk. It feels like all of us belong now. It's kinda interesting that we still have our shields up, but we're slowly lowering them little by little.

I've been trying to get to know Shadow better, but it's been kind of hard. He's so quiet at times, and then other times he gets loud and sarcastic. I know it must be hard for him because he's so shy. I just hope he doesn't mind hanging out with a bunch of gay boys; it's probably gunna make his life hell.

Shadow kept sneaking these uneasy looks at me and Gabriel as we held hands and leaned against each other. I don't know if he thinks we're gross, or if he's jealous about me being with Gabriel. I don't think he's gay, but you never know. One thing I've done is promise myself not to read any of my friend's minds anymore unless it's an emergency. I don't think it's fair, so I don't really know what he's thinking.

☯ 〰

People were staring at us like we were aliens from another planet when we walked into the cafeteria. We've never eaten in this place once, so I'm sure us being there was a weird thing.

Whole tables of people stopped talking and stared at us as we walked to a table in the middle of the cafeteria. It was funny and sad. Some guys started making kissing and sucking noises as we walked by. A few guys even put their fist up to their mouths to simulate going down on dick.

It was so stupid, but predictable. It looked like those guys had some experience sucking guys off..lol Hunter got pissed when they started doing that, so I knew some bad shit was gunna go down. Hunter stopped dead in his tracks, turned and stared at them. Then this one guy said, "What the fuck you lookin at bitch?" Well that was the wrong thing to say O__o

Hunter started making their table shake and bounce all over the fucking place as everyone tried to grab their food trays. Then he started electrocuting them. Their bodies started shaking uncontrollably. Everyone in the cafeteria was watching what was goin on.

All of a sudden Hunter made it all stop and then leaned down and said, "If you say one more fucking word, I'm going to open up the earth below you and let it swallow every one of you mother fuckers up." He smiled, and then continued walking to our table.

Gabriel and CJ laughed as Hunter sat down. "We'll this is starting out well," CJ said.

No one moved an inch or said a word at that table for a few seconds, and then every single one ofem got up and ran the fuck outta there..lmfao Everyone was looking at us and whispering to each other. Some lunch ladies walked over to that table all pissed off because food was all over the fucking place. They had the janitor guy come clean it up.

"Are you sure everyone is gunna come?" I asked.

"Your wish is our command," Hunter and CJ said, at the same time.

"Watch what happens," Gabriel said, as he turned and kissed me in front of everyone.

Some people started groaning because they were grossed out, but I didn't care.

And then it started happening. One by one, everyone that I wanted there started coming through the doors. All of our friends came in on one side of the cafeteria, and all of our enemies came in on the other. It was the strangest thing to see. The looks on all of those thug faces walking in was mad funny. It was like, "What da fuck we doin here?" CJ started laughing as he worked his magic. He made everyone one of those Rican thugs and their girls go stand in line to get the shitty lunch. Man, you don't ever wanna eat that stuff if you can help it :(

I could tell our friends were scared because we were sitting right in the middle of all the haters. The only people not scared were Marco and three other basketball players. They sat across from Gabriel and me talking and laughing like it was no big deal =)

Shadow sat next to Gabriel looking kinda worried about the situation. Sergio sat next CJ, and Jacob sat next to Hunter holding hands under the table. I really felt sorry for Shadow, Drake, and Erik. I knew they didn't wanna be in the middle of all this, and

I don't blame em, but it's important not to be afraid of shit sometimes. Sieko, Vega, and Kerri seemed ok with the stares and stuff even though they were quiet. Jennifer and Christal started getting our table talking, which was kool.

Just as everyone was finally relaxing a little, these five hard ass Ricans walked up and said we were sitting at their table. They told us to "Fucking leave."

"Sorry about that. Do you wanna sit with us?" I asked.

"Are you fucking kidding?" One ofem said.

I was being nice and really did want them to sit with us, but I could tell it wasn't gunna happen. Then Hunter stood up, walked over to them, and said, "Miguel was being gracious by asking you to sit with us. Now, since you've declined his invitation, you need to find another table."

Then CJ and Gabriel got up and stood next to Hunter to show they meant business.

"Me and my niggas is gunna finish dis shit later." And then they left.

Everyone got quiet at our table again and looked like they wanted to leave. I got to thinking that maybe this wasn't such a good idea. I also started worrying because I didn't know where Roberto was. All of a sudden he walked in with this weird look on his face as he came over and sat down next to me. Man, it looked like he hadn't slept or showered. His hair was all over the fucking place, and he had dark circles under his eyes.

"What happened to you?" I asked, all worried.

He looked down at the table for a second, and then said, "I was playing video games and broke night again. I gotta stop this shit so I can at least try ta get some sleep. My insomnia is killing me."

"Are you sure you're ok? You don't look so good."

"Yeah, I'm ok. Don't worry Miguel." I decided not to push him any further, so I dropped it.

I looked around and saw our enemies watching us, like they were sizing up the situation.

Luis and his boys were a couple of tables away. Lucifer's disciples were sitting on both sides of him like they were his bodyguards. Luis looked a lot more brolic and sure of himself. I know those guys are feeding him that powder shit to make him stronger. Cesar and his boys were at the table next to Luis's acting all swag and looking O D stoned. Maya and her friends were at a table on the other side of Luis. They looked like they had just smoked some blunts too. Some ofem were laughing hysterically, and others looked all glassy-eyed and out of it.

Two other tables were filled with lots of people who've also been hating on us. I looked at them and couldn't believe how many people wanna hurt us.

I turned back to our table and noticed Shadow looking nervous, like he was gunna have a panic attack or something. Gabriel noticed too and asked if he was all right.

"Yeah, I'm ok, I think." Then he said, "I'm going to go now. I don't want to be here anymore. I need to play some music so I can relax. There's too much weird shit going on in here."

Erick said he needed to go too. I was surprised that Drake stayed. He was looking down at the table as Shadow kinda waited for him to leave too. Then Drake said, "I'm going to stay.

I'll see you guys at band practice after school." Wow, I couldn't believe Drake stayed.

"Are you and Erick still coming to the party tomorrow night?" Gabriel asked.

"Are you sure you want us to come?"

"Yeah, it'll be kool for everyone to hang out and party. I'm sorry about all this, but it's what we go through every day. I don't blame you for leaving. Do you have the address to CJ's?"

"Yeah, the party starts at six, right?"

"Yeah. See you then."

Shadow and Erik had this look on their faces like they were ashamed. I felt sorry for them because they have nothing to feel ashamed about. Roberto tried to break the gloomy atmosphere.

"Hey CJ, I'm stoked about the party."

"Yeah, it's gunna be a lotta fun."

"Miguel, can I ride the train with you and Gabriel tomorrow?"

"Yeah that'd be kool. Come over around three or so. That's when we're gunna leave."

I asked everyone if they were still coming to our party. They said they were.

"I'm really looking forward to it," Drake said.

Just as everyone started relaxing again, Luis's table started up the typical gay bashing shit.

"Look at all da pretty faggots and lesbos sittin at their princess table like they is fuckin holdin court. You a bunch a little bitch fairies and dykes. Yeah, and you too Marco. I'll bet the only reason you play basketball is so you can take showers with guys."

Marco and his friends started to get up, but I asked him to

ignore them. "They want you to start the fight so we'll get kicked out of school. Please don't."

"Sure, no problem Miguel." They sat back down.

It got quiet at our table again. All of a sudden Gabriel put his hand up behind my head just in time. A bunch of food was in midair coming at us. He stopped time. I turned around and saw all this food stuck in mid-air and people frozen in whatever position they were in. Gabriel smiled and asked, "Are you ready?"

"Yeah, I think so."

He put his hand down and everything came back to life. All the food that was headed our way had reversed course and hit the people who threw it. Everyone at Luis's table and the tables around him were being hit with food. Gabriel flung it back with so much force that it was knocking everyone right out of their seats. Then he made all ofem start hitting each other over the head with their food trays. It was the funniest thing I've ever seen.

Hunter and CJ looked towards the kitchen, and then all this food came flying outta there and hit every one of those haters again. There was so much food all over them. Man, it looked so gross and slimy. People at other tables were laughing their heads off. The whole situation was outta control. A bunch security guards and teachers finally came in and made Luis, Cesar, and everyone else at those tables clean the mess.

They were so pissed. We sat at our table and watch it all like it was a movie. We finally got up and left. I overheard a teacher telling them they were getting detention for trashing the cafeteria, and that their parents would have to pay for all of the food taken from the kitchen.

I was hoping for a different outcome, but I should have known better. I wanted everyone in the cafeteria today so people could see that being around gay people wouldn't hurt them or make them gay, but I was dead wrong. I don't know why people are afraid of what they don't understand.

The idea of friendship is difficult to touch
It can feel warm and real
Or calculated and contrived
Like it's only there for pleasure
Or pain
Or manipulation.
Is friendship just an endeavor so we don't have to look in the mirror?
Or be alone?
It should be an equilateral
Where all sides and faces are equal
But it's not that simple
Because friendship can never be an equation.

♯ ♭

2am on the terrace at CJ's

"Are you ok Michael? You're way to quiet."

"I'm sorry, I'm just thinking. I wanted it to go better than it did today, but I guess I also knew shit was gunna happen. I was feeling something strange at our table today. Maybe I'm just gettin paranoid or something. I'm also worried about Roberto; something's not right with him."

"Your mind is adjusting to the vibrations all around you.

Humans are easy to read most of the time. Just go with it and trust what you feel," Gabriel said, as he put his arm around me.

CJ and Hunter weren't saying much, they were looking deep into the sky in some sort of a trance. I cuddled with Gabriel on a lounge chair and felt the cool breeze swirl around us as we looked into the night sky. All of a sudden CJ and Hunter disappeared.

"Where did they go?"

"Don't worry. Remember, they are your soldiers and are just doing what they've always done throughout eternity."

"Gabriel, it feels like I'm stuck. Why is it taking so long to change?"

"I don't know, but believe me, it will be worth the wait. You're doing great with the powers you do have. We just need to work on refining them a little because we don't really know the true extent of your abilities. We are in new territory on this one."

I finally closed my eyes and lay my head against Gabriel's chest knowing I was safe from those who want me dead.

Journal Entry 44
Sunday morning
October 14th

"One shall have to undergo suffering to reach truth."

The Rig Veda

3:30 am
I'm glad he finally fell asleep. I don't think he's slept for days.
I feel so bad for Roberto because I know what he's going
through.

❤ = ❤

2:45 am
Roberto asked if I would stay with him. He said he was lonely. Of course I said yes, so I got a blanket and pillow and got
him all comfy and tucked in on the couch. I sat on the floor and
leaned my head against the cushion near his chest and listened to
his rhythmic breathing as he began to fall asleep. I thought about
how I could protect him from all the shitty stuff happening in his

life, so I decided I would be his guardian angel. I would protect him at any cost.

It was nice sitting in the dark looking at the city lights through the windows knowing my friend was safe.

"I had a great time tonight," Roberto whispered.

"Me too."

"Miguel, I've never met anyone like you. I think I'm realizing some things, especially after what happened today. Where did you come from?"

"Nowhere really. I've always been here, but no one noticed until you and Gabriel came along."

"Miguel?"

"Yeah."

"I'm sorry I been crushing on you, but I can't help it. CJ wanted me to promise not to love you like that, but I can't do it because I do love you like that. I'm sorry."

"It's ok. There's nothing to be sorry about. I love you too."

"You do?"

"Yes."

Roberto smiled and then gently put his arm around my chest and hugged me as he kissed the back of my head. "Thanks for being here for me."

"I'll always be here for you," I whispered back.

⚥ = ♥

Saturday morning 8:15 am

We were eating breakfast this morning and I could tell CJ was nervous and jittery.

I've never seen him like this; he's always so sure of himself. I think he's crushing on Sergio way more than he thinks. He's been looking all dreamy eyed the last few days ;p

"Hey, what's wrong? You kinda seem out of it this morning, like your head's in the clouds," I said, trying to smile a deviant smile like he always does to me.

"I don't know, I guess I'm nervous about the party. I hope everyone has fun tonight."

"I know it's more than just the party. I think your crushing on a certain someone big time."

"Yeah, you're right. I really like Sergio, but I know nothing can happen between us, and that has me frustrated. Having a relationship with a human is something we're not supposed to engage in, but I can't help it. I really want to kiss him," CJ said, looking kinda upset.

"Man, I hope you're not turning into a human," I said, smiling.

"I just think since we're going to be here for a while, we should be able to have boyfriends; it's only human," Hunter chimed in.

"Are you turning human too?" I asked, jokingly.

"Hunter, have you kissed Jacob?" Gabriel asked, with a serious look.

"Yeah, it just kind of happened. I went to hang out with him when you and Michael were at NYU and I couldn't help myself. He's just so cute and we have a lot in common. I really like him. "You guys have to be careful. You know you shouldn't get sexually intimate with Jacob or Sergio because it could alter their whole existence, and we aren't supposed to do that without a valid reason."

170

"Well CJ, I think you should kiss Sergio and see what happens. You guys make a cute couple. Hunter, I've been waiting for you and Jacob to get together. I'm happy it's finally happened. Keep kissing that cute boy," I said, as I got up to put my dish in the sink. "Gabriel, you said we could do anything we want, right?"

"Yeah, we just have to be careful."

"Thanks Michael, I hope it happens tonight. He's just so cute I can't stop thinking about him," CJ said. "I think I'm in love to Jacob," Hunter said, with this little smile on his face.

It was 8:30 when I decided to leave for art class.

"Are you ok with going to NYU by yourself?" Gabriel asked.

"Yeah, I'm good. Don't worry about me. I'm worried about you guys going after Lucifer.

I wanna help. All this waiting crap is pissing me off because it makes no fucking sense. I feel like our hands are tied behind our backs and God just wants to see how close we can come to getting destroyed."

"We'll be ok Michael. Be patient."

"I'll be listening and feeling your energy, so if something bad is happening I'm comin to help you guys," I told them.

"We're just setting things up in neater fashion. It's really no big deal. We have to travel to a place where you can't come yet, or I'd definitely take you. We'll be back in time to get the party ready. I'll meet you in the lobby at three, Ok?"

"I promised Roberto he could take the train with us to the village. Do you mind if I go back to the apartment after class so we can ride back together?"

"No problem. That actually sounds like a good idea."

I gave Gabriel a nice long kiss, and then told the guys to be careful.

"Yeah yeah, ok moms," CJ said, grinning.

Then I disappeared from Gabriel's arms and was instantly standing in the lobby at Tisch.

I walked into the studio but didn't see anyone there yet. Then I heard some banging in a storage room and out popped Donovan with a box full of paint supplies.

"Hey Miguel, good to see you. How's it going?"

"Hey Donovan, I'm good. Couldn't wait to get back here. Hey, by the way, thanks for making me feel welcome on Thursday, I was mad nervous."

"No problem. Everyone was talking about your work after you left. Sorry the others weren't here. They were on a short field trip to another part of campus to look at some paintings. When they got back and saw what you did, and when I explained how you did it with your eyes closed, they were amazed. I'll introduce you to everyone in a few."

"Kool," I said, as I started getting nervous all over again. I don't know why I get so nervous meeting people. I gotta stop that or ima have a heart attack :/

"Where's the professor?"

"He'll be here in a little while. He likes it when we're alone creating and not being influenced by his presence. The professor wants us to free our minds so we can create in the pure sense. You know how it is, once you get in your zone it's off into the stratosphere. Abrar understands that completely."

"Kool. Donovan, I think you're an amazing artist," I said, as I walked into his area and started taking a good look at his work.

"Thanks. I still have a lot to learn, but it's kool because I get to come here. It's also kool because all of us can learn together."

"Yeah, I know what you mean."

All of a sudden I could hear talking and laughing coming from the hall. "I think they're here."

I could feel my face getting hot as these very artsy looking people walked in. All of a sudden I got shy and looked down at the floor; I even thought about running outta there :/

They walked up to us and said hi.

"Hey everyone, I'd like you to meet Miguel, our newest prodigy."

I looked down embarrassed as I said hi back.

"Miguel, this is Asher, Jude, Liz, and Sameer. They're the other resident prodigies," Donovan said, as he smiled.

All ofem said they liked my work. Sameer really liked the sketch. I told him it was my boyfriend Gabriel, and he didn't even flinch. "Kool. He's very cute."

Liz and Asher were looking at my painting with kind of serious faces. "This painting really draws you in," Liz said. "Yeah, there's some intense emotion emitting from it. I can't put my finger on it though," Asher said.

"Thanks. Yeah, I don't know what got into me when I started painting it. I guess I just got into my zone and went wherever it decided to take me."

We went around to each workspace and looked at what everyone else was creating. I felt like I was in heaven because it all made sense to me. Then Jude put some classical music on and everyone started doing their own thing.

There were a half dozen empty canvases leaning up against my table, so I took one that was about 36 x 48 and put it on my easel. I closed my eyes and started listening to the music as I let my mind float away. All these images came into my head and started playing around with my emotions. I tried to stop em, but couldn't.

All of a sudden I started feeling this real bad headache comin, so I opened my eyes and went to the bathroom to put some water on my face. I could feel that puky feeling come into my throat, so I ran to the toilet just in time and puked. God I hate it when that happens because I feel like my insides are comin outta me, and it smells awful. But puking always makes me feel better for some reason. I flushed the toilet and sat there for a few minutes feeling a little dizzy. Then I heard the bathroom door open.

"Hey Miguel. are you all right? Are you sick?" Donavan asked.

"Yeah, but I'm ok now. It must have been something I ate from that corner stand by the park," I said, lying through my teeth.

"You want me to get you a soda or something?"

"Sure, I could use one about now. I'll meet you back in the studio."

When I walked back in, everyone gave me sympathetic looks. I felt so fucking embarrassed, like I wanted to hide in a corner. Donovan came over and put his arm around my shoulder. "Hope you're feeling better now. Have some fun." He smiled as he gave me the soda. I took a couple of big gulps; man it tasted great.

I got back to my space and closed my eyes again hoping I'd be all right this time. I sat there for a minute until it came to me. Four hours went by like it was thirty seconds. I stepped back and looked at my canvas feeling all these emotions mixing in my mind. I didn't know it, but Donovan said I was crying the whole time I was painting. I stood there lost in my thoughts as he stood next to me with his arm around my shoulder.

"You must have some pretty bad memories."

"Yeah, I guess I do," I said, as I wiped the tears from my face. "I'm sorry about all this. You must think I'm a real psycho."

"No Miguel, I don't think that at all. You're an artist, and artists feel things other people can't. Does it make you feel better getting it on canvas?"

"Yeah, I think so because I at least got it outta my mind. It's been haunting me for weeks, and I didn't know what to do."

"It's really good."

"Thanks," I said, as I gathered my brushes to go clean them. No one else came over because they knew I was a wreck. I cleaned my brushes as I listened to the music in the background tell its own haunting story, like it was trying to let me know that I wasn't alone.

After I finished cleaning my brushes, I started to walk back to my space and saw Professor Abrar looking at my painting. I hesitated for a few seconds, then got the courage to walk up and stand next to him. "I call it Anion," I said.

"The way you have the body on the floor in a fetal position is very interesting; like it is sleeping comfortably, yet in extreme pain. The texture is incredible."

"Yeah, it just kinda happened."

"All of the eyes painted in the broken mirror fragments set against the red splatters are indicative of humankind being wounded and isolated. This painting really does draw you into its emotional quality. Nice work Miguel."

"Thanks."

Then Professor Abrar got all of us together and talked about imagery, texture, and how passionate artists never limit themselves or hold back. Sameer and Jude were saying stuff that amazed me too. They are really smart. They know all about the art world. I stood there thinking how lucky I was to be with these artists.

٦ لجج

It was around 2:30 when I appeared on the Grand Concourse and started walking to the apartment so I could meet up with Roberto. I decided to stop at a corner bodega to get a soda, and that's when I saw Luis and his boys trying to fuck Roberto up. Luis had him up against a wall punching him as the others stood in front of them to block what was going on. I ran over and yelled at Luis to let Roberto go. Lucifer's disciples tried to grab me, but this lightning type energy came outta of my body with such force that all three ofem flew backwards in the air and landed in the middle of the street. They almost got run over by a garbage truck.

One ofem said, "Fuck, I should have known, he's protect-ed." The other Ricans standing in front of Luis looked at me like "What the fuck!"

I got so fucking angry that my tatts started sucking in energy again, but this time the whole city block started rumbling and shaking like mad. I tried to calm down but couldn't, and I knew I was losing it. All these people on the sidewalk started running and grabbing onto shit thinking it was an earthquake.

Then it happened, just like it does to Gabriel, CJ, and Hunter. White beams of light shot out of my eyes hitting Luis and every one of his thugs. They tried to run, but the beams locked onto every single one of them as they fell to the ground screaming in pain. All of them passed out on the sidewalk. Smoke was actually coming outta their bodies. I thought I killed them, but when I ran over to Roberto, I saw that Luis was still breathing.

Roberto stood against the wall and looked at me totally stunned by what I had just done.

"Are you all right?" I asked. "Your lip is cut real bad."

"Yeah, I'm ok. Miguel, what did you just do?" he asked, real quiet and scared like.

"Please don't ask me that right now. Let's get you to my place before they wake up."

I put my arm around Roberto's waist to help him walk. The street finally stopped shaking as we walked away. I didn't want Roberto to see any of that, but I couldn't help it; he was in trouble.

We didn't say anything until we got to the apartment. Roberto finally asked, "Miguel, what happened back there? How did you do all that stuff? There were laser beams coming out of your eyes. You took on every one of those guys like they were nothing."

"They made me mad, and when I get mad, stuff seems to happen. Please don't tell anyone what you saw, ok? Will you promise me?"

"Yeah of course, don't worry."

You need to know a few things. Can you wait till we get to CJ's? I want Gabriel to be there when I tell you, ok?"

"Sure." Then Roberto gave me a little smile and hugged me.

"Thanks for being my superhero." ^__^

"Anytime."

When we got to the apartment I got serious with Roberto.

"Will you tell me what's been goin on? Besides you just getting the shit beat outta you, you look terrible," I said, as I cleaned the cut on his lip and put some antibiotic stuff on it.

"Nothing's goin on. I just haven't slept to good lately."

"You're lying to me, I can tell. You've been wearing the same clothes since Thursday, and I can tell you haven't taken a shower or washed your hair. What's goin on?"

He looked away as I put more stuff on his lip.

Then I whispered, "I'm here for you. That's what friends do." Then I gently kissed him on the forehead. He finally looked at me as his eyes started getting watery.

"Me and my dad got in a big fight and he kicked me out of the house. He said I'm confused and fucked up and don't know what I want or what I am. He actually told me he won't allow me to be a queer pervert, and that I can't hang with you anymore or go to the GSA meetings. He also said he was even calling the school to make sure I don't. I told him it's my life and he has no right to tell me what I am or what I can do, so he told me if I didn't like his rules I could leave, so that's what I did. My mom even backed him up, and that's what hurt the most," Roberto said, as tears fell down his cheeks.

"You shoulda told me. When did this happen?"

"Wednesday. I've been walkin round Manhattan at night so I can be at least a little safe. There's some real fucked up people out at four in the morning," he said, laughing a little.

"You're staying with us now. You shudda come right over after it happened."

"I didn't wanna bother you."

We hugged as I told him that everything was gunna be ok now.

"Why don't you take a long hot shower and I'll get some of my clothes for you. I'll dress you up all emo and then we'll go have some fun."

"Yeah, I could really use a shower. Thanks Miguel."

♪ ☮

We got to CJ's apartment around five or so, and when we walked in, Gabriel ran over, held me in his arms and kissed me.

"I missed you. Are you and Roberto ok?"

"Yeah, we're fine." Then he whispered in my ear, "I'm really proud of how you handled Luis. You showed great restraint even though some people saw what you did. There was even a special report on NY1 about a 2.6 magnitude earthquake in the Bronx. You have more power than I ever thought, so please be careful."

"I couldn't help it. Roberto was in trouble and I'm not gunna let anyone hurt my friends, ever." Gabriel put his arm around me and kissed my pouting lips again. "It's ok Miguel, you did the right thing." Roberto pretended not to hear what we were saying as he walked over to the window.

"Well now, here is our resident earthquake maker now," CJ said, laughing as he and Hunter came outta the kitchen. "Something else happened too, didn't it? I can see it in your eyes," Hunter said, with a sly smile.

"Yeah, I guess it did," I said, looking at Gabriel and feeling a little proud of myself. I could see Roberto looking at each one of us curiously. CJ went over to Roberto and twirled him around, "Man, you look extremely hot, emo boy. Your puppy dog eyes really stand out with that eyeliner. All you need are a couple of tatts and a few piercings."

"Thanks," Roberto said, smiling self-consciously.

I sat on the couch wondering how to tell Roberto who I really was. I didn't know how to start. Gabriel helped out. "Roberto, I guess you're wondering what went on with Miguel today, right?"

"Yeah, no, I mean… "

"I don't really know how to tell you this other than to just say it," Gabriel cautiously said.

Roberto decided to stop him. "Gabriel, you don't need to say anything. I don't think I need or even wanna know right now. All I know is that Miguel was there for me when I needed him. When he's ready to tell me, he'll tell me. Is that ok?"

"Thanks Roberto. I'll tell you some stuff pretty soon," I said.

"Kool. But I hope you'll go on being my superhero."

I gave him a big smile and that was that =D

† Ω

The first people to arrive at the party were Jennifer and Kristal. They were excited to be in such a fancy place. "This is like being in a Celebrity Cribs episode. I'm waiting for Trey Songz or Lady GaGa to come through the door any minute," Kristal said, as she looked around.

CJ laughed. "Why don't you pretend you're Niki Minaj. We'll make a funny video of you taking us on a tour, and then we'll put it on YouTube."

"Very funny CJ," she said, as she playfully punched his arm.

Jennifer asked how many people were coming. "We invited like eighteen or twenty, mostly from the Drama and GSA clubs. Marco and Alex said they were gunna stop by too," I said.

"Kool. I've been looking forward to this all week."

"Yeah, me too. We definitely have to party after all the stuff that went on at school."

Then Jennifer told us that Maya and a couple of her friends overheard her talking about the party.

"She got mad pissed and started telling her friends that us queers were gunna have an orgy in fag village. Then she has the nerve to walk up to me and say, "I hope you get fuckin AIDS and die." I almost punched that bitch in the face, but I walked away instead."

"You did the right thing. Just ignore her. She's not worth it," I said.

"What the hell happened to you Roberto?" Jennifer asked,

181

all concerned.

"Nothing much. Luis was just beating the shit outta me to-day, but Miguel stopped him."

"He's such a nasty ass thug. He gives me the creeps. I can't picture you beating anyone up Miguel. You're so sweet," Jennifer said.

I laughed. "Yeah, you know I don't fight, so I just kinda did some fast talking and then we ran like hell."

All of a sudden Paul the doorman called to get the ok from CJ to let everyone come up.

Having this party was a great idea because it was a chance for everyone to hang and get away from all that intense bullshit in the BX. It's funny though because we're the weirdest mix of people you'd never think in a million years would be partying together.

I was happy to see Ramon show up. He's so little that you just wanna hug and protect him =) Sergio was nice enough to take the train with him so he wouldn't get lost or feel outta place.

Everyone was blown away being in a penthouse apartment seventeen floors up with a gazillion dollar view. They stared out the windows like they were looking at heaven.

Marco stood in the middle of the great room and said, "So this is what the American Dream looks like. Man, its type fire! I hope I make it to the NBA someday so I can have a crib like this."

CJ put his iPod in the docking station, hit the mood lighting, and the party began.

It was the first time I ever hosted a party, so the four of us tried to make sure everyone was having good time.

I was happy that everyone showed up. It was a nice surprise when Shadow, Drake, and Erik walked through the door, especially after what went down in the lunchroom yesterday. I didn't think they'd wanna hang with us anymore. They looked mad nervous when they walked in, except for Drake. He had this huge smile on his face as he said hi and gave me a hug.

He looked around for a couple of seconds and then saw the terrace. "Miguel, can I go out there and look at the city?"

"Yeah. I'll go with you. The view is amazing."

Shadow and Erik followed us out. It was kinda windy and cold, but by the look on their faces, I didn't think they minded one bit.

"I never knew the city looked like this for real; I've only seen it this way in the movies."

"Drake, where are you from? I really like your accent," I said, trying to get him to look me in the eyes.

"Bangladesh. I moved here about a year ago with my mom and dad."

"I bet you miss your friends. I know I would."

"Yeah I do, but I'm really happy to be here. I game online with my friends back home so I don't get too lonely. I think I'd go mad if I didn't have the internet."

"Yeah," I said, as he finally looked at me all shy-like.

"Miguel, I hope you won't get mad, but I told my parents I was going to Shadow's to practice for our recital. They don't like the whole gay thing that's going on here in America. They're super religious and don't embrace some of the freedoms yet. I think they'd think I was turning gay if they found out I was here. I'm sorry. It makes me feel like I'm deceiving you and my parents at the same time, and I don't like that feeling. I just want you to know that I really like you and Gabriel."

"Don't worry about it. I understand all of that kind of stuff, believe me," I said, trying to make him feel better. "I think you're a nice guy. It's great getting to know you."

They stayed out on the terrace talking for a while, and I went back inside to find Gabriel.

I saw CJ and Sergio sitting on the couch real close laughing and talking. I connected with CJ's mind and told him to grab Sergio and just kiss him. I wanted to see what was gunna happen. He turned to look at me. "Don't worry Michael; I plan on it when the time is right."

The music was loud, the food was great, and everyone was having a great time. It was perfect for a change. Hunter had his arm around Jacob's waist as they talked to Seiko, Razi, Tala, Kerri, and Vega. They were kissing each other every chance they got. They make such a hot couple. I'm so happy for them :)

Everything seemed perfect. I did notice one weird thing though. Every once in a while I'd catch Seiko staring at me or Gabriel whenever she thought we weren't looking. Vega was doing the same thing too. It didn't feel right. I tried to put it outta of mind, but couldn't. Then while I was talking with Marco and Roberto, Gabriel connected with me.

"You're right; they've been checking us out all night."

I started worrying because I wondered what the fuck was

going on. Seiko was the only person who'd been nice to me right from the very first day of school. Gabriel said, "Don't worry about it Michael, everything's under control. Just have fun." So that's what I tried to do :/

The one thing lacking at this party was dancing. No one was feelin it. I wanted to dance with Gabriel, so I went over and took out CJ's Ipod and put mine in.

The best way to get people to dance is to put on some Bachata. I suck at dancing, but wanted to try some hot Dominican Bachata with Gabriel, so I put on the Spanglish version of Stand by Me by way hot Prince Royce, then grabbed Gabriel by the ass and started dancing all sexy with him. Then everyone else started dancing too. It was kool cuzz guys were dancing with guys, girls with girls, guys with girls. A couple of other Prince Royce songs came on right after Stand by Me, which got everyone into the bachata rhythm. ^__^

After we danced a while Gabriel and I went to our bedroom to talk.

I told Gabriel what was going on. "Roberto got kicked out of his house on Wednesday because his dad won't accept him being bi. They had a huge fight, so he left. I want him to stay with us till things get fixed."

"He should have come over right away," Gabriel said. "He needs to be protected."

Gabriel got off the bed and walked over to the window. He looked angry for some reason.

"Whats wrong? Why are you so upset? I protected Roberto the best way I could. Shit, I almost killed Luis doing it. All I know is that I'm gunna protect Roberto just like you guys are protecting me," I said. Then I walked over to Gabriel and put my arms around him.

"I know you will. We better get back to the party cute one," he said, as he kissed me.

CJ got his video games out and had both flat screens on so more people could play at the same time. I was sitting in-between Gabriel and Roberto playing when I noticed Hunter, Seiko and Vega head out to the terrace. All of a sudden CJ looked over at us. Gabriel whispered, "Come with me."

We walked out to the terrace to see what was up.

"How do you like the view from here?" Hunter asked Seiko and Vega.

"It's great," Seiko said, looking a little nervous. Vega looked at Seiko but didn't say anything.

"Yeah, I think it's a great view. I feel like I can see all the way to the edge of the universe from here. Sometimes I come out here and lie on the lounge chair and stare for hours," CJ said, looking at both of them with that look of his. Then everything got quiet and uncomfortable for a minute or so. I wondered what the hell was goin on. You ever get that feeling when you know somethin's wrong?

Gabriel finally broke the silence. "I heard they closed the Bronx Pride Center today because the woman in charge got caught stealing close to three hundred thousand dollars. Now they have no money left to keep it open. The government stopped giving the grant money because of this."

I looked at him totally fucking shocked. "I can't believe

someone could be so cold and greedy to take money that's supposed to help us," I said.

"That really sucks," Seiko chimed in.

"Yeah, she took all sorts of expensive trips and even had a
dog walker," Vega added.

Hunter was looking at them intensely. "It really sucks when
the people who are supposed to be your friends turn out to be
your enemies. It fucking pisses me off that people like that bitch
hate gay people as much as many straights do."

"Sometimes we don't know who are friends really are, but
in this particular situation we do know." CJ said, as Gabriel and
Hunter looked at Seiko and Vega. They didn't say a word.

All of a sudden the curtains closed on terrace doors from the
inside as beams of white light shot out of Hunter's eyes hitting
Seiko and Vega. Gabriel stood between us and them to protect
me as their skin started to melt, revealing what they really were;
fallen angels.

Their screams of pain were eerie sounding; like something
not of this world. They tried to escape, but couldn't. Then CJ
shot his light beams deep into the universe and held them steady
as Gabriel held up his hand and turned Seiko and Vega into glowing metallic particles. They were dissolved into CJ's light, and
then a few seconds later, everything went quiet and dark. Then
the curtains automatically opened up and I could see everyone
still playing video games.

"Where did they go?" I asked, totally stunned.

CJ smiled. "Oh, I sent them to visit my good friend Blacky
V404 Cygni."

"Who's that?"

"Actually it's a what," Gabriel said, laughing. "It's a black hole 7,800 lightyears from here. We destroyed those two because they were disciples in Lucifer's army. Seiko and Vega were powerful princes of the underworld. We knew about them all along. Once we got what we needed, they had to be destroyed."

"Man, I thought Seiko was my friend. Is anyone else in there our enemy?" I asked, looking through the door wall at my friends.

"No. They're all humans and real friends," Hunter said.

I kept looking at everyone wondering if they'd notice Seiko and Vega being gone.

"Michael, they never existed in their world. It was all an illusion," Gabriel said.

We leaned against the ledge taking it all in as we looked at each other. Things are so weird sometimes :/

I finally told CJ, "You need to go inside and kiss Sergio. What are you waiting for you chicken?"

"Yeah, I think I'll do that," he said. He kissed me on the cheek and then walked right through the terrace door.

"Jacob looks lonely," Hunter said, following right behind CJ ;p

I put my arms around Gabriel and pulled his body into mine and kissed him nice as the night wind danced around the two of us.

♥ ⚠

The party started breaking up around one-thirty or so. I hate it when good things have to end. Sometimes it feels like it might not ever happen again. Everyone leaving made me a little sad. CJ said that he was gunna have another party soon, so that kept all of us happy.

Roberto tried to sneak out with Jacob and Sergio, but I grabbed him by the arm and asked where he thought he was going.

"I don't want you feeling sorry for me. I'll be all right."

"Roberto, you're staying with us," I said, as we said goodbye to everyone.

After CJ shut the doors, I said, "We're the five musketeers now." Roberto smiled as we went to clean up the apartment and then crash.

Journal Entry 45

Sunday, October 15th.

7 pm

When I let go of what I am, I become what I might be.

Lao Tzu

It was quiet except for the conversation Gabriel's mom was having in the kitchen with Roberto's mom. She was letting her know that Roberto was safe. The five of us were in the living room listening to the sadness in her voice as she tried to explain things in a logical way. Her voice softly echoed throughout the apartment like it was desperately trapped and needed to be set free.

Roberto had tears in his eyes as he looked down at the floor. He was hugging his knees as he rocked back and forth. I didn't know what to say to comfort him, so I started writing in my journal and then passed it on after I finished. It's the first time I've ever let anyone else write in it.

In the Garden of Dreams
there was an awakening of spirit without compromise,
it was hidden between the heart and the mind
and the reality of the journey forward.
The shallow footsteps of his youthful innocence
and those imperfections that would make him human
measured the qualities of things not yet known,
but as always
the haunting melodies played on and on just ahead of the curve.
He wondered what lie beyond the gates
that separated two worlds light years apart
one that was safe from the ravages of time
and one that only the heart and mind could ever imagine.
Those hesitant footsteps were testing his determination
as he walked within the garden walls,
but the voices of the future kept calling to him
and he knew the time had come.
Heading for the gates that had always protected his gentle soul
he thought about how his life would change forever.
With hands firmly griping those slivers of iron
and his eyes staring out to a new world
the squeaking could be heard for centuries
as the gates slowly opened up and let him go.
And he knew with each step forward
it would never be the same
but he also knew that he could never waver
from what he felt deep inside,
and so his journey began.
With his eyes and his heart wide open
his youthful determination proceeded down life's winding path

where the world would begin its cruel and heartless decent
as the deceptions and lies started to cover his skin.
He flinched at the sight of so much hatred
and wondered why people caused so much pain.
They looked at him with overwhelming disgust
as they raped his virgin body
in the alleyways of their dark refined pleasure.
They held his naked body down
destroying his innocence with each touch of his flesh.
They cut his veins with their jagged smiles
until he was almost unrecognizable,
even to himself.
They said it was for his own good
because of what he was
and because his beliefs had no name.
In reality they feared his passion, knowledge, and artistic vision.
They continued to shoot their arrows one by one
but he kept moving forward through all of the ignorance and hate
he had come to know by the age of fifteen.

Miguel

I watched in agony
as he hid all that he believed within his artistic soul
never telling anyone about his gift
for fear they would try and take that away too.
And when their brutality tortured his gentle heart
he longed for that innocent garden as he tried to numb the pain
but he knew he could never return

because it was no longer his reality.
He would lay in his bed screaming out in pain
and yet he vowed to continue on
knowing that love and truth would guide the way.
Hope, Love, and Dreams
Hope, Love, and Dreams.

Angels are visions of pure energy
like the brush strokes on a canvas
so hard to touch or comprehend
but as real as the vapor trails of the imagination.
I could never tell you about the depths
and the constellations I have flown
or the shadows I have walked in silence.
Hope, Love, and Dreams
is all it has ever been in my world
a world I wish you could see.

The perfect atmospheres of advection
knew that it was always meant to be
as I stood silently on the cliffs of immortality
realizing it was a fool's existence if it meant that I was to be alone.
Oh the constellations I have flown just to be here with you,
To have you by my side once again in the sunlight of perfect love.

Gabriel

Oh yeah,
I say I ain't takin no shit from an animal of imperfection

like a fuckin chain reaction of your ignorant shallow satisfaction
you ain't my motha, you ain't my fatha,
cuzz I'm the long lost gay son that you wanna slap the shit outta.
Well I'm nowhere you're ever gunna want me to be, cuzz you see
your world on a pedestal is nowhere near the world up my sleeve
you can't make me return
and you ain't ever gunna make me burn
I'm no token kid who's gunna compromise
cuzz I got a life where you'll never be able to look me in the eyes.
In this world of hate
I will never hesitate
you can try ta grab my wrists
but I'm just gunna pull away.
I'm just like the burnin tree of time
that keeps the fire goin cuzz it's mine all mine.

Oh yeah,
You can wear those rusty medals like that fallen god of truth
or wear the watch of a demented timekeeper who tries to take away
our youth
it ain't gunna work cuzz I'm not a puppet on a string
all tangled up in your hurricane of hatred and insidious lies
that you think I gotta learn.
Well you don't know what the fuck I'm made of
I'm a cherub who's gunna snap those hands
right off the motha fuckin clock
like a long lost nursery rhyme the old once told the young.
I'm no token kid who's gunna compromise
Cuzz I got a life where you'll never be able to look me in the eyes.
In this world of hate

I will never hesitate
You can try ta grab my wrists
But I'm just gunna pull away
I'm just like the hands of fate
That tried to get you to see and re-evaluate,
instead
it was a chain reaction.

Roberto

Once Upon A Time
a long lost world edged a little too close to its sun
and singed its wings as sunspots radiated through
its logic of absurdity.
Illogical knowledge and sleight of hand
were the ways they manipulated and cheated the mind.
And in their clever little ways
they calculated repression, greed, and power as a divine right.
Oh those mighty kings, omnipotent liars, and magicians
who kept the masses ignorant for centuries
through fear, submission, and torturous death;
they are now remnants of a dying sadistic power.
Yes, it is dying by the hand of empirical knowledge
as they still try to justify their relevance.
Like that dead narcissistic Ptolemaic system,
the doctrine of guilt and shame are fallacies
now being swept into the fiery depths of hell.
That innocent kid may only be fifteen
but he has been the recipient of centuries and centuries

195

of hatred, guilt, and shame.
So if you look closely
it is already being re-written.
Once Upon A Time

C J

The purple, black and red hues being painted onto my canvas
are laughing at this world of blue desperation.
Look closely because here it comes
edging onto that temperate horizon
ready to devour the darkness of hateful simplicity.
You've had your chance at redemption
but time and time again
you have thrown it all away
as you tried to destroy the innocence of the young
who dared to be different.
But don't you worry your pretty little head my friend
because you are going to pay the price
oh yes, and it isn't going to be very nice.
Picture life's fallen moments on a high tide
being swept out to the crushing gravity of a black hole;
I am going to place you on that event horizon
and make you wish you had never been born.
He never deserved what you have done to him
but all of you did it with smiles on your faces,
and that is the human disgrace.
So look closely, because here it comes.

Hunter

Journal Entry 46
Monday Morning 4 am
October 16th

I went back because it's been on my mind, and I needed to put things into some kind of logical perspective. I walked out of the shadows from the corner of my bedroom, the corner where I used sit for hours hoping they wouldn't hurt me anymore, and stepped into the light coming through the window that was trying to help me see. Even if I was blind I'd know I was in my bedroom, because the echoes of everything I am come from this room; that can never be erased or forgotten or washed away.

I just stood there for a few minutes as I closed my eyes and listened to the sounds of the street and the whispers of loneliness that covered all that was once mine.

It seemed like a thousand years ago.

Time plays with the mind, and the mind plays with the heart, and nothing ever seems to rhyme other than my footsteps stirring the dust on this familiar squeaky floor.

They were all looking at me as if I had abandoned them without warning, but they could see it coming even as they helped me through it all.

The fan was covered in dust as it looked at me from the corner. I could tell it wanted things to return to the way they were, but the shadows wouldn't allow it because shadows don't believe in empathy.

"I want to comfort your body" the fan cried out to me.

"I'm sorry" I said, rubbing the dust off my little friend.

"Please lay on me just one more time," the bed cried out, "So I can heal your pain."

It wanted to comfort me just like it did all those nights in that now unreal world.

The sketches that were piled at the foot of the bed came running up to hug me. I hugged them and said how much I missed their comforting visions.

"Please remove the blood and take us with you. It's too lonely here," they cried.

And I cried as I stood there knowing how they had saved my life time and time again.

I sat down on the edge of the bed and held each one in my hands as my tears removed the bloody stains.

I walked over to the desk and touched it with my hand. It smiled at me but did not say a word; it knew. That beat up desk someone threw out with the garbage on the curb gave me the strength to create and challenge myself. It was a friend to me when no one else cared if I existed or not.

All of them were crying to take them with me.

There was no broken mirror or blood-stained floor because that part of my existence had been washed away to hide the guilt. They said they tried to stop her, but she scrubbed and scrubbed trying to make my presence disappear. My chair had yelled at her and said she was not human, but she just looked at all of them with disdain.

I sat on the edge of my bed wondering why I could never get any love from the people who were supposed to be there for me. I called to Gabriel, CJ, and Hunter, and they instantly appeared. They looked around my room wondering why God had put me here, but I finally knew the answer; being human is a gift, and with this gift come the realities of being mortal.

"Are you ready to come home now?" Gabriel asked, as he sat down beside me and put his arm around my shoulder.

"Yeah, I just needed to come back here so I could take my friends home. We've missed each other."

Journal Entry 47
Monday Night 11:30 pm
October 16

$\dot{E} = \dot{E}$

I close my eyes and listen to everything around me realizing that the arrow of time can now be altered. This haunts me.

Whenever my thoughts glide through the universe, the same numbers appear in front of me. It gets me tight because I don't what it means yet. $V/W = 10^{10^{123}}$

All I know is that it's filling my mind with weird thoughts.

$$\Sigma \neq \text{\ffi}$$

I wonder if it will ever stop: You know, the centuries of brutality at the hands of the so-called chosen ones. The consumption of countless souls who never had a chance.

Calculated violence.

Random violence.

The indifference of self-anointed conduits to a higher

authority who have said time and time again that our worthless lives on earth are only meant to be a stepping stone to some greater nirvana; The carrot on the stick crap :/

I wonder about love so meaningful that it makes people do anything to find it, and then hold on to it with all their might. Or to be able to trust the friends closest to you and know things are understood without ever saying a word. Or to find the wisdom to let go of the things that have weighed you down as you realize it's time to say goodbye.

t غ گ

It was fun getting ready for school this morning. I was thinking about Gabriel, CJ and Hunter pretending to be teenagers. For some reason that thought made me feel good as we ran around getting ready. Gabriel looked at me with those dreamy eyes of his as he was putting on his skinnys.

"Michael, are you making fun of us?"

"No way. It makes me happy because it's so unreal."

Roberto asked, "What's unreal?" as he stood there in his tighty-whities looking in my closet for something to wear.

"If you only knew," Gabriel said, as he put on a hot looking red t-shirt.

Roberto smiled at both of us knowing to let it go for now.

CJ and Hunter told Roberto they were taking him on a shopping spree in the Village after drama practice today.

"We are going to get you stylin any way you want," CJ told him.

"Thanks. I'd love that," Roberto said, as he got dressed. He looked extremely hot after we got done with him. Gabriel put some red and blue dye in his hair, and I put some eyeliner on to make his dark brown eyes stand out even more than they already do. He has these long eyelashes that make him look way hot ;p

♥ ♥

When we got to school, there was the typical fighting shit goin on. The security guards were breaking up a fight between two girls goin at it over some guy who was seeing both of them at the same time. It was the typical hood fight as they yelled and pushed each other around.

They were pulling each other's hair, and one ofem pulled the other one's weave right off her head. OMG everyone was laughing =D

Two security ladies finally grabbed em and took em to the office.

CJ smiled, "The Bronx is one of the most entertaining places I've ever been. It's better than watching TV."

We were standing there waiting for Jacob and Jennifer to show up when I spotted Sergio coming down the street at like fifty miles an hour on his skateboard. He was weaving in and outta traffic as he rounded the corner and flew up over the curb and through the gates. He stopped on a dime in front of CJ, then leaned back on his board and flipped it up into his hand without even looking. "Hey guys, how's it goin?" He put his arm around CJ and kissed him nice.

As they kissed, we heard the same boring bullshit words like faggot, queer, AIDS breeders, and all the others. We don't pay attention to it anymore.

We walked into the school and found Jacob and Jennifer trying to climb into their lockers for some reason. I started laughing because Jennifer was stuck. It took Hunter to work a little magic to get her unstuck..lol Shadow and Drake walked up to see what was goin on. Shadow started taking video with his phone as Drake did a play-by-play of the situation. Jacob ripped his shirt as he tried to get out of his locker. He got pissed because he likes to look perfect. Hunter told him he looked way hot all scruffy and torn, and then kissed him. I like it that CJ and Hunter have boyfriends now because I get to see the softer side of them.

As all of this was happening, Mr. Bricklin walked up and started yelling at us. He's like this ex-marine gym teacher with big muscles and a crew cut who thinks we're in a military school or something.

"You dam boys stop kissing right now. It's disgusting to watch this kind of perverted crap."

I thought for a second Bricklin was gunna try and separate em by force. Hunter kept on kissing Jacob. "I'm warning you to stop right now," he said again.

Hunter finally turned to Bricklin and said, "I'm sorry that you find two guys kissing not up to your standards of behavior, but I believe everyone has standards that are just as relevant as yours are. Wouldn't you agree?"

"Are you trying to get smart with me you hop head? Because I'll haul your ass down to the office so fast it will make your head spin."

"No, not at all sir, although I think you are discriminating against gay people with your comments."

"I am not discriminating. Boys kissing boys goes against everything in a morally decent society. It's dead wrong."

Hunter smiled. "You are discriminating with your comments and with your actions. You walked past two straight couples who were kissing just to stop us from kissing. You didn't say a word to them. So from my observations, I would say that you have a double standard and an agenda."

Oh man, Bricklin's face turned beet red as he started going at Hunter. He stopped himself from going ballistic and turned around to leave, but turned back around and started yelling at Jacob and Jennifer.

"What in the hell were you two doing trying to climb into your lockers? Don't you know that you can damage school property? I'm going to write all of this up. I think everyone here needs some detention."

He was really getting me angry. "Mister, we're just hanging out having some fun before we go to class. We aren't hurting anyone or anything," I said, without stuttering once.

He turned to me with this disgusted look on his face as he tried to crowd me against the locker. He stopped quickly because he started getting these huge electrical shocks from me.

His body started convulsing wild-like as his eyes rolled up into his eyelids until only the white part was showing. I could smell this metallic smell on his breath and a tar-like smell coming from his body. He backed away real quick and buckled over as he fell down on his knees. I thought he was gunna puke any second.

Bricklin finally got it together a little and gave me this sneering look. "You're the one who is making this school go crazy with all this gay crap. I'm watching you close because I think you're nothing but a trouble maker," He said, almost in a growl.

"You need to leave me alone mister, or I'm gunna report you for harassment."

He looked like he wanted to kill me, but I stared him down as my angel wing tatts started taking in energy. Gabriel got between me and Bricklin real quick because he saw my eyes starting to go white. All of a sudden Atwood came out of nowhere and asked if everything was all right. Bricklin turned to look at him and said, "Everything's fine," and then started walking down the hall. Gabriel hugged me to calm me down.

As Bricklin walked away, CJ made him trip and fall on his face. His clipboard and papers went all over the place. Some students started laughing at him. Atwood went over to see if he was ok. No one said a word for a few seconds. Everyone just looked at each other like, what the fuck. Then Shadow smiled and calmly said, "I have the whole thing on video. We need to show this to the principal. He can't get away with this kind of shit."

"Wow, I can't believe you did that," I said. "Kool."

As we walked to the office, I connected with the guys to let them know what I smelled on Bricklin; we discreetly looked at each other as we walked.

🐦 🐦

We got to English a few minutes late. Atwood had already started the class discussion about the book we've been reading.

It's called *In Cold Blood*. Reading this story has really bothered me. It's a true story about a hard working farm family that gets murdered by two asshole white thugs who think there's lots of cash hidden in their house. They don't find any money so they kill them for fun.

I looked up some stuff on-line and found part of the author's interview with Perry Smith, the guy who actually killed this family. The killer said he thought Herbert Clutter was a nice man with a gentle way about him. Then he tells the writer he slit Clutter's throat and shot him in the head. I couldn't believe how evil this guy was. Then this insane asshole calmly and methodically shoots the guy's wife, daughter, and son in the head too. He showed no guilt or remorse about what he had done. After I read that interview I couldn't read the book for a few days. I even thought about throwing it away. It's made me doubt a lot more things about this world.

As we went to sit down, Atwood was asking the class, "When reading the first sixty pages, what do you think about the idea of randomness versus destiny? Do you believe in destiny? Or is everything around us a random act that we have no control over? Another thing I want you to think about is the concept of a natural born killer. Are there people who can kill and not feel guilty? Are these types of individuals perfectly sane, or are they mis-wired in some way?"

I looked around the class to see if anyone was gunna answer. I could tell some people hadn't even read the book at all because they were looking down at their desks or staring blankly waiting for Gabriel, CJ, or Hunter to start talking. Mister caught

Tasheena texting and told her to put her phone away. Marta said she believed in destiny, but only the good kind like karma and astrology. I had no fucking idea what that meant '___' Mister tried to get her to explain more, but she didn't say anything else. She sounded lost. Mister then called on Tyron.

"This story's wack. Shit like this happens in the hood every day, and I'm supposed to care about rich whitey and his family? It ain't all paradise man. Sometimes you gotta take what you need. This story needs more blood and guts like in Mortal Kombat. Yo, you do that, now you gotta good story."

Atwood looked at him for a second totally stunned. "Tyron, I don't really know what to say, but let's see if we can dissect the concepts of destiny and randomness with a bit more clarity. Gabriel was gunna raise his hand, but I raised mine first, which was like the first time I volunteered to give an opinion. Mister looked surprised as he called on me.

"In my heart I wanna believe in like pre-destiny, but I don't know if it really exists or not. I've been thinking about these murders because it upsets me that stuff like this happens in the world."

Rafael started laughing. "Was you born under a rock or somethin? You is a real retard, retardo."

Mister told Rafael to be quiet.

"Here was a guy who worked hard all his life to become successful. He had a great family, he hired people who respected his hard work and generosity, and then in a matter of minutes the entire family was murdered because of greed and sadistic pleasure. Herbert Clutter and his family were living the American

Dream and making their own destinies, but someone else's evil destiny got in the way. To tell you the truth mister, I can't stand reading this story. It's like watching two cars going a hundred miles an hour head-on into each other. No one deserves to die like they did," I said, with anger in my voice. "The Clutters did everything they could to be good people, and they got murdered for it. It sucks!" Gabriel tried to calm me down because I was feeling this rage inside of me ready to explode.

"Miguel, you offer some great insight about this topic. I agree with you," mister said.

Then Gabriel raised his hand. "If we believe in something beyond this life, then I guess there must be some form of pre-destiny. That's what all religions espouse. But if we believe the life we are living right now is all there is, then even the best laid plans are random. Everything, including this earth, is a random act in a random universe, among a multitude of random univers-es, and random Big Bangs, and on and on. I agree with Miguel, no one deserves to die at the hands of another human being. With that said, it begs the question, is man inherently good or evil? This has been the philosophical mind game people have been playing with for centuries.

This random act of violence at the hands of an evil heartless human is what is so tragic about this particular story. It teaches us that everything can disappear in the blink of an eye without any justification."

Then Hunter raised his hand. "Mister, you've asked if there is such a thing as a natural born killer, someone who enjoys it for kicks. Well, I think there are plenty of people who enjoy killing.

We see it every day. Many people who commit murder show no remorse over what they've done. They either deny it by saying the authorities have the wrong individual, or they smile and say they'd do it again in a heartbeat. The world is full of Perry Smiths, and I personally believe in an eye for an eye to get these people off the planet."

Hunter was looking over at Rafael and Tryon as he said that. Mister stopped the discussion at that point. He wanted us to keep reading the story for the rest of the class period. He sat at his desk looking at little shaken by what Hunter had just said.

☮ ☮

During lunch I went to see Roberto's dad where he works. I wanted to talk to him so that maybe I could get him to understand some things.

"Do you want me to come with you," Gabriel asked.

"No, that's ok. I wanna talk to him by myself. I hope you understand."

"Yeah I do. I'll see you in a few." Gabriel kissed me and then I disappeared.

Roberto's father works in mid-town Manhattan as some kind of manger, or something like that, of a parking garage. I walked into the garage and saw him sitting at a desk talking to a fat guy in this little office area. I was nervous but determined to try and make him understand what Roberto has been going through. When I open the door, he stared at me like I was street trash.

"Mr. Santiago, my name is Miguel Montag. I'm a friend of Roberto's."

He didn't say anything to me, instead he told the fat guy to leave. Fatman gave me a 'what the fuck are you' look as he left. Roberto's dad leaned back in his chair and shook his head in disbelief. "So you're the little gay fucker who turned my son queer. What the fuck are you doing here?"

"Sir, I just want to talk about this thing to see if you can understand what Roberto's going through. He really misses you and his mom."

"I don't have a son no more. I don't know what he is or what the hell you are, but it ain't normal. Look at you. Do you honestly think you're normal? You're the weirdest fucking thing I've ever seen with that hair and your clothes and all the other shit. If you was eighteen I'd beat some sense into you."

"Sir, please calm down. Roberto loves you. Don't you know that?"

"I don't care. I'm so fucking angry at what you done to him. He was never queer until he started hanging out with you and those other queers. How do you think it'll look to my friends and family if they find out I got a queer son. They'll think I'm queer too, or that I did somethin to Roberto that made him queer. I'll be a laughing stock because people will think I'm fucked up and got no control over my family."

"This isn't about you mister, it's about Roberto being honest with you. No one turned him gay. He's known about his bisexuality for a while now. He was born that way, and he needs you to understand that."

"Listen you little queer prick, if you don't leave right now I'm gunna get my guys to make you leave." He started to get up, but

I put my hand up and slammed him back into his chair. He didn't know what was going on because an invisible force had knocked him backwards and held his body so he couldn't move. It made him look disoriented and weak as I glared at him.

"Look Mr. Santiago, you're not going anywhere until we talk some more. You're arrogant as hell to think this is all about you or your pride or your manhood or whatever. Fuck that shit!

It shouldn't matter what other people think about you or your son. If you love Roberto like I think you do, swallow a little pride and try to understand what he's going through right now.

He was wandering all over the city at night and could have been killed, and you just let him leave. That's so fucking irresponsible. Do you secretly want your son to get murdered so no one will find out he's bisexual? DO YOU?"

He didn't say anything, but I could tell he wanted to either punch me or kill me. He tried to get up but I wouldn't let him. I started reading his mind and could see how much he hated his own son, and me.

"I can't fucking move. What the fuck is goin on?"

"Just shut up and listen. You know something mister, it's small minded people like you who have really fucked this world up. History is full of assholes like you. Just because I'm gay and Roberto is bisexual doesn't make us freaks. We feel the same things you do. I hope one day you'll be able to understand that. I want you to know that Roberto is staying with me and Gabriel, and he's going to live with us for as long as he wants. I hope you and his mom think this thing through a little more and ask him to come home. You know, if I had a son I'd never do what you are doing to Roberto, I'd love him with all my might."

We stared each other down for a few seconds. I shook my head in disbelief because of what he was thinking, and then walked out. I made myself invisible so I could watch what he'd do. He came running out of his office to try and get at me as he wondered where I went. He yelled to a couple of his guys, "Did you see that little faggot leave?" One of the guys said, "No, we thought he was still in there with you. Don't you dare hire that kid if that's what you're thinkin. He's the weirdest fuck I've ever seen."

I reappeared at the music room door and then went in to hang with everyone. Gabriel was playing guitar with Drake and Sergio when I walked in. I gave him the 'it didn't go well' look as I sat down next to him. Hopefully Roberto's mom and dad will think this thing through.

♥ = ♥

Drama was fun today. Everyone's getting better the more we practice. I love to act now because I'm not as nervous. I like to pretend I'm different people, and I enjoy watching everyone pretend too. It's kool how everyone can go in and outta character so easily. It seems like pretending is easier than real life sometimes.

Ω Ʊ

CJ and Hunter took Roberto shopping in Soho after play practice, and me and Gabriel went home so we could have some alone time. I needed to be with him and well, you know... ;p

When the guys got back from shopping, we ate dinner and then Roberto put on a fashion show for us. We ended the night by watching Dead Poet's Society.

Journal Entry 48
October 18th

3am Random Thoughts

It was another wild, weird and fun day yesterday: the crazy's protesting, typical school shit happening, another great GSA meeting, being with Gabriel, and hanging out with my friends. I need everyone more than ever right now.

Sometimes it feels like I'm being crowded into a corner as people try to rip me apart little by little, but at least I'm dealing with it without fear now. Fighting back and using my brain is becoming a way of life instead of hiding and hoping no one notices me. It's easy to let people put you down and go crazy on you just to make you feel small. It isn't that way for me anymore. Bullshit is bullshit, and I finally escaped all those depressing fucked up people who were once part of my life. I'm never gunna let it happen again.

I make my own decisions now! Right or wrong, at least they're my decisions.

One thing I'm noticing about the changes I'm going through is how clear my mind is. My whole life up to this point has been nothing but fear, yelling, smacking the shit outta me, violating my body, making me feel like I'm not good enough to be alive, being put in a dark corner so I'd know my place, and yeah, being told ima sin because I'm gay.

Guilt and shame don't work on me no more.

We stayed in last night so we could chill together. After we did our homework the five of us sprawled out in the living room and did our thing. CJ and Hunter were playing chess and listening to music through their headphones. Gabriel was sitting on the couch playing guitar and reading a book on his iPad. He's been reading this book called *All Quiet on the Western Front*. He says it's a book I need to read. I'm gunna read it right after he finishes.

I sat on the floor leaning against Gabriel's leg as I sketched some ideas for art class. It's our way of connecting our energy so others don't notice. Roberto sat next to me with his head resting comfortably against the cushion while he read a book called *A Separate Peace*. He's a lot like Gabriel because he's always reading stuff. I looked at him out of the corner of my eye and noticed the hair on his arms were standing straight up.

He was even glowing a little. I nudged Gabriel to look. He looked at Roberto and then back at me. We both smiled knowing we were accidentally giving him some of our energy, and we knew he was feeling it because he had this contented look on his face.

It doesn't get any better than this.

♂ ♪

1:30am Flying in the Sky

After Roberto fell asleep we went to see what Luis and his boys were up to. They've been way to quiet. As we flew around to findem, I could see how the darkness of the city works as it hides a strange reality. I can't believe all the shit that goes down in the Bronx at night. It's way more nasty than I ever thought. All the gangs and prostitutes are doing their business, which is normal, but I can't believe how many old people are out fucking around too. There's tons ofem my mom's age and older smoking weed, drinking, having sex, and hitting on younger people who are tryin ta be all grown up. The young people who hang out at night are like anywhere from my age to twenty-five or so, and all they wanna do is have sex, score weed, booze, and get some street cred. All ofem use each other to get what they want. No wonder the world is so fucked up. And these people are the ones telling me and every other gay person how screwed up we are. I don't get it :/

I used to hear stuff going on from my bedroom window as I'd lie in bed listening to the outside world. I hardly went out at night because my mom always kept me on lockdown.

She was always telling me I'd be a target for "nasty ass thugs" as she called them. At least she did that right by trying to protect me and my sister from all the shit. She just never realized how easy it was to trick her as they got inside our apartment to do the damage.

All I know is that these streets are really fucked up.

Anyways, we found Luis and his posse hanging with Cesar and his posse by some abandoned buildings near the East River and 149th. Four of Lucifer's disciples were there too.

All ofem were snorting that powder and smoking blunts. I could tell Luis and Cesar were way more brolic than just a few days ago. They don't even know they're being used, but I guess it doesn't really matter to them because they're getting high for free.

We listened to them talk about their plans to get us. One of the disciples who decided to call himself Treymor was saying they need to separate us and get us one by one.

"We gotta be careful cuzz they can fight and they're smart an shit, so we gotta be more smarter." Luis was all buzzed up with this crazy look in his eyes telling Cesar he wanted to kill me. "Yeah, they got somethin on their side goin on, but I'm feelin mad strong and I know I can fuckem up now. I'm gunna get that little faggot Miguel all by myself. Don't any of you mutha fuckas be touchen him. He's mine. He's fuckin mine! I'm gunna fuck with his head first, then I'm gunna make him wish he was never born. Oh yeah, and before I kill that queer, I'm gunna make him suck me off just for laughs. I wanna see him choke on real man dick," he said, as he grabbed his crotch.

They all laughed as he took another hit from his blunt and snorted more powder.

I wasn't afraid about what he was saying, I was just sad he felt that way. All this because I'm gay? Why does he wanna erase me so bad? All these macho Ricans are homophobes because they're afraid they see themselves when they look at gay boys like me.

They don't fucking get it that they're a little gay too.

Luis has gay feelings because he wants me to suck him off O__o and I can tell his niggas wanna watch because some ofem are on the DL. Think about it, they hang out with guys all the time bein all swag and showin off to each other. They're always touchin themselves when they talk, and you can tell they want their niggas to notice how hot they look. That's being gay without the physical sex. It's mental and visual sex, and they know they're feelin it but they can't say anything. Man, there's some real repressed feelings going on.

Luis thinks that by hurting or killing me, he can get rid of those feelings. I know he doesn't wanna kill me, but he's feelin stuff he doesn't understand, and he's got Lucifer's trolls feeding him hate and revenge with that powder.

Gabriel shook his head. "We have to figure out a way to stop these guys without having to kill them."

"In order to protect innocent people, eliminating the enemy is the only option. If you want to defeat your enemy, you kill your enemy. It's what we do when we have to. It's an eye for an eye my friends," Hunter said, looking at the three of us.

"I wish we didn't have to," I said.

Ψ ⚎

Tuesday Morning 7:30am

A lotta protesters were already standing on the sidewalk with their signs when we got to school this morning. We hadn't seen anyone protesting all week so I thought maybe they got bored with the whole thing. As we walked by, this older lady, she looked like someone's nice abuela, tapped me on the arm and gave me a pamphlet that said homosexuality can be cured. It was a religious pamphlet churches give out saying they can turn gay people straight with the help of God. I smiled at her as I took it, and even said thanks. Then I looked deeply into her eyes to show her what real love looks like.

"Can you see it," I asked, very softly. She stared at me like she had just seen a ghost. Then she got emotional and looked away like she was embarrassed.

"It's ok, don't worry," I said. Then I put my hand on top of her's so she could feel what I had just shown her. "Gracias," she said, as her eyes started to tear up. All of a sudden she gave her sign to an angry man next to her and walked away.

"What did you do to her?" he shouted at me. Then he started yelling for her to come back.

"You're turning your back on God." We just kept walking into the school.

"Miguel, that was nice of you to do that for her," Gabriel said.

Roberto watched the whole thing. "What did you do Miguel?"

"Nothing much. Sometimes just looking into a person's eyes is all you need to do."

Roberto decided to look into mine, and I let him see a little bit more. We stood there eye to eye smiling at each other as Gabriel, CJ, and Hunter watched. Then I pressed my hand to Roberto's chest and let him feel what he was seeing. He started to get real emotional, so I gave him a hug to calm him down.

"It's ok. It's pretty kool, isn't it?"

"Yeah, thanks."

Then CJ quietly said, "Hey guys, Atwood's looking for us. He wants to talk." We headed inside to find him. We saw mister opening his classroom door when we rounded the corner.

Roberto yelled to him, "Hey mister, did you wanna talk to us?"

"Hi guys. As a matter of fact I do want to talk to you. How did you know?"

Roberto looked at CJ like "what the fuck?" CJ just smiled and shrugged his shoulders with a blank expression on his face; we followed mister in.

Atwood put on a pot of coffee and started telling us what the protesters were up to.

"I don't want you to worry about this at all because the law is on your side, but some of the parents and the religious leaders who were protesting last week have hired a lawyer and are attempting to shut down the GSA club. They want to sidestep the law by trying to force Principal Rodriguez to shut down all extracurricular clubs."

"I've heard that some school districts have tried to do this recently," Gabriel said.

"You're right. A school in Texas did shut down all of its clubs to stop an attempted petition forcing the school to have a GSA club. The school faculty and the school superintendent spearheaded this, along with many parents. By shutting down all of their clubs, they avoided compliance with the Equal access Act, a federal law that was passed in 1984 to allow clubs such as yours. They are attempting to do the same thing here. Their lawyer sent the principal a letter stating that our school needs to shut down all clubs, citing a lack of funds for other educational needs."

"What do you think we should do mister?" I asked.

"Just keep having your meetings and let us handle this unfortunate situation. You have a lot of support in this school and in our district. Principal Rodriguez has notified the Department of Education's legal staff to handle any potential court action. I do know that some parents have already stopped their kids from attending some of the clubs. They are putting unneeded pressure on their own children to do this. There is going to be a school meeting on Monday after school in the auditorium to discuss the matter."

I couldn't believe what these stupid people were trying to do. "I see we already have our protesters starting quite early today," mister said, with a little laugh.

"We can't let em stop us. We're starting to change things around here," I said, getting angry. The guys looked at me hoping I wasn't gunna start shaking the school to shit.

"These losers are always fucking things up," Roberto blurted out. "Oh shit, sorry for cursing mister."

"Don't worry. Sometimes those words fit the situation," he said, smiling.

"Mister, I was thinking about having a GSA Halloween dance on the Friday before Halloween. Since they're having the regular Halloween dance in the auditorium the same night, I thought we could have ours where we have our meetings. It's a perfect space." Do you think it would be ok?"

"I don't see why not. I'll ask the principal and let you know by the time the GSA meeting starts."

"Kool. Thanks mister."

We sat around, drank coffee, and listened to some old jazz music mister had put on.

After a while Roberto had to leave to get to his first period class. I felt bad for him because he had to leave. Gabriel read my mind. "I'll get him transferred into our class starting tomorrow." That made me smile :)

2:30 After School

We were hanging at our lockers when Luis and his posse rounded the corner and walked towards us. Maya was with him and they were holding hands. They gave us dirty looks as they walked by, but didn't say anything. It was like they were showing off or something. They looked stoned too. I'm sure they broke night partying as usual. I could smell weed on their clothes. I decided to read Maya's thoughts; she was only with Luis for status, and to get back at me. She hates me and she likes me and it's got her emotions all fucked up. I wish we could talk.

"They're trying to size us up," CJ said, leaning against his locker.

"They are the dumbest assholes I've ever seen. Even Lucifer's trolls are unwise. He must be trying to clean out Hell by getting his bottom feeders destroyed," Hunter said.

We went upstairs to the fourth floor to see how many protesters were out front once again. There were lots more than last week. I was waiting for the news trucks to start pulling up any second :/ We had a few minutes before the GSA meeting started, so we just watched them through the window waving their signs and chanting anti-gay crap. I got upset when I noticed this cute little kid, maybe about six or seven years old, holding a sign that said, "Kill the Faggots." I wanted to go down there and yell at the stupid mom of that kid. These people are sick using kids this way. Gabriel put his arm around me. "Michael, don't let this upset you."

"I can't help it. All of this is really sad. It's like an endless cycle that can't be broken. Well, I'm gunna figure out a way to break it, and when I do, look out, because this world will never be the same."

Some of our friends came over to see what was happening outside.

"Hey guys, those people down there are some new GSA members lining up to come to our meeting. Very kool," CJ sarcastically said, as everyone laughed.

Ω ☮

We had another great meeting. Everyone was there from last week, plus we had four new people. One of the new members was another basketball player. Marco and Alex introduced us to Juan, a six-foot-five point guard. Man, I always think I'm tall until I stand next to these guys..lol

We started off the meeting the same way as we did last week with each one of us saying how our week was. I like doing this because it makes everyone not feel sorry for themselves when bad shit happens to them. In each personal thing that's being said, we learn that fighting through all the bullshit is the only way to move forward. I read somewhere online about an old guy named Churchill saying, "If you're going through hell, just keep going." Those are some words I've always tried to live by.

I started out talking about the protestors hiring a lawyer to try and shut down all the after-school clubs. "Mr. Atwood explained that we shouldn't worry about it because the Department of Education supports all extracurricular clubs, including ours. He also said that our club is influencing other schools to start GSA clubs. Everyone here has made an impact by being part of this club. That's pretty kool."

Next on the agenda was the GSA Halloween dance. Everyone loved the idea of a having a dance. Ramon asked if we would have a security cop by our door. I could tell he was nervous.

Mr. Atwood spoke up and said that extra security was already arranged for us.

"As all of you can see, we have our disgruntled crowd out front again. We know this dance is going to cause some anguish with certain parents and students, but you have the same rights as they do to have a dance. We will have plenty of security, so just worry about having fun." Ramon calmed down when mister said that.

We had mad conversations going all at once on how to put the dance together. Jennifer and Kristal said they'd help decorate. Jacob and Roberto said they'd download music on the school's lap top. They took out some paper and started writing songs down. Everyone yelled songs out for em to put on the list =D

Marco said he was going to the main dance, but would also

come to our dance too.

"We got like this tradition about all us b-ball players dressing up in a Halloween theme. This year it's Super Heroes."

"That's kool. Invite anyone else you think might wanna come from the other dance," I told him. Shadow said he had an idea for a kool costume, Drake and Erik said they might dress up like zombies or something. Then Roberto said something that totally shocked me.

"You and Gabriel should be angels."

I looked at Gabriel real quick to see his reaction. Roberto had this humongous smile on his face.

"You know, you could be the archangel's Michael and Gabriel. You already have their names." Everyone agreed.

"That sounds like a great idea Roberto. Thanks for the suggestion," Gabriel said.

Then Gabriel changed the subject quickly by suggesting that Hunter and I draw up posters to put in the halls. CJ said he would take care of the lighting and computer equipment. Mister said once we get a list of people who are going, he'll order snacks, pizza, and soda. He also told us to go to the office to get Halloween decorations. "They have three cabinets filled with every kind of decoration possible."

Everyone offered to do something. We had everything pretty much planned by the end of the meeting. I couldn't believe how much fun we had today. I didn't even think about those people out front hating on us. We decided to all leave together again as a show of unity. Mr. Atwood walked out with us too. We watched everyone carefully just in case bad stuff started happening. There were twenty-six of us walking past the pro-testors. What was kool about the whole thing was the way we handled it. As we walked by, we ignored them and just talked and laughed about stuff like we always do when we're in school. We weren't gunna give them any satisfaction by looking nervous or intimidated. Most of us went to hang out in the park for a while to talk and relax before going home. Whenever I'm in the park, I always like to pretend I'm in a deep dark forest searching for hidden treasure or some other little kid fantasy..lol It takes me back to when I was a kid and my abuela would take me to my cousin's house in Pennsylvania. I loved going there because it was so different from the city. But she disappeared from my life when my dad left. He wouldn't let her come and see me or my sister anymore :(

It felt good to sit on top of the picnic table with my arm around Gabriel listening to everyone talk. I swear I could feel the autumn wind connecting each one of us together.

Nite =D

Journal Entry 49
Thursday morning 3:30 am
October 19th

Do you really think you can surround me by closing the circle
and then beat me until I bleed my way out of this world?
My breath and my flesh and my synapses
communicate in ways you will never understand
I am surprised you can't even see
that the circle has already closed around you.

7:30am Wednesday morning
We met up with Sergio and Jacob when we came outta the subway this morning. They were standing on the corner waiting to cross the street. We caught up with em and walked the rest of the way to school together. Just as we turned the corner to the last block, we saw Luis and his boys walking towards us. There were maybe twenty of them: two Disciples, some older Ricans, probably from Luis's hood, and nine burnout juniors from school. We ignored them when we walked by. They didn't

say anything as they watched us, and then it became clear what was goin on. As soon as we got past them, Cesar and his boys stepped onto the sidewalk about thirty feet in front of us. They were hiding between two buildings waiting for us. We were surrounded by at least forty thugs. Roberto, Sergio, and Jacob were scared to death. Cesar gave a hand signal for them to form a circle around us. Me, Gabriel, CJ, and Hunter got ready to do some damage. No one said a word as we all stood there looking at each other.

All of a sudden about fifteen ofem took out their blades and got ready to strike. Then Luis took a couple of steps forward and said, "See how easy that was? You don't have much time left queer boy." Then he backed away and said, "Come on my niggas," and then left.

We tried to calm Jacob down because he was freaking out. Hunter put his arms around him and hugged him tight. "Nothing is going to happen to you. We've got this covered."

Gabriel's eyes went white for a second; I thought for sure he was going to turn every one of those assholes to dust. Roberto stayed close to me and Gabriel the rest of the way to school. Sergio made jokes about it. We all laughed when he said, "Did you see how little their blades were?"

And so it begins.

♑ ♎

12 noon

We decided to go to Hector's Greasy Burgers for lunch so we could talk about the Halloween dance some more. Jennifer,

Christal, Jacob, and Roberto met us by the front gate at noon. Sergio was skating around doing tricks for everyone. He skated over to us once he saw CJ. He grabbed hold of CJ's shoulder and gave him a kiss. It was so cute ;p

"I'll meet up with you guys in a few. I gotta pick up my latest Yugioh card at the hobby store," Sergio said.

"Which one did you get this time?" CJ asked.

"Black Luster Soldier - Envoy of the Beginning."

"Man, that costs mad dollars and is hard to find," I said, jealous as hell.

"Yeah I know, but I'm tryin ta build me a new structure deck. I want this one to be the best so no one can beat me."

"Kool. See you in a few," CJ said, and then kissed Sergio goodbye.

As we walked to the restaurant, CJ pulled out two Yugioh cards from his pocket. One was an Effect Veiler and the other was Trishula, Dragon of the Ice Barrier, two more rare cards that also cost tons.

"Where the fuck did you get those?" Roberto asked.

"Oh, I have my methods. I thought I'd surprise Sergio with these as soon as he gets back."

"That's sweet. If I can get some money together, will you try and get me a couple of cards?" Roberto asked.

"Yeah, let me know which ones you want and I'll see what I can do."

CJ looked over at Hunter, who had his arm around a nervous looking Jacob, and then at me and Gabriel, giving us his wicked little smile. When we got to our booth in the back of the restaurant, there was a package rapped up real nice with a note that said, "To Roberto, from CJ."

Roberto looked totally surprised. CJ told him to open it up. Everyone was excited to see what it was. He unwrapped it and smiled. Staring him in the face was a kool looking deck box with the two Yugioh cards he had wanted. One was a Dark End Dragon and the other was a T.G. Hyper Librarian. He was totally in shock.

"How'd you know?"

"I listen a lot," CJ said. Roberto leaned over the table and gave him a big hug.

"Thanks. I've wanted these cards for like forever. How the fuck did you do this? I can't take these," Roberto said, as he started choking up."

"Yes you can. Remember that old proverb; don't ever look a horse in the mouth when he's giving you a gift," CJ said, as everyone laughed.

The waitress came over to take our orders. Just as Jennifer started telling her what she wanted, CJ got a panicked look on his face. Gabriel and Hunter immediately knew what was going on. CJ told everyone, "I'll be right back. You guys stay here, but Miguel, Gabriel and Hunter, come with me."

We hurriedly walked outside, disappeared and then reappeared where Sergio was getting beaten and robbed by four of Cesar's thugs. Sergio was crouched down trying to protect himself as they punched and kicked the shit outta him. CJ zapped those assholes with electricity, making their bodies spazz out uncontrollably. CJ made sure their heads hit the sidewalk hard when they collapsed. Sergio was hurt really bad. There was blood coming from his nose and mouth. CJ ran to Sergio and held him in his arms. He was crying hard as CJ tried to comfort him.

"I'm here now. Everything is going to be ok."

Those assholes busted the shit outta Sergio's skateboard, took his wallet, his phone, and his new Yugioh card. I could tell CJ was ready to go ballistic. "They aren't going to hurt you anymore," he told Sergio. CJ stood up and told Gabriel to call 911 and tell them there's a knife fight going on. I knelt next to Sergio as CJ and Hunter went over to those guys to make them pay. With a wave of his hand, CJ lifted their spazzing bodies off the ground and stood them up while they were still unconscious. I could hear the cop sirens in the distance. CJ and Hunter touched each one of them on the neck, which immediately made them wake up. They were bleeding real bad because sidewalks don't move. Then the weirdest thing started happening; the four thugs started punching each other in the face as CJ and Hunter stood back and watched. These guys were fucking punching each other to shit as the cops pulled up. CJ yelled, "They robbed and beat up my friend, and we tried to stop them. Now they're out of control fighting over what they've stolen. I've never seen anything like this before officer."

All of a sudden those thugs pulled out their blades and started stabbing each other. I couldn't believe it. CJ knelt down next to Sergio and kissed him on the forehead.

The cops pulled their guns and told them to stop. I thought for sure they were gunna shoot em, but they held back for some reason. There was blood all over the sidewalk as they finally collapsed on the ground from multiple stab wounds. A huge crowd had formed to watch what was happening.

"They will live," Gabriel said, knowing I was concerned. Then he looked down the street and two ambulances suddenly appeared outta nowhere. The ambulance guys got to them fast, but one of the guys was bleeding so badly that he wasn't showing any signs of life. They were shoving needles into his arms and used those paddle things to try and start his heart. His whole body jumped off the ground when they hit the switch. They had to do it twice before it brought him back. The whole thing freaked me out. I've never seen someone getting stabbed. Believe me when I say it's nothing like you see in the movies or in video games.

An ambulance guy came over to look at Sergio to see how badly hurt he was. CJ was already healing Sergio's cracked ribs and his cuts and bruises without him knowing it. Then a cop came over to take our statements about the robbery and the fight. What a fucking scene the whole thing was. The battle has started O__o

They finally put those thugs in an ambulance and took them to the hospital. CJ knew I was upset. "Miguel, I'm sorry you had to see that, but I know you would have done the same for the people you love too."

"Yeah, you're right. There's going to be violence whether I like or not."

They put Sergio on a rolling bed and took him to the hospital too. CJ went in the ambulance with him. The cops drove the three of us back to school because it was way past lunch. They came inside to let the principal know what had happened. They told Mr. Rodriguez that we saved Sergio's life by getting him away from some gang members they've been after for a long time. "All four are going to be charged with robbery and assault with a deadly weapon," one of the cops said. "You boys were lucky today, but you are also heroes. You should be proud of these students," the other cop told our principal.

"Believe me, I am. These particular students are very unique individuals," Mr. Rodriguez said. Then he thanked us for saving Sergio.

Word got around the school quick about what had happened, and as usual, a whole bunch of wild stories were being told. Someone said Sergio got stabbed five times and was in critical condition at the hospital. Someone else said CJ got shot and died. Some asshole walking down the hall between class was telling his friends, "They shoulda killed all those faggots so we can get this school back to normal."

We got outta there right after our last class and went to the hospital to be with Sergio and CJ. When we got there, Sergio's mom was sitting with him in the emergency room. CJ was sitting there too holding his hand and healing him. The doctor said he was lucky because nothing was broken and there was no internal bleeding. I'm just happy he's ok.

Faced with what is right, to leave undone shows a lack of courage.
Confucius

2am Thursday morning

I wanted to do something nice for Marco because he's put his reputation on the line for us, and because he's been hurting for a lot of years. Gabriel helped me give Marco a special gift when we went to pay him a visit.

We appeared in his bedroom as he slept. He kinda made me laugh because his feet were sticking way out beyond his bed. Man, he's really tall. I quietly looked around his room to see what he was passionate about. His bedroom definitely reflected his personality. Marco had all sorts of b-ball trophies and other sports awards displayed everywhere. There were lots of pictures with the b-ball team, his friends, and I think some of his girlfriends. But what really caught my eye were the pictures of his brother Ronaldo and him on the night stand next to his bed. There must have been at least a dozen of them. Marco was so young when his brother died. I could tell by the pictures that he really looked up to him. Those pictures got to me because two people who really loved each other were separated way before their time; I needed to fix it.

I asked Gabriel if he was ready; he said yes. I nudged Marco on his shoulder to wake him up.

"Marco, wake up. It's Miguel."

"Uh, what?" he said, in a sleepy voice.

"It's Miguel and Gabriel." He sat up real quick and turned the light on and looked at us weird. "What are you guys doing here?"

"I know this seems strange, but someone wants to see to you."

He looked over at Gabriel again totally in shock because his brother Ronaldo appeared out of nowhere and stood next to him smiling. Marco started to cry. Ronaldo slowly walked over to Marco's bed and sat down. They hugged each other as tears of happiness streamed down their cheeks.

"I've missed you so much," Marco said, sobbing hard as he held Ronaldo with all his might.

"I'm sorry I let you down by leaving the way I did, but I want you to know that I've been watching you grow up, and if I had a second chance, I would never have left you. I was so selfish." At that point we wanted to give them some privacy, so we disappeared for a while.

When we reappeared, they were both sitting on the bed talking and laughing about stuff.

Ronaldo looked at us and then back at Marco.

"You have to go don't you?" Marco said, with sadness in his voice.

"Yeah, I think I do," Ronaldo reluctantly said.

I could see the look of anguish on both of their faces. "Hey, you guys can see each other anytime you want, so don't worry," I told them.

Ronaldo smiled at me and Gabriel, and then gave Marco one last hug. "I'll see you tomorrow."

They held each other's hand until Ronaldo slowly disappeared.

Marco sat there with tears running down his face. He wiped them as he stared at both of us. I knew how much this meant to him.

"Thank you. I've dreamt about seeing him again a million times."

"Hey, no problem."

"How did you guys do this? I'm mean, how can you do this?" he nervously asked.

We just kinda looked at each other for a few seconds before Gabriel said, "It's just something we are able to do."

Marco had the biggest smile on his face. "I'm dreaming, right?"

"Sometimes the best things in life are in our dreams, but no, this is not a dream; it's real," I said. Marco gave Gabriel and me heartfelt hugs, and then closed his eyes and went to sleep.

Gabriel turned the lamp off and then we went flying around the city for a while before we headed home.

Nite =D

Journal Entry 50
Friday Morning 4:00am
October 20th

I can feel it swirl around me
It knows the places in my heart where I am most vulnerable.
My mind is open within the mist of a million new thoughts
as I step to the edge
the knife edge of no return
and no remorse over the way it will happen.
I listen to the haunting melodies
knowing the notes and their vibrations have attached themselves to me
like a tidal wave of love.
I want to touch your hand so you can feel it too.

Everyone was staring at us when we got to school yesterday morning because of what happened to Sergio. It was on the news last night, so I guess lots of people saw it.

They reported about Sergio being beaten and robbed, that we helped him, and how those guys stabbed each other.

The news lady said no one knows why members of the same gang would stab each other so viscously, other than maybe fighting over the stolen stuff. She also said the whole thing was being considered a hate crime because Sergio is gay. What really surprised me was seeing the video of those Ricans stabbing each other. Someone must have taken it with their phone.

Man, it was strange seeing it again, and seeing all the blood. Roberto was sitting on the floor next to me watching it.

"Shit's always happening in the Bronx. I fuckin hate this place. I try not to think about this kind of shit, but when it happens to my friends it gets me tight. You guys were real brave saving Sergio. Everything's gettin fuckin crazy around here."

"I'm glad you weren't there because you coulda been hurt again," I told Roberto.

We were waiting for Jacob, Jennifer and Kristal to show up when Luis, Maya, Cesar and some of their posse rolled in. We were hanging by the front steps as they walked through the gates and then went to hang by a side wall about a hundred feet away. CJ gave them a look that could kill. Luis gave us a stupid grin, flipped us the bird, and then started making out with Maya. Cesar was grabbing his crotch while he talked to his amigos. I guess he wanted to make sure he still had his dick with him..lol I decided to listen to Cesar for some laughs.

He was bitching. "Yeah my niggas, I tol my shortie don't fuckin get me goin askin me what I do wit my niggas an shit. My nigga, I punched the fuckin wall right next to her face and tol dat bitch dat coulda been yo face, so shut da fuck up."

I looked at Gabriel and shook my head thinking, what a loser. If his girl puts up with that, she's as dumb as he is. All of a sudden CJ froze everyone where they stood. Then he walked over to Luis and Cesar. We followed and ended up standing in front of them.

He unfroze them, and the show began. Cesar went for his blade as CJ closed his eyes like he was willing all of his powers to come forward. He made both of their bodies rise up off the ground and then slammed them against the school wall with their arms and legs in crucifix position. It looked like they were nailed to the side of the school. CJ held them there as his own body started glowing. Cesar's knife fell out of his hand and hit the ground without making a sound. Luis and Cesar looked like they knew they were gunna die.

CJ's eyes were nothing but intense white light when he finally opened them. He put his hand out and the knife jumped into it. He held it in front of Cesar's face so he could clearly see it and then quickly cut his throat just deep enough to make him start bleeding all over the place.

Then he went over to Luis and did the same thing.

"You refuse to learn, so I'm going to teach you one more time."

CJ stood back as beams of white light shot out of his eyes and entered their bodies, causing them to go spastic. Then Gabriel, Hunter and me connected with CJ and shot our beams into their bodies too. Their screams had a non-human quality I've never heard before, and I knew we were coming as close to killing them as we dared.

All of a sudden they stopped screaming and their bodies went limp. They were still stuck against the wall as smoke came out of their bodies. CJ walked up and put his hands on their chests and gave both of them jolts to make them come to. He stared them down as they looked away.

CJ calmly said, "See how easy that was? You bitches don't have much time left, and I do mean that. Enjoy the time you have left on this little blue planet."

Then we walked back to the front steps and CJ unfroze everyone.

Maya started screaming hysterically as Luis and Cesar lay motionless on the ground bleeding all over the place. The security cops came running over, and so did a bunch of students to see what the hell was going on. Jacob, Jennifer and Christal finally showed up as all this was goin down. Roberto had this stunned look as he looked at Luis and Cesar lying there, so I grabbed him by the arm and asked him not to look.

"Let's go inside because it's already getting crazy this morning," Gabriel told everyone.

As we walked inside, I turned to see the security cops all panicky as they crouched over Luis and Cesar. CJ made it look like they had cut each other. Both of their blades were lying on the ground next to them.

We walked down the hall not saying a thing, like everyone was in shock. I put my arm around Roberto and asked if he was ok. He shook his head no.

"Miguel, what's goin on?"

"Hey, it'll be ok. Trust me."

CJ decided to disappear so he could be with Sergio. His mom wouldn't let him come to school. She wanted Sergio to rest for another day or two. I hope she doesn't panic and try to make him transfer :/

We headed to the music room to see if Shadow, Drake and Erik were there yet. Gabriel wanted to get everyone in a safe place. A few minutes later we could hear sirens at the front of the school.

Σ Ω ♥

Marco stopped by our locker between classes to say hi. He gave me and Gabriel the biggest hugs. He stood there for a second not saying anything, he was just looking at us in almost a pleading way. "Man, I had the most bizarre dream last night and you guys were in it," he said, almost in a whisper. I smiled knowing he wanted some kind of answer. I looked at Gabriel, and then back at Marco. "It wasn't a dream. What happened last night was real. You can see your brother whenever you want. We've opened a door for you and Ronaldo."

He had the weirdest look on his face for a second, and then started smiling.

"I won't say anything to anyone, I promise."

"Thanks, we appreciate that," Gabriel said.

Marco looked at us so innocently. "Who are you? I mean, no, forget it. It's not important. I mean it is, but you don't have to explain. All I know is that you've changed my life forever.

I'll never forget what you guys have done." I felt so happy for Marco and his brother. I wish I could do this kind of thing for everyone.

"Sometimes the tragic moments in our lives need to be resolved in some way. You and Ronaldo should never have been separated. A mistake was made," I said, touching Marco's arm so he could feel my energy. His eyes started tearing up.

Gabriel added another truth. "We are here to help people find their way."

Marco nodded because now he understood. He composed himself and smiled. Then he asked,

"Hey, do guys wanna hang on Saturday? Me and my friends and a couple of cousins are gunna shoot some hoops, and then we're having a barbecue at my house. You can meet my parents and my other cousins and stuff."

"Yeah, that sounds great. What time?" I asked.

"Around two or so."

"I can't make it till after four because I take an art class at NYU," I told him.

"Hey, that's wavy goin to college already. You must be like a genius or something."

"Na, not at all. I wish I was though..lol I just like to draw and paint, so I'm lucky enough to get to work with a professor there."

"Can we stop by for the barbecue?" Gabriel asked.

"Sure, no problem."

Gabriel started laughing. "Yeah, you don't want to see our b-ball skills anyway."

Then Roberto walked up. "Hey guys, I think I just aced my Trig test. Hey Marco, what's up."

"Hey Roberto, I'm having a barbecue on Saturday and I want you to come if you're not busy. Ask CJ and Hunter for me too." Roberto smiled as we all bumped fists and then headed to class.

❂ ☾

We were in-between 3rd and 4th period heading to our locker when we saw Jennifer talking to some new guy we've never seen before. Me and Gabriel ducked behind some people to get a better look so we could see what was goin on. Jennifer was being all giggly and shy, and the guy looked mad nervous.

"Uh oh, I think someone's crushing," Gabriel said. We decided to pretend not to notice them as we walked by, but Jennifer saw us and called us over. Things got awkward for a few seconds because I think he didn't wanna be seen with us.

"Christian, this is Miguel and Gabriel, two of my best friends."

"Hey."

"Hey."

Jennifer asked about meeting up for lunch while Christian stood there looking embarrassed about the whole situation. I could tell he was trying to score with Jennifer and didn't want to be seen talking to gay boys. We decided to let him off the hook. "We gotta go meet up with Hunter. Nice meeting you. Catch you guys later," I said.

"Let's see if our friendship with Jennifer ends this guy's infatuation," Gabriel said.

"Yeah, I wanted to read his mind so bad to see if he really likes her or is just gunna use her.

I don't mind being a cock-blocker when I have to..lol"

I headed to NYU with Gabriel after school. The guys went to see Sergio. I really wasn't in the mood to paint or draw because of all the shit that's happened, plus I wanted to see Sergio too. I also had to go to see the social worker lady again right after art class, and thinking about that was making me sad. I needed to be with Gabriel, so we quickly flew to the apartment in the Village so we could be alone :D

⌗ †

Gabriel came to art class with me. Paul the doorman watched us come out of the elevator and walk through the lobby toward the front doors. He gave us a weird look as he opened the door for us.

"Good afternoon gentlemen. I didn't know you two were here today."

"Hi Paul. Yes, we just stopped in for a few minutes. You were busy helping Mrs. Phelps into a cab when we walked in," Gabriel said.

"Oh yes, that's right. Well enjoy your afternoon gentlemen."

"Thanks Paul."

As we walked to the park, Gabriel told me he placed the cab incident in Paul's mind so he wouldn't keep wondering how we always get past him. "There are too many times lately where we are only coming out of the building, but never going in," Gabriel said, laughing.

Our apartment is just a block away, but every time I get near Washington Square Park I feel like I'm entering another world, kind of like a parallel universe; just like that girl who went through the looking glass. =D I love being in this park because it's where I realized there was a different life for me if I wanted it bad enough, and it's where I got to fall in love with Gabriel all over again. We stood by the fountain holding hands and looking up through the arch to the terrace of our apartment; seeing it that way made me feel like it was heaven on earth.

"Michael, it is heaven on earth," Gabriel said, smiling. "You see, people refuse to grasp the concept that the earth is part of the heavens. It's where the rhythm of a heartbeat can find its dream. It may be a hard thing to achieve, but if people are persistent and true to their core beliefs, it can happen.

It was nice having Gabriel come with me. I really need him to be close by because I've been feeling stuff that doesn't feel right. Professor Abrar has been giving me the creeps big time. He's always watching me, and I don't know why. It's like he's got a laser beam pointed at the back of my head as he stares. I don't know what he's all about, I just know it doesn't feel right. It's the same feeling I've had with some of my mom's boyfriends :/

He doesn't know I'm watching him watching me. I don't like it one bit because it makes me go to a dark place in my mind.

I get the exact opposite feeling when I'm near Donovan. He's one of the nicest guys I've ever met, so his energy counters the professor's. He's brilliant and true to his passions. He has an aura that surrounds his whole body when he creates.

Gabriel talked with the professor while I painted so he could get a better read on him. He said if the professor is part of the other side, he'll be clever in hiding it. All I know is that taking this art class is important to me, so I don't want anything or anyone fucking it up.

I decided to do a painting for Sergio. I painted him racing down a street on his skateboard impressionist style. The image of Sergio on his skateboard made me smile the whole time I put him on canvas. He understands what pure freedom is =] I even inserted some of Sergio's DNA into the painting to give it a soul. I hope he likes it. I took it with me so I could give it to him.

After class was over, Gabriel went to go see Sergio and I went to talk to the social worker :/

☹ ♒

My body floats in the air
as lightning plays with the electrons in my veins
I can see me at the age of seven
looking at me at the age of fifteen.
We look at each other with a curiosity that defies all reality.
I see the bruises on his body
and he sees the bruises on my soul.
We both listen to a haunting melody
From a long long time ago.

246

I've been trying to forget the shitty parts of my life, but having to see the social worker brought all the bad stuff back to the front of my brain again. My mind is like a bunch of drawers that I can open and close whenever I want, and I finally decided to close a few of them for good, but then Mary asked me to reopen certain drawers one more time '___'

"How have you been Miguel?"

"I've been good. Actually, everything's kool even though things are a little crazy at school. I'm really in a good place for the first time in my life, and I like the way it feels."

"I'm very happy for you. You know, I can't believe how different you look from the last time we talked. You look like a normal healthy teenager now. Gabriel and his mother must be taking good care of you."

"Yeah, they are. I love them and they love me, and that's all I've ever wanted. They're my family now."

Things got quiet for a few seconds.

"What do you have in the wrapping?" Mary asked.

"It's a painting I did for a friend of mine."

"I'd love to see it if you wouldn't mind."

"Yeah, sure. I'm still learning so don't laugh." As I unwrapped it she kind of gasped a little.

I thought something was wrong, so I turned to look at her to make sure she was ok.

"Miguel, that is absolutely amazing. I didn't know you could paint like that."

"I'm taking an art class at NYU. I still have a lot to learn before I get where I wanna be."

I put the painting against a chair. Mary kept staring at it. I think she could feel Sergio's emotions coming through or something.

"I'm glad you like it. You're the first person to see it. I just hope my friend likes it." I put the wrapping back on because she was seeing stuff I didn't want her to see.

Things got quiet again for a minute or so as she came out of her little trance.

"Your mother came to talk to me. Let me rephrase that, she was required to meet with me. I could tell that she didn't want to talk about the whole situation."

I just stared at her with a blank look on my face. I was trying my hardest not to have a meltdown.

"I'm really not interested in what she has to say," I said, glaring at Mary.

I think I scared her because she looked away real quick. I closed my eyes because I knew I was was getting angry and didn't want her to see my eyes go white. She started talking quiet-like so she wouldn't upset me.

"Your mom told me she's afraid of you because you tried to hurt her. She actually said you are evil. What happened? I know she broke the law when she went to see you, but did you try to harm her? Did you threaten her in any way?"

"I didn't do anything to her. All I did was tell her the truth. I also told her that she can't come anywhere near me. She's a very sick person who just wants to hurt me again if she can get the chance. I'm not gunna let that happen ever again. I want you to know that I don't consider her my mom anymore." I glared at Mary when I said that. "Look, you might think I'm being cruel or an asshole or whatever, but a real mom wouldn't do the stuff she's done to me. I don't ever wanna go back to that Hell I was living in. No one on this earth is gunna make me," I said, as the room suddenly started shaking. Mary grabbed the desk wondering what was happening. I tried to calm myself down. I heard Gabriel whisper in my ear that he loved me and not to worry about anything. That got me calm enough to make the room stop shaking. Mary looked mad scared.

"You gotta understand where I'm coming from. You deal with kids who are abused every day. We got nowhere to turn and no one to help us. I'm never gunna live with her again, so you gotta help me."

"You don't have to worry Miguel. No one is going to make you go back there. Gabriel's mother has already filed paperwork with the court to become your legal guardian."

Man, I couldn't believe what I was hearing. It meant that I could finally put an end to that part of my life. Then I told her something else that's been on my mind. "I want you to help me do something. I want to press charges against Jerel and Orlando for violatin me."

"I'm happy you're brave enough to do this Miguel. We need to get those two off the streets so they can't harm anymore children."

It felt like a big weight was being lifted off my shoulders when she called the police. They came to her office and I told them everything. They went to arrest them, and I went to Sergio's to see how he was doing. Gabriel was waiting for me. He hugged me with all his might.

Journal Entry 51
Friday evening 7 pm
October 20th

I am pushing against an unknown quantity trying to see what breaks first
like a dark painting that has been inserted strategically into the
psyche of my childhood.
  The bogyman I thought I had defeated has come back to tear me
  limb from limb
    just like the memories that never let me forget.
  They force me to look in the mirror and see
  A gay boy in a brutally staged straight world
    The humiliation of being hated
      Stuttering because of guilt and shame
      Words that will never find the real meaning
        The quiet moments that have slipped through my finger tips
        The loneliness of a hard fought journey
          And quantum particles from multiple dimensions
          that are slowly ripping me away from this world.
          But there is one thing I do know for sure,
          I have found love
          I will always give love
          I am being loved.

"What is an Aegis?" Mr. Atwood asked the class.

Gabriel raised his hand. "It's a type of ancient shield that was used to protect people. It's actually part of Greek mythology mister. The Aegis is a sort of cape with divine powers. It protects the one who wears it from being harmed in any way."

"Yeah, it's kool," CJ said. "Augustus wore one, and Alexander the Great had the image of one on his shield. There's just one caveat mister; Alexander wasn't great. He was a slime-ball who killed thousands of men, women and children just to please his narcissistic ego."

"That's right guys. You are also right about Alexander being a tyrannical ruler CJ, but let us save that discussion for another time," mister suggested.

"The Aegis can also be found in Egyptian and Nubian my-thology. It has been part of mythological history for centuries," Hunter added.

"Hey mister? It would be mad kool to see one of those cape things. Do you think all that stuff about it having special powers was ever true?" Roberto asked.

"Well the world is a mysterious place, so you never know. The Aegis could have had real powers, or maybe people were just superstitious back then, just like they are today, and believed this thing was connected to some kind of higher power. I think people are afraid of a lot of things, so believing in mysterious artifacts with supposed divine powers can be reassuring in some way."

Roberto started talking about all the weird crap that scares all of us. "Yeah, it's strange how people are still superstitious. Like no one wants to live on the 13th floor, or have an address with the number 666, or open an umbrella inside a house, or say Bloody Mary three times while looking in a mirror. That stuff even scares me, and I don't know why."

Then the whole class started talking about the weird shit that's happened to them. They talked about doors opening up and slamming shut on their own, hearing voices and footsteps in the night, cold spots in their bedrooms, and all sorts of other scary stuff.

As we talked, the lights suddenly started flickering off and on, and then went out completely. A huge gust of wind swept through the classroom blowing our papers all over the place. I didn't know what the fuck was happening. Then Atwood's closet door flew open and banged against the wall. There was an intense glowing light coming from inside. "What's goin on," Roberto asked, mad scared. Atwood told everyone to stay in their seats as he slowly walked toward the closet.

A couple of girls yelled at him not to go near it, but he kept walking to it anyways, and then went inside. Then the fucking door slammed shut, which made all the girls scream. I asked Gabriel what was going on.

"Don't worry, everything is fine," he whispered. Roberto moved his desk next to ours real quick. All of a sudden the lights came back on and the closet door swung open. Mr. Atwood walked out with something in his hand and was smiling at everyone.

"Did I scare you? I thought you could use a little Halloween fright this morning," he said, with an evil laugh.

"That was so kool mister. How'd you do all that stuff?" Roberto asked, looking totally relieved.

"Let's just say I have my ways."

"Hey mister, what you got there?" Tasheena asked.

"This is an Aegis," he said, holding up a cape with a kool looking insignia on it. Roberto's eyes got real wide as mister held it up so we could see it better.

"A good friend of mine found this in an out of the way shop in Athens Greece a few years ago. I don't know how old it is, or if it has powers, but I think it is an interesting item to show you."

All of a sudden the Aegis started moving all by itself in mister's hand. Then it flew outta his hand real quick and floated in the air all by itself. Mister stepped back as the stupid girls screamed again, which was annoying as hell :/ Another gust of wind swirled around the room as the cape flew from the front of the class to where I was sitting and then gently landed on my shoulders. Everyone looked at me weird, even Gabriel. What was really strange about the whole thing was that I knew it belonged to me as soon as I saw Atwood holding it.

He had a slight smile on his face. "Well, I guess the Aegis has found a new home."

Mister walked to the back of the class where I was sitting and told us more about the cape.

"The Aegis is the ultimate protector with the power to choose who it decides to protect.

I guess it has chosen Miguel. I personally think it is a very good choice."

Man I didn't know what to think, but it felt perfect on me. Roberto asked if he could touch it, and of course I said yeah. Then everyone else came over to get a good look at it. Rafael and Tyron thought the whole thing was stupid, so they didn't come near me. I think they were spooked out, and I also think they were afraid that touching me would turn them gay O__o

"How do you like it Miguel?" mister asked.

"I like it a lot," I said, as Atwood looked at Gabriel, CJ and Hunter, and then back at me.

He had this weird smile on his face. "It's yours now. You don't have to wear it, just keep it close by. It will automatically come to you whenever you are in danger or need it to do something unique; at least that is what the legend says. Use it well my friend."

Then he went back to the front of the classroom and continued his lecture on mythology.

Σ ☻ Ω

Earlier tonight we went to the village to hang at the apartment so we could get out of the Bronx for a while. Gabriel, CJ and Hunter went out on the terrace to talk about stuff. They wanted to give me and Roberto some space. I wanted Roberto to call his mom to see if anything had changed with his dad's attitude. I've been hoping things will eventually work out so he can be with his family. They need to talk face to face. His dad can't be that much of a dick not to want to talk to his own son. When I mentioned this to Roberto, he thought I was trying to get rid of him.

"Don't you want me to stay with you anymore? It's been awesome living with you guys." Then he got quiet for a few seconds. "Is it because I'm in love with you? Well I can't help it Miguel. I love you."

"Roberto, I'm not trying to get rid of you. Please don't ever say that again. And I love you too. You must know that by now."

"You do?"

"Of course I do. But you also know I love Gabriel and it wouldn't...."

He interrupted. "I know you do. I can tell you two were made for each other, and I'd never do anything to hurt you guys. Look, I don't wanna go back home because it'll mean I can't be near you. Miguel, it's hard to explain, but I feel so fucking lost when I'm not around you. You're different from anyone I've ever met. I'm waiting for you to tell me who you really are. You changed my whole life the second you walked through those auditorium doors at the drama meeting. I wanted to kiss you so bad but I could tell you were already in love."

I looked at Roberto and wanted to tell him the truth, but I couldn't.

"Please give me a little more time, then I'll tell you every-thing. Ok? Things are just a little confusing right now. You're an incredible guy, and I love you. I hope you know that."

"Thanks for saying that Miguel. It means a lot to me. Look, I won't ever pressure you about anything because I'm happy for you and Gabriel, but I can't go home because my parents don't understand anything. They'll never accept me being bisexual. And if being near you is the only way I can love you, then I gotta ac-cept it. I guess I sound like a fuckin idiot stalker now." :/

"No you don't. I know exactly how you feel." I gave him a hug and kissed him on the cheek.

I'm so connected to Roberto and I don't know what to do :/ ♥

He finally called his mom after we talked, but the conversation turned to shit real quick. His dad got on the phone and yelled at him saying the only way he could come home was to get fixed first. He wants Roberto to go to one of those religious places that think they can make gay people straight. Roberto had this sad look on his face as he hung the phone up.

"I know who I am and I'm ok with it. If my mom and dad can't accept me, then this is the way it's gotta be." He started crying, so I held him in my arms.

"It's gunna be ok. Please don't cry. We're your family now, and this is your home. I love you Roberto. We all love you," I whispered, as the guys came in from the terrace and helped me surround Roberto with love.

Journal Entry 52
Saturday morning 3 am
October 21st

I spent last night in bed with Gabriel and Roberto. No, it's not exactly what you're thinking; well maybe just a little bit ;p

♥ = ♥ = ♥

The three of us got all comfy on our bed. I was drawing, and Gabriel and Roberto were reading. It's nice to get away from all the pressures and just be with the guys I love. CJ and Hunter went on a double date with Sergio and Jacob. Sergio's mom said he could finally leave the house even though he was still bruised and sore. It's mad cute to see my angels so in love =D They went to 42nd street to see a movie, and then out for dinner. I can't believe how romantic they are, especially Hunter. I had been sketching for an hour or so when I decided to ask Gabriel and Roberto if they wanted to watch a movie.

"Yeah, that sounds kool. What do you want to watch?" Gabriel asked.

"The Perks of Being a Wallflower. It's finally on Netflix.

"Sounds good to me. I loved the book," Gabriel said.

"Me too. I think Ezra Miller is the perfect actor to play Patrick. That's exactly how I pictured Patrick would look," Roberto said, with this dreamy smile on his face.

"He's really hot," Gabriel said, hoping I wouldn't get jealous. Roberto and I definitely agreed; he is extremely hot ;p

I told Gabriel, "I'm gunna take a shower and then I'll make us some popcorn."

I got off the bed and headed to the bathroom. I stood in the shower all soaped up with my eyes closed as I let the hot water hit my body. Man, did it feel good. I was standing there all relaxed enjoying the warmth of the water, when all of a sudden a pair of hands started rubbing my back real gentle. I kept my eyes closed and let those hands touch me all over. Then some hot pouty lips started kissing the back of my neck making my whole body come alive.

"I love you cute one," Gabriel whispered in my ear.

"I love you too," I said, as I turned around, kissed him, and then.... ;p

After we got out of the shower, I went back to the bedroom with just a towel wrapped around my waist and jumped on the bed. Then I jumped on top of Roberto and started tickling him so I could hear him giggle. Then Gabriel walked in with just his tighty-whiteys on and jumped on me, and then started tickling me and Roberto. I finally got loose, but as I went to stand up,

Gabriel grabbed the towel off me leaving me completely naked.

I stood there as Roberto looked at me with a huge smile on his face. I smiled back as I tried to grab the towel from Gabriel, but he threw it over to Roberto before I could get it. Roberto held the towel and kept staring. I could tell he was a little embarrassed because well, you know ;p

"Do you like what you see?" I asked, as I did a 360, giving both of them a good view.

They nodded their heads up and down and kept smiling. It was mad nice because they made me feel so sexy. I gave them a little show in my excited state, then walked to the dresser and put on some sexy undies. I took out another pair of real sexy ones and walked over to the bed where Roberto was sitting; I smiled as I gave them to him. "Why don't you take a shower while I make the popcorn, then the three of us can get all comfy under the blankets and watch the movie; I think you're gunna like it."

⚥+ ♂ = ♥

It was around one in the morning or so when CJ and Hunter finally got back from their dates. They walked in and saw me lying in-between Roberto and Gabriel and gave me a "what the fuck is goin on" look. Roberto was asleep all snuggled up to my back with his arm around me. I was snuggled up to Gabriel with my head on his chest while we watched TV.

"I'm not going to even go there," CJ said, as he looked at us with a wicked grin. Gabriel put his hand on Roberto's forehead to make him sleep soundly so we could talk.

"We need to go see what our little thugs and trolls are up to," Hunter said, as he grabbed some popcorn from the bowl. Lucifer's disciples are harnessing some energy that is giving Luis and Cesar new powers. This could cause us a problem if we don't take care of the situation," CJ said.

"Michael, this creates a dilemma where we may have to eliminate them, along with this current group of disciples," Gabriel said, looking to see what my reaction was going to be.

"I don't care about the disciples, but I don't want to hurt Luis or Cesar unless we have to. Can't we do something that will make them less aggressive?" I asked.

"I don't think so because it isn't in there nature anymore. You see, they have been physically altered by those disciples. This is the way Lucifer does his work," Gabriel said.

We flew to the Bronx to see what they were up to, and to plan our next move.

Journal Entry 53
Saturday 11:30 pm
October 22nd

Just got back from Marco's a little while ago. Had a kool time hanging with him and his friends. I used to think all the jocks were stupid and stuck up, but I was wrong. They made me realize that I'm just as guilty as anyone about judging people before I even know em. I don't know why we're all labeled anyways. Who started this shit?

Everyone thinks ima faggot emo boy who cuts, is anorexic, and is always depressed. I am gay, and I guess emo or whatever, but all the rest of it is bullshit. Marco and his friends are chill. Like they're really outgoing, funny, and have mad talent in any sport they play. It's also an instant party whenever they get together :D

We did scare Marco's family when we showed up though. Gabriel's Metatron Cubes were goin crazy as we got near his house. It got me worried that shit was gunna go down. I could tell they didn't like us because this one old uncle guy got all pissed when we walked into the backyard. He came up to us and asked what the hell we wanted. Marco got him calm when he came over and gave us hugs. I was glad he did because this guy wanted to hurt us. Everyone there stopped talking and just stared. All those judgmental eyes were trying to intimidate us, but we kept our kool and pretended not to notice. Marco started introducing us to everyone. He even had his arm around me when we met his parents. They seemed nice but didn't say much. I could tell they were still sad about losing Ronaldo. I guess sometimes there are no second chances.

Gabriel and CJ got the conversation going as I studied their faces. Marco's mom and dad looked a lot older than they really were. I know the death of Ronaldo has done that. I could also tell how protective they were of Marco; he's all they got left.

They smiled as Marco told them that I was the guy who started the GSA club at school.

"You are doing a brave thing Miguel," his mom said. Then his dad put his arms around both Marco and me and said, "I'm glad all of you are friends with my son. Miguel, you are way too skinny, you need food." He took us over to this huge barbecue grill and got each of us a plate of the best ribs and chicken ever =D

I could tell how much Marco's dad was still hurting just by the sound of his voice. As we stood around the grill eating, I whispered to Marco, "How's your brother doing?"

"He visits every day. It's kool having him in my life again." Marco's smile was a look of pure love. "I was thinking that maybe your mom and dad need a visit from Ronaldo. I'll let him know it's ok." Marco looked at his mom and dad, and then back at me.

"Thanks Miguel, we need to be a family again."

After a while Marco put some wicked beats on, which made him and his friends start doing lots of crazy dancing. They started showing off to everyone as they tried to outdo each other with hot moves. It was kool watching them do their thing; it was type fire! ;p

We formed a circle around em as they battled each other. Marco had the best moves of all; that's because he is way hot ;p Then all of us started feelin it and danced the night away. A bunch of his little cousins came over and danced with us. They were so cute as they tried to copy us big people. This is what family is all about =D

I watched Roberto sleep this morning as I gently ran my fingers through his hair. He looked like such a little boy as he slept under the blankets. He was even drooling a little outta the corner of his mouth. So cute ;p I love Roberto and want him to be happy. I kinda wish I could sleep like that again because I miss regular dreams.

"Everything seems like it's going too fast," I whispered to Gabriel, as we lay in bed.

"Yeah I know what you mean. But you know you have control over all of this. We have lots of time. You've been given something special by being human. I know it isn't going to be an easy thing to give up, but when the time comes, you will always have the qualities they possess. What is so kool about it is that you will always have the best of both worlds. Even though a person's time is very short in the scheme of things, the human experiment is extraordinary. I wish I could have experienced being human with you. It would definitely help me understand their reoccurring mistakes with more wisdom."

"I want to stop time right now and have everything stay just like it is. I want all of my friends with us forever."

"Well maybe we will just do that when the time is right."

This morning more weirdness happened on my way to art class. I was waiting for the light to change at the corner of 5th ave and Washington Square, when I spotted my dad standing under the arch staring at me. He looked terrible; like a homeless drug addicted bum. I was trying not to lose it even though I felt the urge to hurt him. Instead, I read his mind to see what he wanted. He wanted money from me. Can you believe it? He knows where I live and thinks ima rich boy now. What a cockroach loser '___'

I stood there as energy started entering my tatts. I connected with his mind and told him to leave before I killed him. He looked crazy scared as soon as he heard my voice, but he didn't move. I told him again to leave, and I even made his body start shaking so he would get the hint, but he still wouldn't walk away. All of a sudden the power in the buildings and every electrical thing on the street went dead as my eyes turned bright white. Light beams shot outta my eyes hitting my dad's body with such force that he disintegrated right in front of me. I thought for sure

I had killed him. Gabriel appeared by my side in an instant and asked if I was ok.

"I think I just killed my dad."

Gabriel closed his eyes for a second. "No you didn't. You transported him back to the Bronx. He's actually lying in a dumpster unconscious. Nice!"

"Are you going to be ok?"

"I think so. Will you walk me to class?"

"Of course I will cute one."

"Hey, what are you painting?" I asked Donovan, as I put my book bag down in my workspace and then looked over at his easel.

"Archangels," he said, as he dipped his brush in paint. "I was inspired by a dream I had last night. I couldn't wait to get here this morning to get the whole thing on canvas."

"Wow, that's kool. What was the dream about?"

"Well, it was kind of crazy actually. In my dream I was around twelve years old, which was a little strange, because it felt like I was looking at myself from a distance rather than being in my body. Anyway, it was a perfect summer day, and I was sitting in Washington Square Park sketching and listening to music, when all of a sudden the Archangel Michael and Gabriel walked up and sat next to me."

Donovan stopped talking for a second, looked at me, and smiled. Then he continued.

"It was weird because they looked exactly like you and your

boyfriend Gabriel. I know that must sound strange, but it seemed so real to me. Anyway, the Archangel Gabriel smiled as he put his hand on my shoulder. He quietly said, 'All good things come to those who can see.' Then you put your hand on my chest and I could feel your pulse connect instantly with my heartbeat. An indescribable feeling of love came over me. I've never felt that kind of intensity in my life. I started to cry because I was so happy. Then both of you got up and quietly walked away hand in hand, but you no longer looked like you exactly. I mean, your faces still looked the same, but your bodies glowed and were no longer defined as you walked right through people and objects in the park. I still can't get the whole thing out of my mind."

I stood there not saying anything for a couple of seconds.

"Wow, that's kool to be an angel in someone's dream. I'm honored. I read somewhere that when you are visited by the Archangel Gabriel, you are going to be someone of great importance on earth. And when the Archangel Michael visits a person in their dreams, everything you wish for will come true. Being visited by both of them is rare. I think your life is going to be extraordinary. This is a real gift." He didn't say anything. He just looked at me with a look I'll never forget. Then he put his brushes down and hugged me.

"Thank you Miguel."

"For what? I haven't done anything."

"Yes you have." Then he picked up his brushes and continued to paint me and Gabriel.

Journal Entry 54
Monday morning 3 am
October 24th

It's all so illusive
like a spinning top,
the silent inertia of a tidal wave maniac
spinning round and round to the destiny of a fading day.
Sound the alarm for that cloak and dagger mindset
hiding as it steels the gentle thoughts of the young
just like the crusades that were once the only truth
and then revealed to be a bloody path to nowhere found.
Feel the apprehension
twist your trepidation into the realm of unparalleled possibilities,
fight fire with fire through the eyes of love
and never turn your back on that ghost-written story.

There are times when we think the whole world revolves around us; that we are the only thing that matters. But it is so much bigger than that, and we have to step into those other shoes to feel it, to experience it, to understand the emptiness so many people feel.

We are afraid to love.
  We are afraid to be alone.
    We are afraid to stand on our own.
      We are afraid of what we see in the mirror because
      mirrors always reveal the truth.
It is no use looking away.
  It is a philosophical dream; a theory of what life can be.
    It is a philosophical nightmare as we feel our way in the dark.

$$\Sigma \ \Omega$$

We went to a rally at Union Square for LGBTQ homeless teenagers today. It got me fucking angry to see so many teenagers like Roberto and me living on the streets just because of what we are. Can't parents see what they're doing? Why can't they accept their gay kids and love em just the same? It's sad to see this bullshit situation. I looked around and saw so many people that were hungry, lost, and beaten up by the mean streets ' ___ '

I connected with Gabriel.

"We have to do something."

"We will. It's just going to take some time to change the hearts and minds that are so stuck in the past. This kind of thing has played out so many times over the centuries, and people keep making the same mistakes. We have to remember how brutal humans have been to each other, especially when it comes to the issue of gay people and religion. Gays have been alienated, thrown in jail, put in mental institutions, and tortured and killed all because they were born a certain way. It is still illegal to be LGBT in over seventy countries. There is even the death penalty in a dozen countries right now, which shows barbarianism is alive and well. We need to figure out a different way to teach acceptance before it's too late."

"How do we do that? It seems impossible because hatred happens even at the smallest level. Look at the shit that's going on at our school."

"Nothing is impossible cute one."

I watched Roberto looking at everyone with this frightened look on his face. "Miguel, if it wasn't for you and Gabriel, I'd be homeless just like them. I never told you this, but when my dad kicked me out, I came here to sleep cuzz it seemed at least a little safe. I didn't realize this was where homeless teenagers lived until now."

"You don't ever have to worry about being homeless again. We love you. If you want to know the truth, I would have been homeless too if it wasn't for Gabriel."

Roberto got quiet for a few seconds as he looked at all those lost faces.

"When I was wandering the streets for those few nights, I was so lonely and scared. I just kept moving so no one would talk to me. I picked food out of garbage cans at a couple of pizza places a few blocks from here. I got the idea from some people I saw who were doing it too.

What scared me the most was my second night on the street.

In just two hours, three guys had come up to me and asked me to have sex with them. They said they were gunna pay me and everything, and even let me sleep over. It creeped me out, so I ran fast as hell to get away from them. It felt like I was living in a fucking nightmare.

The next night, I was sitting on that park bench right over there trying to stay warm, and I watched two guys my age, maybe younger, selling their bodies for sex so they could eat and have a warm place to sleep. This one guy I met named Luke tried to turn me on to the ways of the street. He told me that selling myself was what I was gunna have to do to survive. He said he'd even help me get started. That's when I knew I wanted to die. But then you saved me Miguel."

Roberto had this wounded look in his eyes. "That's the kind of stuff we have to stop from happening." I put my arms around Roberto to let him know he was safe.

"Let's figure out a way to help all of these people," Gabriel said.

We walked over to where some people were giving speeches. We stood there listening to this guy talk about how the city had cut the budget for the homeless shelters to the point where there weren't enough beds or food. I held Gabriel's hand as I listened. We were sharing our thoughts like we normally do. "That's the perfect solution," I said, smiling.

"Some of them are here," Hunter growled. My smile faded fast when he said that.

"Let's have some fun and disintegrate the bastards," CJ said.

"Miguel, you and Roberto stay here. We'll be back in a few

minutes." Gabriel kissed me and then disappeared into the crowd.

Roberto and I stood there listening to the guy giving his speech and watching what was going on in the park. I knew a lotta people were trying to help, but it seemed like it was all talk and no action. I also knew all these homeless teenagers were hungry, so I got an idea. I looked at the vendors selling food and got into their minds. All of a sudden one vendor guy yelled out, "Free hotdogs, get your free hotdogs while they last." Then the other vendors started yelling the same thing. All those hungry teenagers ran to get the free food. It made me smile as Roberto and I watched it all go down. "Wow, I can't believe they're giving away free food," Roberto said.

"Yeah, it's mad kool," I said.

Then I started looking around for Gabriel, CJ, and Hunter because I was worried. Roberto went to get a free hotdog and I leaned against a tree hoping Gabriel and the guys would be back soon. As I waited, these two guys, probably about twenty-five-years old or so, came up and started hitting on me.

"Hey, you're way hot emo boy. Do you wanna come back to our place for drinks and, you know, get in-between us?"

"No thanks. I'm not into that kind of thing, and anyways, my boyfriend wouldn't like knowing that you're hitting on me," I said, hoping they'd leave before I got angry.

Then Roberto walked up eating a hotdog. "Is this your boyfriend? Hey boyfriend, you wanna eat my hotdog," one of the jerks said, as the other guy laughed.

"I want you guys to leave now," I said, as my tatts started going crazy.

"Come on emo boy, we're just having fun. We really wanna fuck you. We'll even fuck your little twink boyfriend too if that'll make you happy."

Roberto started to panic.

"Get the fuck outta here now," I said, as I put my hand up and blasted both of them away from us. They flew backwards and hit the ground. Their bodies twitched and shook like crazy. In an instant Gabriel, CJ, and Hunter appeared outta nowhere.

"Are you all right Miguel?" Gabriel asked, looking at those two assholes lying on the ground. "Yeah, I'm fine. They were hitting on Roberto and me. I told them to get lost, but they wouldn't leave, so, you know, I fucked em up a little."

"Way to go Miguel," CJ said, as he slapped me on the back.

Gabriel held me in his arms to calm me down. "I was worried about you," I whispered. "Did you get rid of them?"

"Yes. There were nine of them. Lucifer is getting closer," Gabriel whispered back.

"I'm not afraid of him."

"I know you're not."

I looked outta the corner of my eye and saw Roberto looking at all of us weird again because of what I had just done, and because the guys appeared out of nowhere. I turned and gave him a sympathetic look hoping he'd understand. He slowly smiled at me. Then Hunter froze everyone in place, Roberto too, for a few seconds so he could figure out what those two assholes were. He quickly scanned them. "What we have here are two pedophile procurers, or in layman's terms, pimps. They were trying to lure you and Roberto to become prostitutes."

"That's really fucked up," I said, looking at them lying on the ground unconscious.

CJ told me and Gabriel to stand back, then they disintegrated them in an instant.

"They are people who no longer belong on earth. They have been judged and will never hurt anyone again," Gabriel said.

"Thanks guys. All this shit is outta control, and we have to fix it," I said, looking at everyone frozen in time.

"Should we let Roberto remember what happened?" Gabriel asked.

"Yeah, because he trusts us. I have this weird feeling that he needs to see our reality little by little."

"Okay then." Gabriel unfroze everyone and things got back to normal.

We were just about to leave when we heard a bunch of sirens coming toward the park. All of a sudden five Cadillac Escalades came round the corner and pulled up near where we were standing. Out jumped the mayor and some of his guys. It was kool because he stopped and shook our hands.

"What's goin on?" Roberto asked.

"I think help is on the way," I told him.

The mayor walked up on the little stage and told the crowd that he wasn't cutting the budget for the shelters. "We are expanding our help for all homeless teenagers. It will include counseling, quality shelter accommodations, counseling, and educational opportunities. Our goal is to get all of our gay and straight homeless teens off the streets and eventually back to their hometowns so they can be reunited with their families."

Everyone started applauding like mad. I hugged Gabriel.

"Thanks for doing that."

"Anytime cute one."

♥ ♥

After Roberto fell asleep, Gabriel and I went to see my sister, and then we flew around the city so we could be alone. We ended up on the top of the Chrysler Building lying next to each other completely naked as we looked deep into the universe. It's our special place. We made love for hours under that comforting night sky ;p

After we were done making love, Gabriel and I talked about stuff that was going to happen soon. It seems strange how the forces of the unknown have so much power over everything. I feel like I'm stuck in quicksand and I'm slowly sinking. I need to have some control over my life. I hate the waiting.

"Things are gunna start happening soon, aren't they?" I asked.

"I'm not quite sure yet, but I think so. We are taking all the necessary precautions until you become the archangel again."

"It's all so weird. The visions I see when I meditate are making me aware of so many things. All this intense stuff' has been filling my brain for the last couple of weeks, and I'm trying to put it all into some kind of context. There is battle between two worlds going on inside of my mind and body. I'm so close. I can feel it."

Gabriel held me in his arms. "You are going to get through this, and then the world is going to see what a gift you are to them. It really is going to be different this time because of the kind of archangel you will become. I can't wait until it happens to you Michael."

I didn't say anything, I just held Gabriel real close and stared into those beautiful haunting blue eyes that found me when I was lost and alone.

Journal Entry 55

Tuesday morning 2 am
October 25th

So we got to school yesterday morning and saw that Mr. Bricklin asshole violating Ramon.

He was yelling at him because Ramon didn't wait outside like everyone else until it was time to be let in by the security cops. I've read Ramon's thoughts before; he's scared outta his mind because of Luis, Cesar, and all the shit that happens in front of the school. He likes to sneak in to get away from it.

Bricklin had Ramon backed up against the lockers as he hovered over him like a mad dog.

I told CJ and Hunter to get the principal. Then I gave my iPhone to Roberto and told him to video what was going down.

"Roberto, use the zoom to get everything up close. Me and Gabriel are gunna stop this shit right now." We ran down the hall and confronted Bricklin.

"Hey Mr. Bricklin, stop yelling at Ramon. Can't you see you

got him upset?" I said, trying to stay calm.

"This is none of your business punk. Get the hell out of here now before I write you up for interfering with official business. GET OUT OF HERE NOW!"

"Look Mr. Bricklin, all Ramon did was come into the school early so he could be safe. He's not doing anything wrong," I said, getting more pissed off.

"Look you little queer, I'm going to give you three seconds for you and this other queer to leave."

I looked at Gabriel and then told Ramon, "Go to the office and get the principal." I grabbed him away from Bricklin and told him to run. Bricklin tried to grab Ramon's arm, but he was too quick and got away. He ran as fast as he could. Bricklin started running after him, but stopped, turned around, and walked quickly back to me and Gabriel. He grabbed me by the arm and shoved me against the locker real hard. The protection around my body started electrocuting him, but he was still yelling at the top of his lungs all crazy, and even slammed his hand against the locker right next to my face. Gabriel was gunna hurt him, but I got to him first.

"Get the fuck away from me!" I said, pushing him away. He started coming at me again, so I kicked him in the balls as hard as I could. He fuckin went down like a shot and started puking all over the place. "Two seconds later, Principal Rodriguez came around the corner with the guys to see what was going on.

"Bricklin was picking on Ramon like a wild man, and he grabbed me and slammed me up against the locker," I said, as I looked down at Bricklin moaning in pain.

"It's true mister. Mr. Bricklin was verbally and physically

violating Ramon and Miguel. He even called Miguel and I queers," Gabriel told him.

Bricklin tried to defend himself, but couldn't get any words out.

Then Roberto walked up. "Mr. Rodriguez, I have it all on video," Roberto said, showing the principal what had just gone down. The look on mister's face said it all.

"Mr. Bricklin, as soon as you've composed yourself and cleaned this mess up, come to my office immediately. Boys, I want to thank you for helping to make our school a safe and respectful environment. Roberto, please email the video to me, I'll need it for my report.

Guys, please come to my office during first period so I can get your statements. And don't forget, we have that meeting after school in the auditorium about the GSA club situation. I think you'll be pleased with the outcome."

"Thanks for everything Mr. Rodriguez," I said.

We headed to the music room to hang for a few minutes.

Gabriel put his arm around me. "That was fucking brilliant Miguel."

"Man, I thought Bricklin was gunna punch you in the face," Roberto said, looking upset.

"Yeah, a kick to the balls always does the trick," CJ said, as he and Hunter laughed.

❁ ↘

We stopped by English Lit to tell Mr. Atwood that we had to go see the principal.

"I just heard about the unfortunate situation in the Teacher's Lounge. Are you and Ramon okay?"

"Yeah, I'm good, and so is Ramon. Mr. Bricklin is crazy coming at us the way he did. All we did was protect ourselves," I said, knowing I coulda easily killed him if I had wanted to.

My acting skills are getting better =D

When we walked into Mr. Rodriguez's office, Bricklin was sitting in a chair off to the side next to some guy from the teacher's union. Two cops were standing by the door ready to take our statements. We told them what happened. They recorded it and also wrote it all down. I could see Bricklin outta the corner of my eye looking really pissed off. I started smelling that metallic smell on him again. The four of us connected our minds. "Michael, we will take care of him today," Hunter said, as he looked over at Bricklin and smiled.

Ω ♨

A bunch of us went out for lunch to our favorite restaurant. The usual shit was happening as soon as we walked out the front doors. Luis and his posse were hanging by one wall, and Cesar and his posse were hanging by another watching us. It looked like the parting of the sea.

Both ofem still had bandages around their necks and still didn't know what had actually happened to them last week. CJ erased it from their minds.

The crazy protestors were out on the sidewalk too. The security cops kept them off to one side so students could get through. It's all intimidation shit tactics by everyone, but it ain't gunna work. They can try and close in on us, but they're in for a big surprise. We walked past the people out front as they yelled the usual stupid stuff. Luis, Cesar, and about ten other Ricans followed us to the restaurant, but stayed about a block away. I could tell they just wanted to let us know they're never far away, and will strike when we least expect it. Gabriel asked if I was okay.

"Yeah, no problem."

☮ ♯ ☾

The meeting in the auditorium was tense. Everyone who's been coming at us was there.

The angry parents and religious nuts had a lawyer guy to represent them on why the clubs should be closed. Principal Rodriguez had two lawyers and a guy high up from the Department of Education there to discuss our rights by the state and federal government to have a GSA club. They were also there to explain the funding that supports all of the clubs in New York City.

It was nice to see everyone from the GSA, Drama, and Music clubs. Marco and four other b-ball players showed up too. They sat right in back of us. Marco put his hands on my shoulders, then leaned in and whispered, "Hey Miguel, I told you I got your back man. Anything you need just let me know."

I turned around and smiled. "Thanks Marco. It means a lot knowing you're with us."

As I talked with Marco, I noticed Luis, Cesar, and a bunch of their boys quietly walk in and stand in the back of the auditorium. It looked like they were sealing off all the exits so no one could leave. I knew they wanted us to think we were surrounded.

Roberto, Jacob, Sergio, and Ramon looked mad nervous as they looked around at all the angry people. They are being real brave just by being seen with us. Gabriel turned around and looked at all the thugs in the back. I could see his eyes starting to go white.

"Don't worry about them Gabriel, they can't hurt us."

"I know. We've protected you on many levels, but something isn't quite right, and I can't put my finger on it." CJ and Hunter turned to look at Luis and Cesar, and then back at us. I connected with them and said I was safe, but I could feel an extra force field go up around all of us as the arguing began.

Some parents and two religious dumb asses started yelling stuff at us, but their lawyer told them to be quiet. It made me laugh. A game of chess was going on as their lawyer tried to argue with the school's lawyers about why all of the after-school clubs need to be closed. The school board guy explained how school funding works, and how the law is on our side. It was interesting to watch how it all played out. The principal was trying to smooth things and get everyone together, but it wasn't gunna happen. I felt sorry for him.

After a lotta of talking, it became clear that the school was winning the argument, so the parents started walking out of the meeting as they yelled shit at us again. The security cops made sure they stayed away from us as they left the auditorium.

After the meeting was over, the principal asked me and Gabriel to come onto the stage so we could meet the school board guy. He was real nice. We thanked him and the lawyers for helping us keep all the clubs going. We thanked Mr. Rodriguez and Mr. Atwood too, and then headed to play practice.

Sergio and Jacob came over tonight to have dinner and watch a movie with us. Gabriel's mom made roast beef. Man, it was so good =) She also made some killer mashed potatoes and gravy, and three kinds of vegetables. Gabriel made his mom sit at the table and relax while we served everyone. I loved the look on her face as she listened to our friends rant and rave about stuff. Roberto, Jacob, and Sergio had us all laughing hysterically with their conversations and impressions of people from school. I was laughing so hard that I started choking on my food. I took a drink of milk, but I swallowed wrong, and some of it came outta my nose. They thought that was funny as hell and kept laughing at me as I choked to death..lol It was one of the best dinners I've ever had. After we ate, we spread out on the living room floor with pillows and blankets and snuggled up together. We watched a movie called Edge of Seventeen. Gabriel held me close because I was quietly crying through most of it.

Journal Entry 56
Tuesday 10 pm
October 25th

Random Thoughts:

The last couple of days I've been feeling like I'm fading in and outta this world. I can't stand the feeling because I don't have any control over it. I haven't said anything to Gabriel because I don't want to worry him. I figure this weirdness is part of what's gunna happen pretty soon. I can see it playing out in my mind's eye; I just wish it would happen already O__o

My mind keeps filling up with all this stuff I never had a clue about. Everything around me finally makes sense. That's pretty kool. Knowledge is a weird thing. I can't believe how fucking clueless I've been most of my life.

My sketches and paintings are mad intense; they're getting more intricate and emotional by the day. It's a reflection of both my old and new life. What's kool is that I still lose myself easily in that special place I always go when I create. At least I know that will never change.

I'm trying to forgive the people who have hurt me, but it's hard. I hope I can do it someday.
I'm scared that I'm gunna forget what it feels like to be human once it's over.

Living forever means that I have to accept that everyone in my life is gunna die. All of them will leave this earth, and it makes me sad. I can't believe everyone I know will be gone one day. Am I always going to be the one who gets left behind just because I'm a protector? The only good thing about it is that Gabriel and I will always be together.

Can we love more than one being at the same time, with the same intensity? Is that considered cheating, or is it a part of who we are? I've been feeling guilty about some feelings lately.

I wonder if Gabriel still has intense feelings for CJ. They were together when we couldn't be. I understand what he was going through when we were apart, but every once in a while I get a sick feeling in my stomach. I wonder if he's been getting that feeling lately too.

♥ = ♥

Luis and Cesar stepped it up at school today as they continued trying to fuck up weaker kids.

CJ, Hunter, Gabriel, and I separated so we could stop them. I can tell Lucifer's disciples are trying this stupid divide and conquer thing to find our weaknesses. I want them to think we are weak. They've been harassing everyone who's been coming to the GSA meetings. They're pissed because the parents couldn't shut down our club.

Jennifer's new boyfriend got punched in the face and had his phone stolen by two of Luis's boys. Hunter found the assholes hiding in a bathroom and broke their arms. He didn't break just one arm each, he broke both of them. They were screaming at the top of their lungs like someone who was being tortured. The security cops ran into the bathroom to see what was going on. Hunter had already reappeared and stood next to us as we watched it all go down.

"How did you do it?" CJ asked.

"It was very simple really. Javier was taking a piss and Leon was checking out his new stolen phone. I walked through the wall, turned the lights off and broke their arms on the counter.

Here's the phone. Let's give this back to Christian," Hunter said. We watched those two guys come outta the bathroom screaming and crying. Broken arms look really strange.

"Well, that's two down," Gabriel said.

We saw Jennifer and Christian standing off to the side, so we walked over to them. Hunter gave the phone back. Christian looked at Hunter weird for a second as he took his phone.

"Thanks for getting my phone. How did you...?"

"I found it on the floor," Hunter said.

"You better have that eye checked out. It's almost swollen shut," I said.

In-between fourth and fifth period, Cesar and two of his boys tried to get into Marco's shit just because he's friends with us. Well that was a mistake..lol We arrived just in time to watch the bloodbath. We didn't have to help Marco at all =D

"Hey Marco, what da fuck you doin hangin wit doze queers? That's fuckin O D man.

You queer too or somethin?" Cesar asked, as he tried to crowd Marco and two other b'ball players. It was so fucking funny looking because Cesar is like 5'-4" and Marco is at least 6'-6"

"Why don't you get the fuck outta here before you get hurt," Marco told him.

"Fuck you man," Cesar said, standing there grabbing his crotch and bobbing around all swag. Marco let loose and punched Cesar so hard that he actually bounced a foot off the fucking floor. Blood shot outta his mouth and nose like water out a hose. Cesar was out cold before he even hit the ground. I've never seen someone get punched that hard. Cesar never saw it coming. The other two thugs ran down the hall as fast as they could to get away. Marco and his friends walked away like nothing had happened, leaving Cesar sprawled out on the floor. Marco said hi as he walked by.

"That was fucking awesome what you just did," Roberto said, as he bumped Marco's fist.

"What an asshole," Marco said, shaking his head and laughing.

"Are you coming to the GSA meeting today," I asked.

"Wouldn't miss for the world Miguel. See you guys after school.

$$\Sigma\ Z\ \mathfrak{d}$$

During lunch period we walked to the music room to hang. Just as we were about to go in, I saw in my mind's eye that Luis, Maya, and some of his boys were picking on three of the quiet smart kids just outside the Chem lab. I told Roberto to go on in. "We'll be back in a couple minutes." As soon as Roberto was in the music room, Gabriel and I disappeared and then reappeared on the third floor where it was goin down. A bunch of people had formed a semi-circle and were helping to taunt the guys who were backed into the corner by Luis. One kid was crying, and the other two looked scared outta their minds wondering why Luis was picking a fight with them. Just as Luis and his boys were about to start punching them, I made all of them start pissing in their pants. Their jeans started getting soaked with piss as it dripped all over the floor. Everyone started laughing at them. Luis looked down at his jeans, and at the huge puddle on the floor. He didn't know what to do. They were trying with all their might to stop pissing themselves, but I made them piss uncontrollably. They panicked and started running down the hall, leaving a trail of yellow behind. Gabriel started laughing. "I love it Michael."

"Thanks. I think pissing your pants in front of everyone at school is a humbling thing."

$$\text{\small ≈}\ \text{\textcircled{\tiny ♪}}$$

287

The GSA meeting was pretty intense today. Everyone was talking about all the shit Luis, Cesar, and their gangs have been doing to harass people, and how they are always the ones who end up getting hurt instead. Everyone had some sort of story to tell as the four of us innocently smiled at each other.

Jennifer was the first to say something. "Two jerks came up to us while I was walking to class with Christian. One asshole pushed me against the locker, and the other one punched Christian in the face. They took his brand new phone and ran down the hall, and then into a bathroom. Like thirty seconds later we heard mad screams, so we went to see what was goin on. Those two assholes came outta the bathroom with their arms broke to shit. It was the weirdest thing I've ever seen. It's like someone's watching over us or something."

Roberto and Marco looked at me when she said that. I turned and smiled at both of them as I put my finger over my lips so they'd get the hint. They understood.

Then more people started telling their stories of weirdness. I guess maybe we have to be more careful about how we help out..lol

After everyone shared their stories, we talked about the meeting in the auditorium and how upset the gay haters were about everything. I thanked everyone for showing up. "It was great that all of you were there yesterday. It let all of those people know we aren't going anywhere."

We ended the meeting by finalizing the Halloween party for Friday. Everyone is excited about it. I can't wait to party with all my friends again =D

Journal Entry 57
Wednesday morning 2:30 am
October 26th

Without boundaries
we can follow those footsteps into that young forest,
into that land of unknown possibilities
where pure dreams with no remorse
are feelings that were always meant to be,
that is eternity to me.

The barbed wire of these city streets
hold so many in layered ignorance
as it cuts and tears the flesh.
Those blood droplets underneath the trash on the streets
are reminders of desperation without a final equation,
nothing but circular arguments on a razor's edge.

I went with Gabriel a couple of hours ago and stood outside
on 138th street in my old neighborhood. We just watched and

listened to one stupid sad thing after another. It's disgusting what people do to each other. I wonder how anyone makes it outta the hood without being damaged forever.

We stood in the doorway of an empty storefront so no one would notice us. This loud annoying mom, probably around twenty or so, walked by cursing like a big booty street ho right in front of her little daughter, who was like maybe five. She was dragging her by the hand and yelling at her. She was also talking to a friend at the same time. Her friend was cursing mad crazy too. It was "fuckin this and fuckin that, and she a bitch, and dat thug a dick who be stealin my shit," and on and on. This is the reality that little girl is growing up in; she doesn't have a chance.

Then we watched an ambulance pull up to the corner bodega where this old black guy was lying on the ground drunk and stoned outta his mind. He was around sixty, but looked ninety. His drunk friends were standing around pointing and laughing at him. The guy's face was a bloody mess from falling face first on the sidewalk. There were some guys about my age standing off to the side smoking a blunt and laughing at the old men. As the ambulance guys lifted the old man off the sidewalk, some high school girls came outta the bodega, which made the young guys get all swag. They started grabbing their crotches and showing off as they walked up to em hopin they'd be able to tap what they got. The girls played em easy; they knew exactly what they were doing. A couple more blunts were lit and then they all walked off together down Brook Avenue.

Then I saw something that made me real glad I don't live here anymore. I saw my mom come outta the Rico Bar & Grill with three guys. I could tell all ofem had a nice buzz going. They were laughing and staggering around in front of the bar. My mom lit a cigarette and then took turns kissing each guy. I read her thoughts and it got me sad. She was taking all of them back to the apartment to have sex.

Gabriel looked at me, held my hand, and then gently kissed my cheek.

"Let's get out of here Michael."

"Yeah, I've seen enough."

Journal Entry 58
Thursday morning 3 am
October 27th

Friendship is a single soul dwelling in two bodies.

Aristotle

Wednesday Morning 5 am In Bed

"Gabriel?"

"Yeah?"

"Nothing. Forget it."

"What's wrong cute one? Is something bothering you?"

"No...Yeah... I guess a little. Man...I don't know."

"Michael, talk to me. I love you."

I was silent for a few seconds as I tried to find the right words. They always seem to disappear when I need them most. I started stuttering when they finally came to me.

"I-I've been feeling confused about stuff, you know, about me, you, CJ, and Roberto.

Will you tell me about what you and CJ had when I wasn't

around? Do you still love him that way?"

Gabriel didn't say anything as we both lay there looking up at the ceiling. He slowly moved his hand on top of mine. His silence made me jealous. Roberto broke the silence when he turned sideways and gave a cute little snoring sound underneath his blanket. Gabriel's mom bought a bed for him and we set it up in our room so he wouldn't have to sleep on the couch anymore.

"Let me ask you something," Gabriel whispered. "Do you love Roberto more than...well, you know?"

I could feel the tears welling up in my eyes because I didn't know how to answer.

"I don't know, but I feel something emotional between us."

"Let me ask you again. Do you love Roberto more than... you know?"

Now I was the one who was silent because I knew my answer was gunna hurt him.

"Yeah, I do love him. Can you forgive me?"

"There's nothing to forgive."

I was crying now because Gabriel understood. "I just know I'm connected to Roberto more than just as a friend."

"It's ok Michael. You don't have to cry because of what you are feeling," Gabriel said, as our fingers interlocked. We were silent again for a while, then I felt Gabriel's body start shaking; I knew he was crying.

"I love CJ like you love Roberto. All of us are connected on different levels emotionally, and I know it's causing a lot of confused feelings right now."

"I guess I've been jealous and hurt ever since you told me about it. I know I shouldn't be, but I am. And then I start having the same kind of feelings for Roberto, and I know it's been hurting you. I never meant for it to happen. I hope you believe me. It has me feeling so guilty because it feels like I'm cheating on you."

"Michael, you aren't cheating on me, you are just feeling love. You are being you."

"I am cheating on you because I love him. I even kissed him."

"Don't be sorry Michael. I understand why you kissed Roberto; you love him and he was hurting."

"Why aren't you mad at me? I'm mad at you."

"Do you want me to be mad?" Gabriel asked.

"Yeah...No... I don't know. My emotions are all over the fucking place. But yeah, I guess I do want you to be mad, but you aren't. I don't get it."

I sat up and looked at Roberto quietly sleeping away. "Aren't you jealous? Aren't you pissed at me and him?"

Gabriel sat up too and put his forehead against mine. We both had tears running down our faces.

"Look, I know exactly what you're going through emotionally because I went through the same thing with CJ. I wanted to destroy myself because I was cheating on you, and because you were here and I couldn't do anything about it. I tried to be with you. And then just as I was about to defy you know who, CJ asked me to think the situation through rationally. He told me that I needed to be patient. And that's when he told me how much he loved you too. We both love you, but couldn't be with you, so we.... you know, that's when we kissed, and then things just happened. Love is very complex sometimes. CJ loves both of us.

"Do you still love him like, well, you know?"

"Yes. It's exactly what you feel for Roberto."

Gabriel leaned over and kissed me. I slowly pulled his naked body on top of me and held him tight.

"What do we do?" I asked.

"Let's just take it one day at a time. We're together and that's all that matters to me."

"Me too."

7:30 am In the Music Room at School

Gabriel and Shadow were drinking hot chocolate and talking about Yugioh. Shadow was showing Gabriel all of his latest cards. Drake was patiently showing Roberto and I some new chords on guitar. I haven't said anything, but Gabriel and Drake have been teaching us how to play. We are actually trying to learn bar chords. We suck big time, but the more we practice, the better it sounds..lol

CJ and Hunter went to talk to Mr. Atwood about a home-work assignment or something. They've been edgy all week. I've been worried about them. I think CJ has been staying away from me and Gabriel to give us some space. I want to talk to him alone to let him know I understand about stuff.

Well anyways, while we were practicing, Sergio walked in, came over and sat next to Drake and watched me and Roberto struggling on our guitars. He had this huge smile on his face.

"Are you laughing at us?" I asked, with a sarcastic grin.

"Miguel, can I talk to you alone?"

"Yeah sure. Let's go out in the hall." I got worried as we got up and walked out.

I saw Gabriel discreetly looking our way.

"Hey, what's up?"

Sergio looked nervous as he took a small box out of his jacket pocket.

"I want to ask CJ to go steady with me," he said, opening it and showing me a beautiful ring. "Do you think I'm being too pushy, or rushing into this? I think I love him."

"No you're not being pushy..lol, You definitely need to ask him," I said, as I gave Sergio a big hug.

"Gabriel and I are going steady. He gave me this subway to-ken," I said, showing him my necklace. "Real love is hard to find, so you have to go for it when it happens. I know CJ really likes you."

"I hope so. Thanks. I'm real nervous, but I'm gunna ask him to go steady at the Halloween dance."

"That's so romantic ;p"

When we walked back in, everyone kinda stopped what they were doing and looked at us.

Sergio had the biggest smile on his face as I playfully asked what everyone was staring at.

"So what's going on? What's the big secret?" Shadow asked, with a grin.

"Can't two people talk alone without it being a big deal?" I said, pretending to be mad.

"You'll find out Friday night anyways," Sergio said, blushing mad crazy.

♥ ♥

12 noon

It was a quiet day for a change. Luis and Cesar weren't at school. They must have been skipping or something. It was nice not to have to see their faces or stop em from picking on people. I know something's up, but Gabriel didn't seem too worried, so that made me feel better.

No one was outside protesting either. I hope those people get it by now :/

I told Gabriel I wanted to skip school too and go fly around the city, but he jokingly said that I shouldn't go around breaking the rules..lol

"Hey, let's go to the Chelsea Piers after school. Do you want to go with just me? Or do you want to see if anyone wants to come with us?" I love hanging out on the Hudson."

"That sounds awesome. Let's see if any of the guys wanna go." I said, all excited.

We cruised the halls for a few minutes, and then went to visit Mr. Atwood. Sometimes he grades papers in his classroom during lunch, and that gives us a chance to talk about stuff.

He always has students stopping by. I like talking to mister because he lets us be us. He never judges anyone. I also like that he's been pushing me to think differently since the first day of school. And since he gave me the Aegis, I've been way more relaxed about things. I'm glad it found me.

When we walked into his room, mister was talking with Roberto. It surprised me a little.

I could tell they were having a serious conversation. Mister looked our way. "Hi guys, what's up?"

"Hey mister, we'll come back later. We don't wanna interrupt you," I said.

"Hey Miguel. Hey Gabriel," Roberto said, looking at us nervously. "You don't have to go."

"That's ok. You guys talk. We'll see you in a little while," I said, as our eyes locked onto each other knowing what we've both been feeling.

We left and then went to find CJ and Hunter. They've been busy angels..lol They're always protecting me, and I know they're protecting Gabriel too. I can tell because even when they're gone to wherever, if a problem starts happening, they appear in an instant. The other thing about them is they are both in love. Sergio and Jacob are the nicest guys.

We found them hanging out in the GSA meeting room.

"We'd love to," CJ said.

"You'd love to what?" I asked.

"Go to the Chelsea Piers after school. You want to go, don't you?" CJ said, giving me his look. "I haven't hung out there in a while and the weather is perfect. I called my mom already and she said she would make us dinner."

"Thanks CJ. That'd be awesome. I think all of us need to get outta here for a few hours," I said.

"Can I go too?" Roberto asked, as he walked through the door.

"We wouldn't have it any other way," CJ said.

I sat down and curled up on the couch to relax. Gabriel said he was gunna get a guitar from the music room. "I'll be right back. Sergio, do you want a guitar?"

"Yeah, that sounds good."

Roberto seemed a little down as he went and sat by the window.

"Roberto, will you sit next to me?" I asked, scrunching over to make room for him.

He got up, came over, and sat next to me. He looked nervous for some reason.

The guys were sitting on the couch opposite us talking. I leaned my head back and relaxed for a change. Roberto did the same thing. It was nice.

"Miguel?"

"Yeah. Is everything ok?" I asked.

"I heard what you and Gabriel were talking about this morning. I'm sorry about everything."

"Roberto, there's nothing to be sorry about. We'll figure it all out, ok?"

"Ok...but I am sorry."

"What's wrong?" Jacob asked, looking concerned.

"Nothing, it's all good," I said.

Roberto and I sat there wondering what was gunna happen next. We didn't say anything else; we just leaned our heads against each other and closed our eyes.

3:10pm

We got off the 5 train at Union Square and walked down 14th street to the piers. I wish all of New York was like Chelsea and the Village because it's so gay friendly. No one ever looks at us thinking we got a disease. Whenever Gabriel and I hold hands or kiss at school, it's like the whole world is coming to an end every time. It sucks having to deal with that kind of shit. Being in Chelsea gives me hope that things will eventually get better in the Bronx.

We stopped at a couple of art galleries along the way. It was very kool to see the work of other artists. Gabriel told me I would have a gallery showing one day. That was so sweet of him to say. I secretly want it to happen so bad =)

It was nice to walk down the boardwalk along the Hudson River. It's such a kool place.

I could see the Freedom Tower in the distance as it reached into the sky like a giant sword protecting Manhattan. Certain parts of this city are Heaven, and other parts are Hell. I think this gleaming tower represents knowledge and progress; that we are always reaching into the sky for that hard to reach dream. It's like Gabriel always tells me; it has always been knowledge versus ignorance throughout this world's history, and knowledge must win out every time.

It was nice watching Sergio and CJ, and Jacob and Hunter walk down the boardwalk holding hands. I leaned against the railing and listened to the water crash against the pier. It made me feel calm and alive. Then I looked at Gabriel and Roberto and thought about how lucky I am to have them in my life. I know things are complicated between us, but there must be a reason why it's this way. Gabriel gave me a kiss. "It's ok cute one. It's ok."

Roberto looked away embarrassed, but I scooted over to him and put my hand in his. Then Gabriel did the same thing. We walked together hand in hand and eventually caught up with the guys.

After we left the piers, we walked through the West Village on our way to CJ's apartment.

It was nice to see his parents and have dinner with them. We cabbed back to the Bronx because I knew Roberto was tired. He had a long emotional day, and so did I. When we got home, Roberto took off his clothes and collapsed onto his bed. Gabriel and I did the same thing. The nightlight was the only light that was on in our bedroom. It gave the room a nice warm glow as we relaxed. I lay there silently listening to the three of us breathing as I thought about stuff.

And then the silence was broken.

"Roberto, will you sleep with us tonight." Gabriel softly asked.

There was another moment of silence that was filled with tension and confusion.

"I don't think that's a good idea," Roberto whispered.

"It's ok," Gabriel whispered back.

"Roberto, Please?" I asked nicely.

"Are you sure?"

"Yeah, I'm sure."

I turned and watched him slowly get out of his bed and walk over to ours. We looked at each other shyly through the dim light. I put my hand in his to let him know everything was ok. He smiled as he lifted the blanket and slid his warm naked body next to mine.

Journal Entry 59
Friday morning 3 am
October 28th

And I looked, and behold a pale horse: and his name that sat on the horse was Death, and Hell followed with him.

Revelation 6:8

Thursday Morning 4am

"Michael, Michael, come back to me! Can you hear me? It's Gabriel. I love you.

Please come back."

I could hear Gabriel calling me, but I was lost in some other place where there was no light, no reason, no love. It was so cold and lonely. I felt like I needed to die; like it was my destiny.

I could feel Gabriel shaking my body in a panic, but I kept slipping away like I was in quicksand. And then in an instant Gabriel frantically reached through the darkness and pulled me back to this world. He held me with all his might against his warm body.

"I thought I had lost you Michael. I love you so much. Please don't ever do that to me again," Gabriel said, as tears filled his eyes.

"What happened? I was so scared. One minute I was lying in bed with my eyes closed letting my mind wander like I usually do, and then all of a sudden I was being sucked into a darkness I never knew existed. I tried with all my might to get back, but I couldn't until you found me."

Gabriel ran his fingers through my hair and kissed me. His whole body was shaking as he held me in his arms. He looked into my eyes with so much love. He didn't say anything, but he began to glow like the stars in the sky.

And then very gently, he hugged me and started fusing our energy together. Gabriel gave me a part of himself. I could feel it immediately. I felt less human all of a sudden, which made me realize that I had been worrying about nothing after all. I had a feeling of peace beyond anything I had ever felt.

"He knows we are protecting you, and he knows you now have an Aegis. He also thinks he knows how to manipulate you. He's trying to destroy you from within. I just gave you another layer of protection to stop it from happening again."

"Are you talking about Lucifer?"

"Yes."

We have to go to your art studio right now. I need to see something," Gabriel said.

CJ and Hunter suddenly appeared right behind him looking like they were ready to kill.

"What's wrong?" I asked, as the three of them looked at me sympathetically.

THE FOUR CORNERS OF EARTH

"Something has happened, and it's not good."

We flew in a flash to Tisch and entered the studio. What we found made me so fucking angry.

The studio looked like an atomic bomb had gone off in it. All the paintings we've been creating over the last few weeks were destroyed and scattered everywhere. Tubes of paint had exploded, making the room look like an abstract painting from Hell. All but one painting was laying on the floor. Sitting on the easel in my space was the first painting I had done; Pandemonium.

The four of us looked at it as it looked back at us with pure hatred. There was a huge burned out hole in the center of it. Smoke was still coming out, and it smelled like burning metal.

There was also this eerie vibration all around it. It creeped me out because I knew the painting was alive.

"We just missed him," Gabriel said, angrily. "The painting is now summoning the underworld to prepare for an attack."

Gabriel, CJ, and Hunter immediately sent beams of white light at the hole to seal it off. Then the painting disintegrated right before my eyes.

"Michael, we have closed the portal. Now Lucifer cannot return to his world. He is locked in this one and has no way out now. The Metatron Cubes won't let him escape. We have to destroy him, and then we have to destroy all of the other fallen angels. There is a new battle on the horizon," Gabriel said, as he walked to the window and looked out.

"What happened? What did I do to fuck this whole thing up?" I yelled.

"You didn't do anything, you were just being you. We were

too blind to see that he would use your artistic soul to manipulate your human vulnerabilities. Somehow he got you to paint his world without you knowing it, and then he used the painting as an entry way into this world. This has been the danger all along. He was able to get past the Metatron Cubes we set up by using your soul. We have failed you," Gabriel said, with sadness in his voice.

Then Hunter told me something that shook me right to the core.

"We haven't done our job Michael. The whole world hangs in the balance with you being able to transform from a human back to the archangel. If you are destroyed, then this world will no longer exist. If Lucifer is able to kill you before you change, then he will have won. He will then destroy this world and this universe. We can't stop him without you and the new powers you will soon have. We can destroy his army, but you are the one who has been chosen to destroy Lucifer."

Everything seemed to be going in slow motion as I listened.

"Michael, you are the gift. God has chosen you as the final protector of this world. You will also be the protector of this universe and all of the others the moment your transformation is complete. God has other experiments on his horizon, so he needs you and us to watch over everything he has created so far," Gabriel said, hoping I would understand the importance of what was going to happen soon.

I walked over to the window and stood next to Gabriel as I tried to take it all in.

"I'm not afraid of Lucifer. If he's stuck here without a way out, then we can destroy him. I'm ready." I looked at Hunter and apologized. "I should have let you destroy him the last time we had the chance. I'm sorry. You've been right about Lucifer from the beginning. I'm not going to make that mistake again. We need to stop this world from being destroyed."

Hunter put his arm around my shoulder and gave me a hug. "Now you are talking my friend."

"Let's put this room back together," Gabriel said. I watched the room magically reverse the damage and put everything back in its place. The studio looked just like it did before, with the exception of one painting.

$$\sum \Omega \odot$$

12 noon

We started putting the Halloween decorations up for the party. We didn't get much done though because everyone was bouncing off the walls for some reason. Just about everyone was there to help. Marco and Alex walked in with Ramon. They looked cute together because Ramon is so little compared to them. Marco and Alex looked like Ramon's bodyguards..lol

Gabriel set up the P.A. system and lights, and Roberto and I set up the DJ equipment.

Ima dumb ass when it comes to electronics, so I was no help to Roberto at all. He's a genius with that kind of stuff.

"Miguel, can we be the DJ's for the party?" Roberto asked.

"You know I'm no good at that sort of thing, but I guess so if you'll do all the talking.

I'll help you select songs."

"Yeah, that'd be kool. We can set the mood for the party,"

"I know you'll get everyone all charged up. You're good at that," I said, giving him a sly smile.

I'm excited about this party because it's a way to show the Bronx that gay people are normal too.

Decorating the room with all my friends helped get my mind off of what happened this morning. I'm worried about everyone now that Lucifer is back. The four of us have to figure out a strategy and then make it work. I'm frustrated because I'm stuck being half human half angel. We gotta plan this thing good if I'm gunna beat Lucifer at his own game.

God hasn't talked to me at all, so I don't know what his exact plan is. I don't even know if I'll ever know; nothing is ever simple with him. I guess I have to figure it out on my own :/

I can tell that Gabriel, CJ, and Hunter are in overdrive protection mode now; we all know what's at stake. Gabriel and I were having a conversation in our minds as we continued putting up the Halloween decorations.

"Gabriel? Why won't God talk to me? He talks to you, CJ and Hunter. I don't get it.

And why haven't I changed yet? I was almost killed, and it was you who saved me, not God.

Why is he putting me in danger?"

Gabriel gave me this sad look. "Honestly, I don't know. He refuses to give us a reason. All he says is that we know what we have to do, and that he will see you when the time is right. He always has. This is obviously some sort of test. All I know is that earth's destiny is in our hands. Humans call it the apocalypse, and there is going to be one. There are only two possible outcomes, so we have to make sure the right one prevails."

"I guess I just want to know where I stand in all this. I feel like I'm going into it blind, and I don't think that's fair. You guys having to protect me makes all of us easier targets for Lucifer. Why would God do that to us?"

Gabriel didn't say anything; he just stopped what he was doing and looked at me like he was sorry about everything.

After my rant, I tried to figure out a strategy. "Lucifer is clever and powerful and all that, but he also has weaknesses. I want to use those weaknesses to defeat him. We need to use me as bait. You know, make it easy for him to get to me. Would you be willing to do that?"

"I don't think that is a good idea at all. I will not put you in that kind of situation Michael."

I could see that Gabriel was getting angry. I've never seen him like that before.

"Gabriel, nothing will happen to me, I promise." He didn't say anything as he came over and gently touched my chest with his hands so we could feel each other's warmth.

♌ ♍

There was a new person helping us decorate today; Jennifer's new boyfriend, Christian.

It was nice getting to know him. He's a real nice guy. I felt bad because the whole gay thing is new to him. I'm glad he was brave enough to come and help. It was so sweet of him to be there for Jennifer. He followed her around like a little puppy dog. I know a lot of straight guys always think they might turn gay if they talk to gay people, and maybe he was thinking that, but I hope not.

3pm standing in front of Tisch

"Guys, I'll be all right. Please don't worry about me."

"We aren't going to let you out of our sight," Gabriel said.

"Lucifer isn't dumb enough to come back here, is he?" I asked.

"I think he might try to kill you here. He takes sadistic pleasure in taking souls where a person finds passion and happiness in life. Lucifer loves to see the look on people's faces just before he rips out their soul and sends them to Hell," Hunter said, as his eyes started glowing wildly."

"Fuck him. I hope he tries to kill me here then. I'll be ready for him," I said, as everything started shaking around us. Gabriel grabbed me real quick. "Calm down cute one. We need to be patient."

I hugged Gabriel and kissed those beautiful lips of his.

"Do you mind if we watch you paint today?" CJ asked.

"No, not at all."

"Thanks. I like the look on your face as you create. It's Magical. And don't worry, we will stay invisible so we won't bother the others," CJ said, as he gave me a hug.

We stood in front of Tisch enjoying the nice weather and watching the college students come and go. Something had been on my mind for a while, so I hoped the guys could help me with the answer.

"Can I ask you guys something?"

"Sure," Gabriel said.

"This has been bothering me since the beginning of school. Who is Mr. Atwood? I know he knows stuff. I've been feelin it since the first day of class. He has some kind of power or something. I know it. Is he an angel?"

The three of them smiled at me big time.

"So you've noticed," Gabriel said.

"It's kinda hard not to, especially after the Aegis magically floated to me."

"Well, he's not an angel, or even immortal. He's a human who has tapped into our energy source somehow. He is one of a handful of people on earth who have evolved to what people will be like thousands of years from now. He is using this gift to help us any way he can," Gabriel said.

"He knows we are angels? That's mad kool."

"Yeah, he recently figured it out. We are lucky to have him on our side," CJ said.

It made me smile knowing he knows. Like Gabriel says, I have to trust my instincts about the stuff I feel.

"Well I gotta go in now. I'll see you guys in a few."

I put my hands up and touch the wind
I can feel the vibrations of earth
Knowing I am one with truth

Journal Entry 60
October 29th

5am Saturday Morning

And The Story Is Told With Simple Words

I'm sitting on the terrace mentally exhausted and numb. I feel intense anger, loss, and an emptiness that overwhelms me. I can't stop thinking about what happened at the party last night, so I need to write it down. I need to put everything into a calm and rational perspective before I lose it and do something I'm going to regret.

Within the blink of an eye it happened, but it came at a cost. Yeah, I was finally cured of that insidious disease known as death as I crossed into the void that haunts each and every person who has ever wondered if their last breath is final bleak darkness.

My transformation from what I was to what I am has given me a new understanding of how fragile all of this is. But even though the world is finite, it is a wondrous moment in time.

So why must there always be dopplegangers that haunt each rotation of earth?

Why must there always be people who kill for their own pleasure?

Why must there always be people who refuse to see the truth?

Why have the lies gone on for so long?

Ancient logic and rhetorical fallacies have starved the brain for centuries. This is a sad truth. Empirical knowledge, on the other hand, lovingly reveals that you are made from stardust in a universe made of strings that play the most beautiful haunting melodies; you can hear them if you listen closely. But I have been looking around this world with real sadness because so few people dare to listen to this undercurrent of wonder.

Even though I had lived on this planet as a violated human being, I always felt that I could get through those horrid moments and find my way. It had been a struggle on so many levels, but I did finally make it. You can too if you really try :)

I see so many cruel carbon entities who have diminished this wonderful gift to the lowest common denominators of HATE, FEAR, IGNORANCE, GUILT, SHAME, JEALOUSY, RESENTMENT,

PSYCHOLOGICAL RAPE, TORTURED HUMAN FLESH, and EMPTY VISIONS OF SADISTIC HYPNOTISTS.

' __ '

It was supposed to be a celebration, you know, a party where gays and straights could have fun together, but they ruined it. They ruined it because they hate what we are. They hate us because we are different, because we are gay, because we see the truth about their righteous indignation. Their hate is deep, it comes from within, and that is the human shame.

And because of this intense hatred, they killed someone I love.

♨ ≋ Ω

7:00am Friday morning

We decided to go to school early so we could finish putting up decorations. As we walked to the subway, CJ was telling Roberto how he was gunna rig some stuff so he could scare everyone. "I'm going to have realistic looking ghosts coming right through the walls."

"How are you gunna do that?" Roberto asked.

"Well, I'm going to use a special lighting technique Hunter and I have devised," CJ said, as he winked at me. "Believe me Roberto, it's going to scare the shit out of every single person at the party. Don't tell anyone, ok?"

"I won't. Can't wait to see everyone's reaction =) Are you gunna use the same kind of magic Atwood used when he pretended to make the Aegis fly to Miguel? That was so fucking kool. Miguel, you shoulda seen the look on your face when that was goin down," Roberto said, as he playfully nudged my shoulder.

"Yeah, I'm going to use a little of that," CJ said.

Just as we got to the the subway steps, Sergio and Jacob yelled from down the street to wait for them. CJ and Hunter had huge smiles on their faces as we waited for their cute boyfriends to catch up. It always makes me happy when all of us are together =)

THE FOUR CORNERS OF EARTH

I could feel it was gunna be a special day.

Well, it all went to shit as soon as we got to school. The security cop told us to go to the room where our party was gunna be. I knew immediately that something bad had happened.

We walked in and saw Mr. Atwood and Principal Rodriguez talking to a cop. The whole room had been destroyed. All of our decorations had been torn down, the couches were slashed, the Smart Board was ripped off the wall and smashed all over the floor. The DJ equipment and lighting were smashed to shit too. Gabriel put his arm around me to calm me down. On the back wall were spray-painted words "FAGS DIE TONIGHT."

The seven of us stood there looking at the mess. "I knew something like this was gunna happen," Roberto said, as he started to clean stuff up.

"I'm sorry this has happened guys," Mr. Rodriguez said.

"Mister, we still want to have the party. We'll clean everything up. We don't need music to have a good time. We need to show everyone we aren't afraid," I said, as I helped Roberto. Gabriel and Hunter walked over to the music equipment to see how bad the damage was.

"I think we can make some of it work," Gabriel said.

"Mister, can we stay here and clean the room?" CJ asked.

"I want to take a few more pictures before you guys start cleaning. All of you are excused from your classes today," Principal Rodriguez said.

Then Atwood walked over to me. "Miguel, don't worry about this. It is small frightened people who do this kind of thing. You have them running scared."

"I know who did this."

"I know you do, so please don't do anything rash, ok?"

I didn't say anything; I just looked at him hoping he would understand my anger.

After the cop left, we got to cleaning and fixing as much as we could. Atwood brought us more Halloween decorations, and the janitor guy came and painted the wall where the graffiti was. Sergio and Jacob got some duct tape from the janitor and taped the slashed up couch cushions. We all got in better moods as things started coming together again.

Gabriel and Hunter worked their magic and got the DJ equipment to work.

"Luis, Cesar, and their boys are skipping school again," CJ said, knowing they were up to something big.

"Yeah, I know those assholes are the ones who did this," Roberto said.

"We have to be careful tonight," Gabriel said, with a look of concern.

A bunch of our friends came by between classes to help us redecorate.

12 noon

Marco and Alex stopped by during lunch to see if they could help out. Marco said that a lot of people were in front of the school getting ready to protest again. I thought for sure they'd get bored with all of it by now. I looked at Gabriel for a moment and then walked down the hall to see what was going on. I went to the window and looked at all those supposedly virtuous people. I was trying to feel some compassion for them, but I couldn't feel anything. Honestly, I was so angry that I didn't care if they lived or died, and that scared me. It scared me because I'm their protector, their archangel, and I'm supposed to love them. Dark thoughts began to enter my mind. I thought, do all these people really matter in the scheme of things? Maybe I should just let Lucifer have them and be done with it because it didn't feel like it was worth all the trouble. That's when Gabriel walked up and stood next to me.

"Hey, are you all right?"

"I don't know."

"Don't let all of this get you down, ok?"

"Why should we help them? They are never going to change. They never have. How many times do we have to come back here and save this planet?"

"Nothing is ever easy Michael, you know that first hand. It takes time. Look at what you did for that old lady the other day. You changed her."

"I don't know if it will ever be enough. We can't do that for every person because then this human experiment will have failed. In many ways it already has failed."

"It hasn't failed yet. And you're right, we can't show miracles to everyone, but sometimes a little glimpse for certain individuals can go a long way. If we can show them little moments of love and kindness, then maybe some of those people will change. I least I hope so."

"I just don't feel any kind of love for them right now. Look at them down there thinking they are doing God's work. They don't have a clue; they just want to burn us at the stake. I guess Lucifer has it a lot easier than we do."

"You're right; he does, but only for a little while longer. We just have to fight that much harder to get these people to see."

"What if no one shows up tonight, then they will have won." I honestly feel like the balance between good and evil has been tipped to the point of no return, and that maybe we should bring this world to its end. That might be the compassionate thing to do."

"Please don't think that Michael. Don't let Lucifer get to you. You alone hold the fate of this world in your hands, and that is a responsibility that takes wisdom and complete love. God is putting his trust in you to make the right decision, so try to forgive them for what they are doing."

I didn't say anything to Gabriel as I closed my eyes and tried to calm down. I took his hand in mine hoping he would help me find the strength I needed to overcome what I was feeling.

"You know, those people down there are afraid. They are afraid of differences. They are afraid of the unknown, so they try and make everyone else feel afraid so their fear will make sense to them. They don't know any better Michael, so we must show them a path out of the fear that is tearing them apart. Come on; let's get back to our friends."

We went home after school to relax, eat some food, and get into our costumes. I wasn't worried about the room getting destroyed again because Principal Rodriguez had a security cop sitting right outside the door. Hunter also put some protection around it too. He said if anyone tried to mess it up again, they would be disintegrated. Gabriel thought he was going too far, but I told Hunter it was the right thing to do.

I thought about Luis and Cesar as I sat on the couch sketching. It's been nice not having to see them at school. I wish they'd just quit or go away. All they do is fuck with people. They never do anything except skip class. School's one big playground for them to harass the shit outta everyone. But not knowing where they were had me worried too. I tried to find them in my mind, but I couldn't see a thing. I figured Lucifer was protecting them because I came up blank. So did Gabriel, CJ, and Hunter. I was getting a bad feeling about them, so I tried to mentally prepare myself for anything. The four of us were worried because we figured Lucifer probably had discovered some new power that we didn't know about.

Anyways, Jacob and Sergio came over so we could get ready and go to the party together. Gabriel's mom made pizza rolls, cheesy bread, and burritos for us. I was starving. I hadn't eaten anything all day because I was so upset. Roberto was starving too. We were kinda wired up as we ate, played video games, and got into our costumes. A bunch of people were also texting mad crazy, which was a good sign everyone was gunna show up.

"I really like your costume Miguel. You make a hot looking angel," Roberto said, as he put on his skeleton makeup.

"Thanks. Can I be your guardian angel tonight?"

"Yeah, I'd like that," he said, as we both shyly looked at each other in the mirror.

I smiled and then looked away, but Roberto kept staring at me, like he was trying to see if I really was an angel.

"You look hot in them bones, skeleton boy," I said, breaking the silence as I shyly looked back at him. Then everyone else started wandering into our bedroom to put on their costumes and talk about how awesome the party was gunna be.

I really liked everyone's costumes. Roberto was the one who suggested that Gabriel and I be archangel's. That was pure karma..lol. CJ and Hunter decided to be themselves too.

CJ was the Archangel Metatron, and Hunter was the Archangel Rafael. We were the four emo archangels from the other side intentionally trying to let our friends see the truth ;p

Jacob dressed up as Bruno Mars. He looked way hot with his pompadour hair, aviator sunglasses, and his shiny grey sharkskin suit. Jacob's long skinny body in that suit made him look like he belonged on the cover of a fashion magazine. I know he wants to be a fashion designer someday. He hopes to get into the Fashion Institute of Technology in Manhattan. Jacob even had a microphone as a prop so he could pretend he was performing. He does have a great voice by the way :]

"I'm gunna stay in character all night, so if anyone asks me anything, I'm gunna answer in Bruno Mars song lyrics..lol"

Sergio decided to be Dracula. "I'm really sick of the whole sparkly vampire scene," he said, laughing. "I wanna be a Stoker vampire with an edge of darkness and mystery." Then he tried to give CJ a hickey on his neck ;p

Gabriel's mom took pictures of all of us together. We looked really good; like a bunch of misfits going off on an adventure. She told us to be careful and to have fun as we were leaving. Gabriel gave her a nice long hug as we stood in the hallway. I got worried because she looked worried as she watched us leave.

♥ ♥

It was kool seeing everyone in their costumes when we got to school. Usually people don't like to play dress-up, but everyone was really into it this time. I kinda smiled when we walked past the protesters because we were actually showing them the truth. They tried to get in our face by yelling at us about desecrating their religions because we dressed up like angels.

I guess if you're emo and gay you aren't allowed to be religious O__o

As they yelled shit, CJ and Hunter decided to levitate off the ground about five feet in the air.

They even made their angel wings flap a little for effect. You shoulda seen the looks they got. Even Roberto, Jacob, and Sergio were shocked by what they were doing =)

Everyone got fucking quiet real quick.

"How do you know we aren't really angels?" CJ asked them.

Then, as they lowered themselves back to the ground, these huge explosions went off behind the building across the street. People ducked down like shots were being fired at them, then they turned around to see what was going on. All of a sudden a bunch of fireworks started going off like it was the 4th of July. CJ and Hunter were really playing with their minds.

"That should keep them busy," Hunter said, as we continued walking into the school.

"How did you guys do that? That was fucking kool," Sergio said, with a stunned look on his face.

"It's just a magic trick," CJ said, as the guys looked at him weird.

"Hey, don't be shocked, it's Halloween. Anything can happen, right?

Then CJ stopped and put his arms around Sergio and lifted him off the ground.

"Feels pretty kool, doesn't it? You make me float on air," CJ said, as he kissed Sergio nice ;P

The halls were filled with people in all sorts of wild looking costumes. I wish we could dress like this every day. I like the idea of everyone being different; that's what life is all about.

We walked down the hall by the entrance where the regular Halloween party was being held so we could see their decorations. They did a really good job decorating. A bunch of people were standing outside the doors waiting to go in. A couple of guys started giving us shit about being faggot angels as we walked by.

"Hey bitches, can we crash your party later to get some head just in case our girls ain't up for it?" I stopped, turned around, and stared at them.

"Come on Miguel, they aren't worth it," Gabriel said.

I kissed Gabriel right in front of those two assholes, and then turned and smiled at them.

All of a sudden their pants and boxers drop to the floor. Everyone started laughing hysterically as they stood there naked from the waist down. CJ laughed. "Hey guys, look at those little dicks." They panicked as they reached down to pull their pants up. They were trying to pull em up, but couldn't because I made them stick to the floor..lol Everyone kept laughing as we headed up the stairs.

Just as we got to our room, Jennifer yelled for us to wait up for her and Christian. The security guy let us in so we could get stuff ready. We put up a couple of long tables in the far corner for the food and drinks. Mr. Atwood showed up a couple of minutes later with a cart that had like fifteen large pizzas and a bunch of soda. Jennifer and Christian got out the bags of chips, jars of salsa, popcorn, and Halloween candy. I couldn't believe how much food we had. Everything looked perfect.

Shadow, Drake, and Erik walked in just as we were finishing up. I loved their costumes. Shadow was dressed as you guessed it, Shadow the Hedgehog, He was all in black except for his hair and shoes. He had a red Mohawk and was wearing bright red Nike Air Max Hi Tops. He looked hot ;p Drake and Erik looked very kool as zombies. Their makeup was awesome. It looked like their faces were rotting away as decaying flesh hung from their cheeks. They also had dark circles under their eyes, and blood around their mouths and on their chins. They even tried to grab us for effect =)

Once we got everything just right, Gabriel turned the room lights off and turned the dance lights on. He put some music on, then walked over and put his arms around me and kissed me nice. The room felt magical, like we had just stepped into another world. It felt so good as he held me against his body.

"Gabriel, thanks for making this happen."

"Anytime cute one."

Then Roberto started practicing his DJ skills. "Here's a song for those two hot guys over there making out." He put on Cosmic Love by Florence and the Machine. I took Gabriel's hand and led him to the dance floor. We were the first to dance on this special night.

I got pretty emotional because everything finally felt right. We held each other close as we slow danced. I could feel Gabriel's warmth surround my body, and I could feel the heartbeats of everyone in the room as CJ, Hunter, Jacob, Sergio, Jennifer, Christian, Shadow, Drake, and Erik slowly formed a circle around us. I listened to the words closely because they reflected exactly what I was feeling. I looked over Gabriel's shoulder at Roberto knowing he had chosen this song for a reason. All of a sudden everyone started dancing as the party officially began.

Mr. Atwood stood by the door with the security cop checking names off the list as people showed up. Within ten minutes just about everyone was there. I was so happy to see all my friends. Even the people we invited from the Chess Club showed up.

I knew Ramon had a crush on a girl from that club. He even got brave and asked her to dance. It was cute seeing them dance together because she was at least six inches taller than he was. They were having a blast dancing to Let Yourself Go by Green Day.

Everyone's costumes looked awesome. People were taking pictures and video of each other posing and dancing all crazy. About an hour into the party Marco and the whole b-ball team walked in. Their girlfriends came too. It looked kool seeing a bunch of superheroes walk through the door. Marco saw me and Gabriel dancing, so he came over and gave both of us a hug.

"Hey, thanks for coming?" I said.

"No problem. I hope you don't mind, but the team wanted to come up here and party.

It's been wack downstairs. Everyone's been talking about you guys, how you ruined their party.

I told them they were full of shit and to just get over it. They were being stupid assholes, so we decided to leave."

"Kool. There's pizza and stuff over there. I'm really glad you're here Marco." He hugged me again and then started partying.

Roberto put on My Body by Young The Giant just as all these crazy weird ghosts suddenly appeared out of nowhere. They scared the shit outta everyone. People screamed as the ghosts flew around the room making spooky noises and chasing everyone. A couple of ghosts even asked some people to dance, but that just scared them even more as the screaming continued. CJ and Hunter were laughing their heads off. CJ asked Roberto to crank the music up. The ghosts started dancing on the floor, ceiling, and walls. One ghost even went up to Jonathan, this guy from Drama Club who's still in the closet, and kissed him on the lips. "You're cute! I wish I were alive so I could ask you out on a date."

Jonathan stood there totally stunned not knowing what to do. A few minutes later the ghosts thanked everyone for inviting

325

them, and then flew through the walls and disappeared. Everyone thought it was the best magic trick they'd ever seen..lol

Gabriel and I got a couple of sodas and stood off to the side so we could take it all in. It felt good watching everyone have fun. We were leaning against the wall relaxing when Gabriel noticed Roberto. "Hey Michael, Roberto looks a little lonely. You should ask him to dance."

"Yeah, he does look a little down. I told him I was gunna help him DJ tonight. I think I'll go see if he wants some help. Do you mind if we dance together?"

"No, I don't mind. He's wanted to dance with you all night, and I know you've wanted to dance with him too. Michael, you know I'm ok with everything, right?"

"Yeah, I do. Thanks." I gave Gabriel a kiss and then went to hang with Roberto.

Roberto smiled when he saw me walk up. It was kool helping him DJ because he really knows how to keep a party going. We stood next to each other trying to talk over the music while we picked out songs and watched everyone dance.

"Are you having fun?" I asked.

"Yeah, this is the best."

I started feeling real nervous and shy as I watched him sync up some songs. I finally got the nerve to inch closer and put my hand in his. Roberto turned and gave me this serious look for a second, then he gave me a half smile and squeezed my hand softy. He put his fingers in-between mine. We were both nervous as we looked into each other's eyes. I leaned in close to him so he could hear me. "It feels nice," I said, as our fingers stayed intertwined.

We listened to the music and watched everyone party as the lights swirled to the rhythm and pulse of every person in the room.

I got nervous again as I leaned in and whispered into Roberto's ear. "Will you dance with me?"

"Yeah, I'd love to."

All of a sudden CJ and Sergio came over and said they wanted to DJ for a while, so I took Roberto by the hand and walked to the dance floor. CJ put on The Long and Winding Road by The Beatles. We held each other close as we slow danced.

"Thanks Miguel. This means a lot."

"It means a lot to me too."

As we danced, I looked to see where Gabriel was. I smiled when I saw Gabriel trying to get Shadow to dance with him. It was so cute because Shadow was looking down at the floor shy-like and shaking his head no. I knew he was feeling self-conscious about dancing with another guy. Gabriel leaned in close to Shadow and said something that made him put his hand in Gabriel's, then they came over and danced next to us. Gabriel and I smiled at each other knowing how special this moment was.

When the song ended, CJ put on In The End by Black Veil Brides, and then he, Sergio, Hunter, and Jacob joined us on the dance floor. The lights got mad intense as we all danced together. It was nirvana in the mortal world; the way it was always supposed to be. We were eight shining stars in a universe that was meant just for us.

Gabriel and I went out in the hall to talk to Mr. Atwood. We wanted to see if he knew how the party was going downstairs, and if the protesters were causing any trouble.

"Most of the protesters have left according to Mr. Rodriguez. I think that is a good sign they might be giving up," mister said. "Everyone is behaving themselves downstairs, even though they are angry that the GSA party has received more attention," he continued.

"That's too bad. I hope they're having a good time anyways," I said.

We headed back into the party and ran into Sergio, Roberto, and Jacob just as we got to the door. They said they'd be right back. "We're going to pee and make sure our costumes still look good. See ya in a few," Sergio said. Then he whispered in my ear, "I'm gunna ask CJ to go steady with me as soon as I get back." I gave him a hug. "CJ is a lucky guy. I know he's gunna say yes."

I watched them go down the hall knowing this was a special moment for him.

We went to find CJ and Hunter to see what they were up to. They were talking to Marco and his girlfriend. We talked for a few minutes and then I went to get Gabriel and I something to drink. As I was filling our cups, Shadow came over to get some soda too.

"Hey Shadow, are you having a good time?"

"Yeah. This is one of the best parties I've been to. Thanks for the invite."

"I'm glad you came."

"Miguel, I just wanna say that I really like you and Gabriel. It's kool hanging out together."

"I like hanging with you too. I think you're really talented, and I know Gabriel likes you a lot. I'm glad you two danced together."

"You are?

"Yeah."

"You know I'm straight, right?"

"Yeah. That's why I'm glad you danced with Him. You were comfortable enough to dance with another guy. That takes a lot of nerve," I said, as I poured him some soda.

Shadow stood next to me with this curious look, and then said, "There's something about the two of you that I can't figure out. It's like you have a secret or something. I get these weird feelings every once in a while, and I just know you guys are way different from anyone else I've ever known."

"Na, we're just a couple of guys comfortable with who we are."

"No, there's something more going on. I feel more aware whenever you and Gabriel are around. I can't explain it, but I can feel it."

"That's kool. Gabriel always says to trust your instincts." Shadow smiled.

All of a sudden I started feeling sharp pains in my chest. I grabbed the side of the table to hold myself up because it hurt so bad. Then a cold empty darkness started entering my body as I looked at Shadow for help. It felt like I was dying.

"Miguel, are you all right?" he asked, as he grabbed my arm to steady me.

"I don't know. Please get Gabriel," I said, as I tried to figure out what was happening.

I fell to my knees as Gabriel ran over to see what was wrong. "Miguel, are you ok?"

"It feels like I'm being stabbed in the chest, and I can feel that dark place trying to take me again."

Gabriel held me close as I whispered in his ear, "I'm connected to someone else. I can feel their pain." I started getting sick to my stomach. Gabriel looked at me and then down at his Metatron Cubes. They were spinning like crazy. He tried to visualize what was happening.

"Something terrible is happening, but I can't see what it is," Gabriel said, all panicky.

CJ and Hunter tried to see what was happening, but they came up blank too. I got it together a little as I closed my eyes and concentrated as hard as I could. And that's when I saw him.

"It's Roberto. They're hurting Roberto."

I willed my body to move with all my might as the four of us ran out of the party and down the hall to see if Roberto was in the bathroom. Sergio and Jacob were yelling and screaming as they banged on the wall from inside the bathroom. Someone had sealed the door completely into the wall, making it look like it had disappeared. Hunter found the door by putting his hand through the wall. He yanked it right out of the bricks and threw it on the floor as we rushed in.

"What happened? Where's Roberto," I yelled.

"They took him. They took him," Sergio said, crying hysterically. "We were just talking and fixing our costumes, when all of a sudden the lights went out. Then there was this weird noise that started vibrating the whole fucking bathroom. All of a sudden we were slammed against the wall and held there. The lights started blinking on and off, and that's when we saw three guys in devil costumes punching and kicking Roberto. They must have knocked him out because his body was limp as they dragged him out. What the fuck is goin on Miguel?"

"We have to find him before it's too late," I screamed.

I closed my eyes again and concentrated as hard as I could. "He's in the park. They've taken him to the park down the street." I looked at Sergio and Jacob. "Go tell Atwood what's happening, he'll keep you and everyone else safe. Please don't leave the school, ok?"

"Ok."

"Go. Now!"

Sergio and Jacob ran down the hall, but stopped for a second, and turned around to ask us something. That's when they saw us disappear right before their eyes.

We reappeared at the entrance of the park and saw this glowing red dome-like structure in the middle of it. We flew to it and tried to break through, but it was no use. We couldn't penetrate its exterior. I flew to the top of it so I could try to see where Roberto was. And that's when I saw the most horrific thing I had ever seen. Luis and Cesar were stabbing Roberto repeatedly in the chest as his half naked body lay there lifeless and bleeding on the ground. I was crying hysterically as I tried to break through to save him. I was watching him die right before my eyes. With each thrust of their blades into Roberto, I could feel it in me. I was getting weaker and weaker by the second. Luis and Cesar were actually laughing as they stabbed him.

"How does it feel now you fucking queer?" Cesar said, with a twisted smile and blind rage in his eyes.

"We got to fuck your queer ass and kill you all in one night," Luis was yelling, as he grabbed Roberto's hair with one hand and continued stabbing his lifeless body with the other. All of a sudden Luis looked up and saw me hovering at the top of the dome.

"Michael, take a good look at what we done to your faggot bitch friend. Yeah, I know who you are motha fucka, and you're next," Luis yelled at the top of his lungs.

I looked at Roberto lying there in a pool of blood and knew he was gone.

Gabriel, CJ, and Hunter were desperately trying to break the dome with me. I started screaming at the top of my lungs for God to help.

"Where the fuck are you? You let this happen. You killed him," I screamed over and over. Roberto and I were only fifty feet apart, but it seemed like a million light years because I had let him down. I was his guardian angel and I let him down. I hovered overhead as I watched Roberto's soul leave his body and start to ascend. His soul brushed against my body as it found me, and that's when I knew I was dying too. It felt right, like all the pain in my life would now go away. I felt myself getting weaker and weaker as I closed my eyes. All I thought was that Roberto and I would die together, and we could leave this horrible place in peace. But just as I was ready to take my last breath, my angelic energy flew out of my body, separating my divine existence from my human existence.

I felt so lost as I watched my soul quietly leave the body I had lived in for fifteen years. It flew to Roberto's soul and started to light up the sky. Then our souls started to ascend together. It made me feel so sad that we were leaving this earth at such a young age. Roberto's lifeless body lay on the ground as his murderers looked at it triumphantly.

My body floated lifeless in the sky as a mirror image of Roberto. His stab wounds were my stab wounds. God had connected us together for some reason, and I didn't know why, but I was glad he did. Gabriel was crying hysterically as he flew over and cradled my body in his arms. He kissed me over and over as he tried to bring me back to life.

"Michael, please don't leave me. Please don't leave me," he screamed, as he held me and looked up at the sky in a rage. "It wasn't supposed to happen this way. You promised. You said there was another way. You said Roberto would help transform Michael without having to die, but you lied to me."

I knew who he was talking to, and I got so fucking angry that God was doing this to all of us.

I frantically tried to let Gabriel know that I was ok, but he couldn't hear me because he was in a blind rage. CJ and Hunter tried to console Gabriel, but he angrily pushed them away with his energy shield.

"Why are you taking Michael away again?" Gabriel yelled.

I didn't know why it was all happening this way, and I didn't know how to let Gabriel see that I was still here, but I knew I had to stop our souls from leaving this world before it was too late. I called out for the Aegis to come to me. It came out of nowhere with blinding speed and rapped itself around both of our souls. It stopped them from ascending. Once Gabriel saw what the Aegis had done, he knew I was somewhere close. He wiped his tears away as my lifeless body started glowing in the most beautiful bluish color imaginable. He let go of me and flew back a little as this brilliant white light suddenly appeared from the deepest reaches of the universe and hit my body with a blinding jolt.

The hand of God had finally found me.

My soul was released from the Aegis and flew to me. Then we were both instantaneously placed back into my body, connecting all three entities once again. I connected with Gabriel to let him know what was needed for my final transformation into the archangel. Gabriel smiled as he, CJ, and Hunter positioned themselves into a divine triangle. They started shooting their beams of angelic energy into my body, along with God. I was centered inside this triangle as it lit up the universe for all to see.

And then it was done.

I immediately smashed Lucifer's death shield and paralyzed Luis, Cesar, Lucifer's disciples, and all of the gang members. I flew down and held Roberto's lifeless body in my arms. "I love you Roberto," I cried. "I'm so sorry I couldn't protect you."

His blood was my blood, his death was my death, and I was going to avenge it.

I heard the words 'An eye of an eye' screaming in my mind.

Gabriel, CJ, and Hunter hovered above to protect us in case Lucifer decided to show up.

I turned and looked at Luis and Cesar with disgust, and then I looked at all of those other evil people who played a part in this murder. I sent multiple beams of piercing blue light racing out of my eyes, hitting them one by one. I disintegrated every guilty human and every fallen angel.

I also made each one of them feel the same pain Roberto felt just before they ceased to exist.

I wanted Luis and Cesar to witness the deaths of their friends so they could see what their hatred had caused as a result of murdering Roberto.

With Roberto still in my arms, I released Luis and Cesar from their paralyzed state and watched as they stabbed each other in the heart. They both died instantly. This was the only compassion I could show them. Then I made their bodies disappear from earth.

There would be no afterlife for any of them.

I turned back to Roberto. "It is time to make you one of us. I need you by my side."

My body started glowing again as I gently placed my hands on Roberto's bloody chest.

I wasn't going to let God take him to Heaven; he was going to become an angel just like Gabriel, CJ, Hunter, and myself. I kissed Roberto and whispered in ear, "I love you with all my heart. It's time to wake up."

The Aegis floated down with Roberto's soul and covered both of us. As I healed Roberto's body, I watched as his soul quietly found its home once again. Roberto suddenly started breathing as I gently held him in my arms. Then I transferred my divine energy into his human form and made him an angel. He was now one of us.

"You did it Michael," Gabriel said, as he flew down and stood next to me.

CJ and Hunter continued to protect the three of us until we made sure Roberto's transformation was complete. Roberto slowly open his eyes, looked at me and smiled. I started crying as I kissed him on the forehead.

"I thought I had lost you," I said, holding Roberto gently in my arms.

"I knew you would save me Michael. I didn't want to die. I didn't want to leave you."

"You don't have to worry about that anymore. We will always be together."

"You, Gabriel, and I are now one. This is the way it was always meant to be."

I took a deep breath and then exhaled, like a huge weight had been lifted off my shoulders. Gabriel and I helped Roberto slowly get up and make sure he had his balance. Roberto looked at me with tears in his eyes not knowing what to say. He hugged me and whispered, "Thank you for bringing me back."

"I need you to be with us. We have a lot of work to do."

We stood there and listened to the sounds of the Bronx night for a minute or so before Roberto finally asked, "What am I?"

I smiled. "You are an angel just like us."

"I am?"

"Yes you are. Look at your arms." Roberto looked and saw angel wing tattoos moving on his arms. "How did I get these?"

"Just like I got mine. You became an angel like you were always meant to be," I said, as we compared our angel wing tatts. "So how does it feel?"

"It feels perfect." Roberto had the biggest smile on his face.

Gabriel put his arm around me and kissed me on the cheek. We were smiling at Roberto because he was in awe as he looked at his glowing body. He slowly turned and looked at us with this innocent grin. "Michael, I have one little question. Will I be able to shoot light beams outta my eyes like you?"

"Yeah, you will. And you'll be able to fly and do all sorts of other kool stuff. We have a lot of stuff to teach you."

Roberto got quiet again. It looked like he was trying to find some sort of memory in his mind. "So, I really died? Because if I did, I can't remember how it happened. I don't even remember how I got here, I just remember getting punched and kicked in the bathroom by someone, and then I must have passed out."

I hesitated telling him the truth because of how brutal his death was. I was happy that God had spared him the pain of that memory. I needed to find a way to give him some closure.

"Yes Roberto, you did die tonight, but there was a very good reason why, and I'll tell you why when we get back home. Do you remember anything other than getting beaten up?"

"No. The only other thing I can remember is my mind speeding toward a distant light, but then some kind of powerful force grabbed me and pulled me back here."

Hunter and CJ finally flew down to check out our newest angel.

"Nice job Michael. It's good to have you back. And it's nice to have another angel on our side," Hunter said.

Roberto had the biggest smile on his face. "What does it all mean?"

"It means the five of us were always meant to be together. This has been the plan all along," I said, hoping it would soften the reality of his death.

It was quiet and peaceful as Roberto looked around the park and saw the trees gently swaying in the wind. He had this contented look on his face. Tears welled up in his eyes as he took it all in. I knew I still had a lot of things to tell him, but I thought I would take it slow. Gabriel agreed. "Hey, we should probably head back to the party. I'm sure Mr. Atwood is worried about us."

"Yeah, I guess we should," I said. I turned and kissed Gabriel, and then I put one hand in Gabriel's and the other in Roberto's as the five of us flew into the night sky.

Listen To The Haunting Melodies

End of Journal 2

A note to my readers:

This book is dedicated to all the gay and straight people who understand. This is the second of seven books in this series.

If you have any questions or comments about book 2, please email me at avzeppa@gmail.com They are greatly appreciated.

Please tell your friends and family about this series :)

Peace,
A.V. Zeppa

CPSIA information can be obtained at www.ICGtesting.com
Printed in the USA
BVOW08s1605190913

331613BV00001B/20/P